The Pity of the
WINDS

Robin Timmerman

Order this book online at www.trafford.com
or email orders@trafford.com

Most Trafford titles are also available at major online book retailers.

Printed in the United States of America.

ISBN: 978-1-4269-9793-8 (sc)
ISBN: 978-1-4269-9794-5 (hc)
ISBN: 978-1-4269-9795-2 (e)

Library of Congress Control Number: 2011918138

Trafford rev. 10/25/2011

 www.trafford.com

North America & international
toll-free: 1 888 232 4444 (USA & Canada)
phone: 250 383 6864 ◆ fax: 812 355 4082

For Jan

PROLOGUE

Four p.m. A chilly afternoon in late April. The day is already darkening over the lake. Here and there in the sky there are large blots of darker shadows. Clouds that aren't clouds, but great dark circles of birds. Large birds with wide wingspans and fierce profiles.

Hundreds of hawks.

The hawks are on their last leg in a journey of thousands of miles, all the way from South America. Today they've been crossing the northeastern U.S. states. Riding the thermals in the cold blue April air.

Now the birds are wearied, fatigued, their wing movements slowing. But they can smell the land ahead in the dusk. They are born with the knowledge of this destination, they carry the maplines in their blood, in their brains. Almost there ! Usually this brings a final surge of strength, of energy.

But today on this chilly dark afternoon, there's an unease flowing back from the lead birds, an unease that moves like a ripple along the air currents. The unease moves through the group. Something's coming. Is it a storm? They've coped with storms on this lake before.

But no, the danger is something new, something outside the ken of knowledge built up through millenia of migration.

The lead birds at the front never even see the towers, the huge spinning, merciless blades. They have no time to react. They just go down before the relentlessly spinning scythes . . . . falling maimed and helpless to the ground.

Behind them, other birds turn and fly into the night, their lost, stricken cries echoing off the bloodied shore.

The sleeper awakes, gasping with frightened anger.
It's only a dream, it's only a dream.
No it isn't. It's a warning, a dreadful warning.

1

"Ummm." Ali Jakes stretched langorously in her slinky silk pyjama top and walked maroon-tipped tipped fingernails across her husband's chest.

"Officer," she purred throatily. "I need some help here. I think I've lost a button."

Pete dropped the manual on Community Policing to the floor.

Later, they lay looking at the moon through the uncovered bedroom window. She'd meant to make a curtain but now thought she wouldn't, preferring to view the dark starry arch of the uncluttered country sky. She snuggled against Pete, as he read out loud,

"It is important to estabish a good relationship with members of the community. Officers should make every effort to extend the hand of friendship and assistance."

She grinned. "I'm for that."

"Yes, but you're a push-over," he trailed a finger along her bare back. "It was a lot harder to impress the teen-agers at the high school this afternoon."

"What were you talking about?"

"The perils of drunk driving."

"Oh, that could be a little grim."

But he seemed to like the job, so far anyway. From a soldier to a cop. It wouldn't have been her first choice but he was happiest out of doors and he told the stories of his training with humour. Not laugh out loud humour, that wasn't Pete. But a dry enjoyment. So the move to the Island seemed to be a good thing.

"How was school today?" he asked lazily. Ali taught the grade one class at Middle Island elementary.

"Fun, we're starting outside dodge ball. Crisis of the day was Britney Halloran's scraped knee."

They both enjoyed these accounts. So different from the crisis of the day in the school at the Kandahar reconstruction project, where they had met. Pete's detachment was assigned to the project, an experimental mix of the army and various international aid agencies. Although the soldiers' chief responsibility was protection of the camp, they spent many hours helping in other ways. Pete found it a heartening change to be part of building something, rather than watching the destruction of the Afghanistan countryside.

He particularly enjoyed working on the schoolhouse where the pretty young Turkish teacher taught in the Classrooms Across Culture program. He was captivated by her infectious liveliness with the children, her big dark eyes that sparkled with laughter as she clapped her hands and encouraged the children to sing or play games.

One day after school, she asked if he would help her put up a shelf for some books. While he worked, they started to share words they knew in Afghani. She knew many more words than him. She thought the schoolroom could use a couple more shelves, he thought he could scrounge some more wood. Every afternoon for a week, he appeared with boards and tools. By the end of the week, he was in love.

Danger always loomed. Pounding of gunfire and shelling from the surrounding fields. Armoured military vehicles on the grounds, men in combat gear patrolling the perimeter. Still, the dusty, tense surroundings were the background to their budding romance. As Ali neared the end of her assignment, he found it difficult to speak his feelings, he hadn't had much practice at that in his life. The day before she was to leave, he had resolved to talk to her whatever the outcome, because life would be meaningless if he didn't. That was the day he was assigned to escort a visiting diplomat to the Kandahar airport. The day his world literally blew up.

Ali came to see him in hospital. She said she would be waiting for him in Canada. He realized then that he had been needing to leave for some time. Unlike the other men though, he had no home to go to.

Until now. Now, miraculously, he had Ali. The lonely times seemed far off.

She came out of the bathroom, swishing her toothbrush, then stopped, frowning by the window.

"Speaking of estabishing good communications in the community, I'm not having any success with our neighbour across the road. I've tried waving and saying hi but she just glares at me."

She used the word neighbour in the narrowest dictionary definition. As in the witch who lived across the road., not a friendly and welcoming presence who brings greetings and a home-baked cake to the young couple who have recently moved into the house with the long muddy driveway. So much for legendary country hospitality. Ali would cheerfully have settled for cool disinterest. Anything but the old woman's cold, critical scrutiny.

"And she's *always* there," she said. "As faithful as any soldier at her post. Believe me, I know, I've tried to find a time when I can sneak away without her watching."

"She's tending her chickens," Pete said.

"Not twenty-four hours a day she isn't."

"She's probably lonely," he soothed. "Old people get lonely. Watching the road is something to do."

"No wonder she's lonely," Ali's look was dire. "She'd scare anybody off. And she has a scary dog that barks at any car that passes by."

Pete kissed her. "Not much happens out here. Try to think of yourself as entertainment, as a celebrity on one of those reality shows. *Gorgeous middle eastern woman moves to the country.*"

"Gee thanks but nobody's filming this. It's not a reality show, it's just real."

"O.K. if I turn out the light?" he asked.

She hoped he would sleep and not be plagued again by one of his dreadful nightmares. Some soldiers came home missing limbs. Others like Pete, had injuries of the soul.

She wasn't exactly thrilled though, that he had decided to become a cop.

"What else can I do?" he asked. "I'm not going to open a dairy dip somewhere and sell ice-cream cones."

She had reluctantly accepted his plan, her secret wish that they would eventually get some a nice posting in a quiet rural area where a missing cow was a big event. And here they were. Just as she'd hoped. She thought she could like living here on the island. It was just what the Jakes needed. A quiet peaceful community where nothing much every happened. Though the countryside sure was dark at night and the wind did rattle these windows in their old frames. Very Emily Bronte-esque. Made you glad to be inside.

She snuggled closer to Pete.

Officer Kevin Ragusa drummed his fingers on the dashboard in an impatient tattoo. Sweet birdsong from farmers' fields drifted in through the open cruiser window but his city conditioned ears didn't hear it. Instead, he fiddled restlessly with the radio dial.

"Geez," he complained, "All you get is country, or cheesy rock for the old folks." He slumped back disgustedly in his seat. "Another thrilling day in hick-land and I haven't even written a speeding ticket this week. Yesterday it's the big robbery, a carton of smokes stolen from the Island Grill. Today we've got some vandalism at a fence. Wow, that's a real terrorist threat."

Pete Jakes ignored the daily rant.

You wouldn't wish for that kind of excitement if you'd ever seen the real thing, buddy.

Ragusa was twenty three years old, a city boy bored with his current cop training assignment. He was chafing to get back to the city. At times Pete felt a gulf far greater than the six years difference in their ages. But that's what serving in the army as a peace-keeper could do to you, he guessed. It could take away your youth.

He wondered if Ragusa had any idea how lucky he was to be driving on this boring Ontario gravel road without any risk of being blown up. In Afghanistan the soldiers called the roadside bombs IED's, short for Improvised Explosive Devices. The homemade landmines were the main cause of Canadian losses and injuries, not firefighting with the enemy.

The fear of stepping on an IED or driving over one was the terror that haunted soldiers' dreams, as Pete and the therapists at the army hospitals well knew. The diabolical devices and their suicide bomber counterparts made driving on the few passable roads a nighmarish experience. At least in the case of a suicide bomber, one of the enemy died as well. But most of the IEDs did their deadly work all on their own.

Kevin was playing his tattoo again. "Nah the worst that can happen out here is a cow breaks through the fence and leaves a flapjack on the road."

But Pete had stopped listening, his gaze caught by the sight of a solitary hawk circling in the sky above. Living freely up there in the air, high above the troubles of earth. He wondered what that was like.

Hawks Nest Point Wind Energy Project. The sign hung on a chain link gate.

Pete checked the directions he'd received from Jane at despatch. "We can walk from here," They came upon the spot quickly. "Man," Kevin gasped involuntarily. "What the hell is that?"

The thing hung from the fence, twisting leisurely in the breeze. A bloody torso, if you could call it that, making a soft thudding noise against the chain link strands. The two men approached warily and found not a body, but a dummy made of a stuffed burlap bag. There was a crudely drawn face and red splashes over the fabric. Paint not blood, but it was effective. A joke, but a well-executed one, definitely achieving the desired grisly effect. A sign was pinned to the dummy's scratchy chest, a rough sketch of a hawk-like bird in red and black paint.

Past the fence, the rocky spear of Hawks Nest Point stretched a half-mile out into the surging cold waters of the lake. Pete shivered involuntarily. A bleak spot, at least on a raw afternoon in late April. There would be no jaunty saiboats of summer out for some time yet.

"Shoot," Kevin spat out his gum. "It ain't nothing but a bunch of junk. Some kids having a joke."

He gave the thing an impatient shove, "Coming out here was just a pure waste of time."

The dummy bobbed obligingly, like some kind of weird pinata, its grin ugly and raw. Kevin laughed shortly and shoved it again. Not for the first time, Pete wondered at Ragusa's utter lack of empathy with his surroundings. He hadn't decided yet whether this was more an asset or a liability in police work. For now, he just said mildly, "Careful. We'd better take some pictures first before you knock it down. And we should get a picture of that hole in the fence too. There's bound to be a damage report from the owner."

The hole was wide, the raw edges of the wire curling back. He took a half-dozen pictures of the gap, the surrounding clumps of burdock making it scratchy work. Then he directed his attention to the garish dummy. It had no proper legs, just tied off ends of the sack. He reached up to touch the 'foot', when a voice barked behind him.

"Bout time you fellers got here. I phoned the station an hour ago."

He turned to see two men. The bigger one, fiftyish, beefy and red-faced in slacks and a brown blazer, brandished a cellphone like a weapon. Obviously the barker.

Pete could brandish too. He pulled out his notebook. "Could I have your name please, sir?"

"Burt Sousa," the man snapped. He obviously had little respect for the police, even though he'd called them for help. The type of man who resented having to stop at a red light.

"And what is your connection to this incident?"

"My connection is that I'm a partner in *WindSpear*, the company developing this goddamned piece of land," Sousa said scathingly. "Didn't your boss tell you anything? I don't know why he didn't come out himself instead of sending a couple of cop trainees out here."

He was about to sputter on but Pete ignored him and turned to the other man.

"Jim Keen, site manager," the man smiled apologetically for the behaviour of his boss, probably a regular duty. He wore a shirt and tie beneath a navy blue windbreaker that bore the company logo, an artistic rendering of a wind turbine tower with the distinctive three white blades. Women likely used to call him boyish looking but he looked nearer forty and had a certain resigned look about his eyes.

He chuckled now, though. "Jeez, that dummy thing sure gave young Gillies a start this morning. I guess he just about set the brush on fire racing back to the trailer to tell us about it."

Pete grinned too at the mental image. "And what time was that, Mr. Keen?"

"Near eight o'clock, I figure. Brad had just set out to check the west fence. He's an engineering student working here for the summer. Clearing brush away from the fence lines, jobs like that."

Sousa brushed aside such necessary detail. "So what are you fellers going to do about this?" he cut in.

"Seems like this might be more of an insurance claim to me, Mr. Sousa," said Pete. "The damage to the fence anyway."

The beefy man scowled. "This here's a crime scene officer. Take your pick, Trespassing, breaking and entering, destruction of property. Whoever cut this fence could have got in to steal some equipment."

"Is anything missing?" Pete asked reasonably enough.

The site manager answered. "We checked, it doesn't seem as if they took anything. The tool shack lock hasn't been fooled with. And all the vehicles look O.K." He turned to his boss. "As soon as these fellas are finished here, I'll send a coupla men to fix the fence."

"Any idea who did this?" Pete asked Sousa.

"You could start with the troublemakers who took up that petition against the wind farm last fall."

Pete had only been assigned to the area in January but he knew a bit of the opposition to the wind turbine project. It seemed wherever they went, the turbines brought controversy and bitter divisions in the surrounding communities. Many people felt that wind power was the long-sought for answer to the world's energy problems.

Others were concerned that the huge turbine towers would upset the delicate natural balance of their quiet rural areas. And nobody, not even the proponents of wind energy, was lining up to live next door to the huge structures.

"So there's been a lot of opposition?"

"Not of any account," Sousa said dismissively. "Just a bunch of know-nothings who can't see a good thing when it's right under their noses. We're putting up the demo turbine tower on Saturday and that's just the beginning. Next month we start putting up another twenty towers, to the tune of a quarter million dollars each. This project is going to put Middle Island on the world map."

He looked past the fence to where the long rocky finger of Hawks Nest Point jutted out into the lake, his chunky face alight at his vision of wind-driven riches. Pete saw only crumbling limestone cliffs, the few scarce trees with their roots bared like naked limbs by erosion of the sparse soil. But there was wind all right, he noted, lots of wind.

He gestured to Kevin to help him cut the dummy down. "Want to give me a hand here?"

Illogically, he braced himself for the weight of a real person but the dummy was light as a balloon, stuffed with batting he guessed. It bobbed disconcertingly in their grip and he was aware of the bizarre picture they must be making. He tugged and the sacking split, spilling out batting like intestinal coil against Sousa's jacket. Involuntarily the man recoiled. "Jeesus!"

The note had come free too, floating like a colored leaf before their eyes. Pete plucked it from the air. There were words too, under the crudely drawn hawk picture. "Sousa you'll be next!"

Even Sousa stopped his bluster for a moment and was silent.

So maybe not just a dumb prank.

Kevin held out the sacking head, still attached to its tether. The painted staring eyes and yawing red mouth looked grotesque. "Anybody want this as a souvenir?"

*　*　*

WindSpear Energy Technologies, said the blue lettered sign. *Using Natural Solutions to Create a Cleaner, Better, World!*

Maybe someday. Sousa let the way across the site which was noisy with the racket of a couple of bulldozers and a gravel truck. A brown and white killdeer ran before one of the dozers, in a desperate decoy move to protect its nest.

"We're building access roads to get the trubines in," Keen explained.

For the moment, the makeshift offices of *WindSpear* were housed in an unprepossessing thirty foot trailer. Inside, the space was well supplied with computers, fax and telephone equipment. The walls were covered with site maps of the area dotted with thumbtacks indicating the positions of the coming turbines. Pete picked up a model of a turbine from the desk, where it was being used as a paperweight. The model looked like a kid's little spinning toy, but he knew the real machines were going to be a lot bigger than toys. He'd seen them when he was stationed in Germany. Three hundred or more feet high with blades over a hundred feet long.

"Where's the kid who found the dummy?" he asked.

"Brad's coming," Keen said. "Here he is now."

Gillies was a tall gangly kid, whose skinny jeaned legs seemed weighted down by heavy workboots. He had recovered from the shock of his morning discovery and was eager to tell his story, which had already gained some embellishment Pete was sure. By the end of the day he'd be telling folks the thing was alive and dripping actual blood, not paint. His freckled face alight, he described the morning drama.

"It was real wet and misty like it always is here in the morning when the mist comes off the lake. You have to wear boots because the grass is soaking wet . . . ."

Sousa grabbed up a hard hat and grunted impatiently. "Enough with the song and dance, just tell the cop what you saw."

The kid looked embarrassed and hurried on. "So I could hardly see anything. That's why I was keeping so close to the wire fence, so's I had something to hold on to, something to guide me along."

He stopped, and shook his head a bit dazedly. And who could blame the kid, Pete thought, it must have been quite a shock.

"That's when I bumped into the . . . body thing. That's sure what it looked like and felt like anyway. I bumped my face right into its stomach, if you know what I mean. Then I looked up and saw its head and all that red paint dripping over its face. Only I thought it was blood," he said defensively.

"I didn't stay long after that, I just took off."

Keen grinned. "Like greased lighting. You must have been going forty miles an hour when you ran into us."

"What time was this?" Pete asked.

"About quarter after eight," Gillies said.

"Is that your regular route?"

"No sir, I don't really have a regular route."

"But somebody would have found the dummy this morning?" Pete asked the question of Keen too.

The site manager looked to Sousa who impatiently agreed. "Sure, it's likely someone would have been along that part of the fence sometime today. It's like I told you, it's those petition loonies again. They wanted us to find the damn thing."

"Again?" Pete asked. "There have been other incidents?"

Keen shrugged. "Nothing much. A dead seagull left outside the equipment shed. And one of the backhoe guys said he heard weird noises from the field a couple of times when he was locking up his machine. There's never been any damage before this."

"What security have you got here?"

"The security system hasn't been installed yet," Keen said with a frown directed at Sousa, as if the topic was a bone of contention.

Maybe you should hire a watchman in the meantime, was Pete's unvoiced thought. There was no good reason why the local police should act as the company's own private security force, especially not when millions of dollars of profit were no doubt involved.

Sousa scowled. "Maybe you guys could leave the coffee shop and drive a patrol car down this way once in a blue moon."

Pete ignored this. "When did these other incidents happen—the dead seagull and the noises?"

"Months ago," Keen said. "Way back last fall."

On the surface, the incidents looked connected but maybe not. Or was the dummy the beginning of a stepped-up campaign? And how serious would it get?

Sousa stomped angrily across the floor, the trailer rocking with his movement and jabbed his finger at the calendar.

"Next Saturday, we're erecting that turbine tower. A quarter million dollars worth of equipment will be on this site. I hope you guys will be out in force because we sure don't need any screw-ups."

Outside the grimy trailer window, a bright orange bulldozer crawled like a giant beetle across the scraped parking lot.

"Can I go now?" asked Brad Gillies.

3

Middle Island Police Chief Bud Halstead was a busy man, at least on paper. And what a lot of paper. A month ago, after weeks of wrestling over figures, he'd submitted the annual policing budget for the district. The Council was not pleased.

Township Clerk Vern Byers had looked downright sorrowful "It's not that we don't appreciate what a great job you've done for us over the years, Bud. But as usual, it's all about money. We're one of the smallest municipalities in the province that still has it's own police force and we're thinking we just can't afford it anymore. We're looking at switching over to the Provincial Police."

The process was a common one and was happening all over the province as policing methods became more sophisticated and more costly.

Halstead scowled. "Jeez, Vern. You're saying the community can't afford the salaries of four cops? How are the provincial boys going to be any cheaper?"

"They're not actually cheaper," Vern admitted, "not the police salary costs anyway. But they will take over all the administration costs, pay their own dispatcher and clerk, buy their own vehicles and equipment. We had to buy a new cruiser for you last year," he pointed out.

"You think OPP cops don't drive cars too? You think they ride horses?"

Vern didn't smile. He was too much the accountant, had never had much of a sense of humour behind that melancholy horse muzzle of a face.

"Look around you, Bud. The station needs $100,000 in renovations. The roof, a wiring update, a plumbing overhaul."

"We have a secretary. Jane's worked here for fifteen years, what will happen to her?"

Vern shrugged. "She'll get some kind of severance package."

"That might last her a year. What about after that? What about my officers?"

"Fred's in the hospital recovering from a quadruple by-pass surgery. I doubt that he'll be coming back to work anytime soon. That's why we got you the two trainees remember?"

Halstead subsided in his chair and looked around the empty council room for an inspiration that didn't come. Dusty light from the window illuminated the chairs and table. On the wall behind the furniture, hung the nation's flag and a picture of the Queen on her coronation day, fifty years ago. The sound of singing came up from the ground floor of the town hall. The weekly meeting of the local Girl Guides troop.

He began again. "The station is a part of Island life, Vern. People around here like having a local cop, it makes them feel safer that there's a cop in town, that they don't have to wait for somebody to come over from Bonville."

"They might just have to get used to it."

"You have no soul Vern."

"I can't afford one." This time the Clerk smiled thinly, at his own joke. He added helpfully. "You'll likely still have a job if you want it."

Likely. Maybe.

The one thing that was sure was that he wouldn't be his own boss anymore. Hell maybe it would be relaxing for a change, to hand the reins over to the provincial boys and forget it all. Or maybe just retire, though fifty-two was earlier than he'd planned.

There was time to think of all that later though. For this year at least, he still had a police detachment to run. True his force was small—only himself and three other officers and two of them were the new probationary recruits. And the area was large, with a population of 4500 people. Most of them lived and farmed on Middle Island which was barely technically an island, joined as it was to the Mainland by the causeway. There was lots of open water on the other three sides, however, all the way to the United States. The other two islands in his domain were considerably smaller. North Island was little more than a rock sticking up into the bay. South Island though, was the base of a former lighthouse and in the summer he had to spare an officer for daily boat runs to check the island out for illicit parties and drunken boat drivers.

His detachment station was hardly grand, even Vern the penny watcher couldn't argue that. A one story brick bunker at the edge of town, functional being the operative word. A parking lot out front for the two cruisers and any visitors. A pot of petunias on each side of the door, Jane's work. Inside, a reception desk, Jane's territory of computer, phones and dispatcher lines. Her cubicle wall was plastered with yellow sticky notes and pictures of her two daughters and several grandchildren. Jane had been at the station for twenty years, longer than Halstead. She knew the Island people and history like the back of her hand.

His own office was across the narrow hallway, superior to Jane's area only by virtue of a cubicle wall and a window overlooking open fields out back. There was also an interview room and the common room with a couple of desks for the constables. A closet-sized space with a coffee pot and sink was euphemistically dubbed the lunch room, but normally the officers ate their sandwiches at their desks. Finally, a holding cell not much bigger than the coffee pot accommodations. Admittedly, it wasn't used very often, and then usually just to house a Saturday night drunk. On the rare occasion a woman had been the involuntary guest of the facilities, Jane looked to her personal needs or requests.

He leaned back in his chair, cranked well back to accommodate his long limbs. He liked his ever changing view of the neighbouring field. Today a swath of soft green winter wheat planted last fall, now just coming up. A restful view and peaceful, or it had been in the past. He could find no peace today though, with Vern's comments rankling in his mind. With council on his back, it was not a time for any screw-ups. Not when he was shorthanded, his second in command in hospital, and two trainees learning the ropes.

He could only hope for a quiet year, the usual round of domestic disputes, the occasional smash and grab robbery, and court appearances for impaired drivers. Nothing out of the ordinary.

When Officer Pete Jakes came in, Halstead gratefully shoved aside the pile of budget estimates. Busy as he was, once he had apportioned an officer some time, he gave his full attention. And let the man know he'd better not waste it.

So he listened attentively while Jakes gave a concise report of the situation out at Hawks Nest Point.

Jakes seemed a smart lad and was an interesting case himself, more than a bit out of the ordinary. He'd come to the profession by a somewhat different route. In the army since he was nineteen, he had served in postings with the peacekeeping forces in two of the word's most unpeaceful hotspots, Iraq and Afghanistan. Usually when a kid enlisted that young, the army became home and he signed on for the next twenty years. But not Jakes, he'd said in his interview that he'd got married and his wife wanted to settle somewhere. That's what he said but Halstead sensed there was more to Jakes' decision. A look in his eyes, some bad memories there.

Probably had a lot to do with that road bombing near Kandahar a couple of years ago. Jakes had been in the same vehicle as the Canadian diplomat who had been killed, along with three soldiers. Jakes had been the only survivor. The man had been badly banged up. Physically he was in great shape, sturdy, five ten, blond hair still clipped army short. But he seemed older than his years, there was a look in his eyes, some bad memories there. Still, he certainly had law enforcement experience and if Halstead was any judge, the makings of a good police officer.

"So, what do you think?" Halstead asked. "Is there any serious threat in this dummy stuff?"

"Maybe, maybe not," Jakes said, with his disconcerting straight-up gaze. The man hardly ever cracked a smile. Though with the attractive Ali as his wife, he should have lots to smile about. Halstead got a kick out of seeing exotic Ms. Jakes going about her shopping on Main Street. She wore a stylish red coat, high leather boots and her dark hair set off her olive complexion and big dark flashing eyes. So different than the local women in their jeans and faded pink and grey winter parkas. They were an interesting looking couple, stalwart, reserved Jakes and willowy Ali, lively and bubbling with life.

Ah to be young again. He reluctantly pulled his thoughts back to the business at hand.

"Somebody put some work into it," Jakes continued. "The dummy was well made, and whoever hung it up was aware there is only limited security out there. The note was pretty creepy too."

"Creepy?" Halstead grinned and Jakes looked embarassed.

"It bothered Mr. Sousa anyway."

"That's Mayor Sousa by the way. Burt's the Mayor of the Island this year." And the biggest proponent of closing down the local police detachment. In the name of progress of course. "He lives in town but runs a construction business in Bonville."

"Well Mr. Mayor seems to think it might be someone in the group who organized the petition against the wind turbine project."

"He could be right, but Lord I hope not. I thought those folks had licked their wounds and left the battle last fall."

He sighed. "The Point used to be pretty quiet. There was the Crown land down at the Bluff and Burt's parents owned the property up at this end. They ran a fishing resort in the summer. Not a big operation, just a dozen little cabins. The Bluff takes a dip there and there was enough accessible shoreline for the boats.

A couple of years ago old Mr. Sousa died, his wife got old-timers' disease and was put in a nursing home. Burt's been holding on to the land with the faint hope that some developer might want to build a resort there someday. He'd probably have sold it just to get rid of it soon. Then the wind people came along and they needed the Sousa land for access to the Point. I heard the *WindSpear* company offered him $900,000 if the project expands as planned."

Pete whistled. "That's a nice piece of change."

"I believe he's taken it as shares in the company. Anyway, Burt's hit the jackpot and a lot of folks around here aren't too pleased about it. Of course it doesn't help that Burt has to rub their noses in it."

"Seems like somebody is fighting back," Pete said. He flipped through the folder in his lap. "I picked up a copy of the petition list from the files. I thought I could go and talk to the organizers. Just to let them know we're on our guard."

Halstead nodded. "You could start with Andy Poltz, he's the nearest neighbour to the wind site. He was pretty hot under the collar about having those turbines next door, said they'd upset his cows. They're some kind of special heritage breed, from Scotland. Then you could drop in on Stephanie Bind, she's on the other side of the road, down the lane. She runs a yoga retreat for women but she's a pretty sensible type."

Privately, Halstead sympathized with Sousa. The protestors had their chance, democracy was served. You lost the battle folks, now live with it. Guess what, you'll be needing energy too.

But as a defender of the public peace, he directed Jakes. "You could also ask them if they saw or heard anything suspicious out there on Wednesday night. Lights, car motor noises, that kind of thing. If they'll tell you."

He didn't envy Jakes his assignment. But the task required somebody mature and competent and Jakes would have a defter touch than young Ragusa that's for sure. He'd better find that one some action.

"What should we do with the dummy sir? It got kind of banged up when we cut it down."

"Tag it and put it in the prop room for now. Maybe we can haul it out next Hallowe'en to decorate the station."

"A dummy covered in bloody paint?" Ali looked out the Island Grill window at the noon-time traffic jam, a couple of pick-up trucks whose drivers had stopped in Main Street to chat. "That sounds pretty creepy."

She took a huge bite of her club sandwich. "So long as it hasn't affected your appetite," Pete said dryly.

"What does your boss think?" Ali had only met Chief Halstead a couple of times. A middle-aged widower, the lanky laconic man with melancholy eyes touched her feminine sympathies.

Pete crushed his straw. "He doesn't seem too worried. He says this Mayor Sousa is always making somebody mad. The wind project is just the latest thing."

Ali leaned forward, her eyes teasing. "We've got a witch across the road, you find a creepy dummy up on the Point . . . . da da da da . . . . she hummed the famous theme from The Twilight Zone. What's next? A pit of snakes? A ghost on horseback?"

"Almost as bad. I'm visiting some of the chief protestors this afternoon and one of them actually is our neighbourhood witch."

"Poor you," she sympathized. "Watch out for the chickens, they look more murderous than the dog."

"What about you, how's your afternoon?"

"I've got spelling and a discussion of bullying."

"Maybe I could send this Mayor Sousa to your class."

* * *

Highland Cattle, Registered Scottish Herd, said the sign by the gate.

With their long curved horns, the animals looked almost prehistoric. And curious, shaking their big shaggy brown heads at Pete from behind the fence. They were huge beasts, looking more like buffalo than the typical, placid Ontario Holstein cow. He doubted these animals would be spooked by the swoosh of a wind turbine or much else.

He found Andy Poltz out by his barn. A big old man in a farmer's overall and rubber boots stiff with cow dung. Poltz was nearly seventy the file said, but he looked strong and fit, the result no doubt of an active, hard-working life. He stood straight and nearly unbowed, glaring out at the world from under lowering grey brows. As mean and shaggy as his weird looking cows.

Pete introduced himself.

"So Sousa's got another knot in his breeches," Poltz said with grim satisfaction.

"What's buggin' him now?"

"Why do you think I'm here about Sousa?" Pete asked.

Poltz's scowl deepened, the age creases in his weather-ravaged face like roadside ditches.

"You're driving a cruiser, not a road maintenance truck. I don't figure you're here about fixing that hole out there in the road," he pointed to an axle-breaking trench in the gravel. Pete had noticed it on the earlier trip out to the Point.

Poltz started walking back towards the house, leaving Pete with little choice but to scramble after him.

"So what's up at Blow Us All Down Acres?" he asked, his tone bluffly casual but his look watchful.

Pete answered with a question of his own.

"Did you hear anything unusual on the road last night? Or see anything suspicious at the Point?"

"You mean like goblins or something?"

"Or something," Pete said dryly. "Something like a car or lights."

Poltz tired of playing his game.

He shrugged his huge shoulders. "I get up early, I go to bed early. I wouldn't hear or see anything after eight o'clock."

Pete looked towards the barn. "Do you have a dog?"

"I live alone. Like it that way."

They had reached the porch steps. Pete could see into the kitchen through the screen door. A glimpse of a counter top crowded with cups and plates, a table piled with newspapers. It looked as if Poltz had lived alone for a long time. Though a scruffy orange cat skulked abut the unpainted porch.

The barn and fence along the road seemed in good shape though, to his inexperienced eye. He'd looked up Highland cattle on the Net before he came out. Originally bred in ancient Scotland, the animals with their thick double coat of hair were well suited to cope with the Canadian winter. Farmers had been importing, then breeding them since the 1920s but they were still a curiosity in the countryside. They could get most of their nutrition from browsing even on rough land and were prized for their hardiness and flavour.

Poltz looked bored, ready to retreat to his lair. "So what did these people in the car with the lights do?"

Pete told him about the damage to the fence but didn't mention the dummy.

Poltz received the news with a grunt of satisfaction.

"Trespassing is a crime you know." Pete pointed out. "So is destruction of property."

Poltz scowled. "Tell that to Sousa. He's about to destroy this whole end of the Island. You should be prosecuting him."

"There are legal avenues of protest, Mr. Poltz. Courts, lawyers."

The old man spat on the ground. "A lot of good they are. Or the police." He grabbed a porch post as if to physically hold the house up. "This farm has been in my family for five generations. My grandparents' bones are in the cemetery up the road. And Sousa the bastard offered to *buy* the place. As if I'd ever sell to him. Over my dead body I told the money-grubbing bastard."

Pete left instructions for Poltz to call if he heard anything on ensuing nights. As he pulled away, he thought he'd have had more success interviewing the cattle.

* * *

YourSpace
Hawks Point Women's Retreat.
The door knocker was a carving of a stylized nude woman goddess. Pete bypassed this and tapped warily on the wooden panels. He wondered who might open the door and what she might be wearing. Hopefully something.

In fact Stephanie Bind looked brisk and business-like in black slacks and a rust-coloured blazer. Or did until she paled at sight of the cruiser.

"My daughter—the bus—has anything happened . . . ."

He quickly explained the purpose of his visit and her expression hardened. "So Burt Sousa has a problem with vandalism and you've come to interrogate *me*. As far as I'm concerned, *he's* the vandal. The way he's run roughshod over his own fellow Islanders . . . ."

She stopped herself and forced a small smile. "But I said my piece at council and I'm done with that. And you're only doing your job. Please come in and sit down at least. You must be new on the force."

She led him to a kitchen island where he politely refused a cup of coffee. She was really a very good looking woman. In her forties with an intriguing blaze of white in her glossy black hair. He knew from Chief Halstead that she had operated a local motel with her former husband and after their divorce had apparently invested her settlement into the retreat venture.

"That was my plan anyway two years ago," she said, with a rueful smile. "Now after months of contractor and building hold-ups, the dream is finally becoming a reality. I'm just about ready to launch."

"You've got a nice-looking place here," Pete said.

The kitchen area opened up into a large room with a fireplace surrounded by several comfortable leather sofas. Floor to ceiling windows on one side overlooked what would soon be an extensive blooming garden and beyond that, the lake.

"Thanks," she said. "I'm trying to appeal to business women who need a break from their laptops and cellphones. I've hired a yoga instructor to give daily classes and I thought that a soothing landscape of seasonal birds and butterflies, would lead to peaceful contemplation and introspection. Or so it promises in the Hawks Point Retreat brochure," she added, with a return of her earlier anger. "That was before I found out that Burt Sousa was planning to build thirty wind turbines next door."

She clapped her hands in a dismissive little movement.

"Ah well, take a deep breath Stephanie as my accountant would say. I'm told that some people even find the turbines an attractive view." She held up her hand. "Fingers crossed and pour them enough wine . . . ."

He thought she wasn't nearly as flip as she pretended.

"But you did help organize a petition against the project," he prompted. "What's happened with that?"

She shrugged. "We got one hundred and fifty signatures and went to the council meetings. A lot of people on the island depend upon summer tourism for a part of their income. They feel people come here to see beauty and wildlife, not industrial wind machines. But it's a big company behind the project and we were simply blown away, pardon the obvious imagery."

"Your neighbour Mr. Poltz doesn't exactly seem resigned to the project," Pete pointed out.

She smiled wryly. "You've got that right. Andy really kicked up a fuss at council the night of the vote. They had to call the police to usher him out. Not that I approve of his behaviour but he was just having the tantrum that all the rest of us actually wanted to have."

"I've met the man, not a friendly fellow." He was thinking that Halstead might have warned him.

She nodded. "I went to school with his daughter Melissa. He was always a miserable old grump. His wife left him years ago, taking Melissa and her sister. Since then the old man's been on his own, stewing in his misery I guess. But he's hardly an eco-terrorist. None of us are. And Andy raises good cattle, on his own organic feed."

"He's an organic farmer?" Pete was surprised. "You'd think he'd be in favour of wind power."

"Actually he's had his own smaller windmill for years. He says that's the way to go, rather than the big monster towers." She sighed. "He's probably right but there's a point when you just have to accept a decision and go on."

"So you don't think that any members of your group had anything to do with hanging up this dummy?"

She laughed shortly. "I certainly didn't. The parts for the demonstration turbine are being delivered this week. I'm a busy woman and I can't see frittering my energy in a lost cause. What you can't change, you live with, that's my motto."

Still, he sensed the anxiety beneath her words. He had some idea of construction prices these days and she had obviously invested a lot of money in her new business. Maybe everything.

He asked her the same questions he'd asked Poltz.

She shook her head. "Sorry, I'm even farther away than Andy. And in my office here, I have no view of the Point."

"But you'd hear a car go by."

"There seem to be trucks going by all the time. This used to be a quiet road."

"At night?"

"If I did hear anything, I'd probably just assume it was Burt or one of the staff going to the site office."

The front door slammed and she frowned, "Oh dear, here's Livy."

A girl moved quickly across the dining room. About sixteen, long dark hair streaming over hunched shoulders. She obviously had no intention of stopping in at the kitchen but Stephanie called out, her voice sounding high-pitched and over-anxious.

"Hi darling, come and meet Officer Jakes."

The girl stopped her headlong rush but still looked poised for flight. She wore a black capelike coat that fluttered like feathers about her small slim body. Her streaming hair framed a face unnaturally pale. Pete could see the girl was torn between wishing to escape her mother and struggling to be polite.

Meanwhile Stephanie was babbling nervously on. "Officer Jakes is investigating some vandalism down at the Point. Somebody cut the fence and hung up a dummy covered in blood."

The girl's pale skin seemed to blanch even further, if that was possible. Pete thought she was going to faint.

"It wasn't blood," he corrected quickly. "Just paint."

"Well it was obviously supposed to look like blood." Stephanie said. "I can't imagine Andy pulling such a trick but who else could it be?"

"I don't want any tea," Livy said, shrinking even further into her shoulders and looking around desperately. "I have to go."

Stephanie sighed. "I can't say the right thing these days, as far as Livy is concerned. Oh pardon me, Olivia, I'm not allowed to call her 'that baby name' anymore."

She looked unhappily after her daughter's stormy wake. "I thought she'd be interested in the news. In the old days we used to natter happily about everything. Now she never talks to me, and when she's home which is rarely, she just holes up in her room for hours at a time."

He could think of nothing comforting to say, remembering his own unhappy adolescence. The army had been his escape. He had enlisted at nineteen, anything to get away from home.

*   *   *

Stephanie walked the officer to the door and watched the cruiser pull away.

She looked at the stairs, thought about going up, then hearing the blaring music from Livy's room, changed her mind. Still, she wondered why Livy seemed so upset about the dummy. Most kids were into the whole goth, vampire, blood thing at that age. The teens all seemed to love those gory horror movies. But she probably wasn't upset about that at all. More likely that her Livy was suffering from unrequited love. That was usually the culprit when a girl spent hours mooning over sad songs.

She wondered who was the unrequiting fellow. But Livy didn't talk to her anymore so that was just another thing she didn't know these days, the mystery that was her daughter.

5

Miranda Paris, said the name on the mailbox. Ali's nemesis. The witch across the road. The house was of a similar vintage and style to his own. A two-story clapboard with some gingerbread woodwork on the gables. The Paris house was green, the Jakes place was a cream colour and both houses could use a fresh coat of paint. The Jakes had taken their house because there was nothing to rent in town other than rooms and the motel where Kevin was staying.

The chickens were out in the yard, about twenty vari-coloured birds pecking in the dirt. He'd have to push his way through. He thought yearningly of the beer he'd have when he got home, and his wife's long, smooth honey-coloured limbs. But onward into the breach.

He felt like a fool. Had called *Hello, Mrs. Paris*, three times now. The woman must know he was there, he could hear the dog barking in the house. What if the old girl simply refused to answer to his knock? But no, the door was opening, she was probably letting the dog out. The way things were going, the animal would be an attack Doberman. He braced himself and tried to look authoritative but the dog didn't look too bad. Smallish, white and black, with a feathery tail that looked too big for the rest of it. And curious rather than aggressive. He reminded himself to introduce Ali to some dogs, she obviously hadn't known very many.

Her description of Miranda Paris seemed fairly accurate though. Close up she seemed about seventy, like Poltz. A bit stooped but still tall and wiry in jeans and something he thought a gardener's magazine might call a smock. Gray hair scraped back under an old straw hat and mouth pursed like she'd swallowed a lemon.

She didn't invite him in, just stood there with the door barely ajar. She said nothing either, as the dog settled companionably around his feet. He introduced himself, and feeling certain that any small talk would only bring on more disdain, he started straight in on the questions he'd been asking all afternoon.

"There's been a vandalism incident down at the Point. We're checking to see if the neighbours heard or saw any strange activities last night."

She crossed her arms and leaned against the lintel. "It's a strange world. There's strange activities going on all the time."

"I meant at the wind farm site," he said patiently.

Her pursed lips almost disappeared. "Don't call that place a *farm* around me. It's going to be an industrialized site. A wind factory. Anyways I don't see why I would hear anything more than you. You're right here on the same road."

"So you're saying you didn't hear or see anyone?"

"If you say so."

He plowed doggedly on. "Do you know of anybody who might bear a grudge against the project?"

"You mean other than me?" she drawled.

Right at the moment, he had no difficulty imagining her as a saboteur, hacking away with garden clippers at the *WindSpear* fence. In fact, as suspects went, it was a draw between her and old rancher Poltz. He smiled tightly. "I know that you were one of the people objecting to the project. There were others."

"I signed a petition," she said dryly. "I haven't been attempting any sabotage if that's what you mean. I heard about that dummy thing, it's just a prank, some children getting up to nonsense."

"News travels pretty fast around here," he said. He wondered how she'd heard already.

"The mail lady told me," she said scornfully.

"It was a pretty ugly prank," he said. "Did you hear the fence was cut up too?"

Her bony shoulders lifted in a shrug.

"So you support that kind of vandalism?"

"What about you?" she asked. "Do you support that bully Sousa and his tactics—whose side are you on?"

"I'm on the side of peace and order. Aren't you?"

She tutted. "Most of the time. But the briefest read of history will show that some of humankind's noblest thought has come from men and women who were breaking some law. Tom Paine was chased out of Engand, early American suffragettes were jailed. And Andy Poltz was dragged out of our own local council meeting."

He couldn't believe he was having this discussion with a possible suspect but there was something about the woman. He felt he had to answer.

"And you're putting Andy Poltz on the same level as Tom Paine? By all accounts Poltz is a brute, he drove his wife and daughters from home years ago."

She shook her head in irritation. "Maybe he's not the champion some people might choose. But change is hard, and it isn't always right. Andy can't just up and leave his land, it's taken him years to earn that organic certificate. He's only speaking up when other people aren't brave enough to do it."

"I believe in free speech too," Pete said. "But the man's hardly been persecuted. He's had his chance to object to this project, lots of chances."

She looked with her wintry gaze up the road towards the Point.

"Well I didn't hear anything last night. Other than the wind of course. Wind always talks strange." Adopting a mock dramatic tone, she quoted. *Ill blows the wind that profits nobody.*

From Shakespeare, he guessed.

Ali was right, she did look a bit witchlike. And liked playing it up, he thought. At least to newcomers.

"I'd appreciate if you'd give me a call at the station if you remember anything that might help us in our investigation."

He handed her his card which she was loath to take. For a minute he thought she might just let it drop to the porch floor.

She retrieved it with lank fingers just in time.

"Good day," he said and made his ungraceful exit back through the grazing chickens. He felt the sharp sting of her gaze upon him as he crossed the road.

*   *   *

Miranda watched the young policeman leave. She didn't particularly like having a police car parked across the road all the time. It wasn't as if she got any benefit, she already had the dog for protection. And who was going to bother an old woman, anyway? Still, he was a good-looking lad. She would have fancied him in the past. Sometimes the past seemed very long ago. Up the road, she saw Andy coming in with his cows. She had retained her perfect eyesight, one blessing.

She sighed. Times had been pretty peaceful for a while but now things were getting stirred up again. If you lived long enough though, you learned one thing. Peace never lasts forever.

"So when are we going to do it?" demanded Sean.

"The turbine is going up on Saturday," Gavin Sousa said. "We'll wait a few more days after that, till their guard is down."

Livy frowned as Sean slumped angrily back in his seat. Sean was so impatient, it could be a problem. Like when he had wanted to call up the *WindSpear* office to tell them about the dummy, instead of waiting for someone to find it. Gavin had won that time but Sean had been teed off.

"I think it's dumb to wait to put up the banner," Sean said. "They could start putting in the security monitors any day now."

"Like I wouldn't know when that happens," Gavin reminded him. "My father phones his foreman every night and talks about the next day's work."

"I still think it's dumb." Even though Gavin was pretty much the leader of the group, Sean knew he could have an opinion. Gavin couldn't hang that banner up on the turbine tower himself. And neither Livy nor Kelly was going to make that climb, they would be the lookouts.

Livy looked at Gavin. She knew he was teed because his face went kind of still and tight but he just went on talking about the details, the things they'd need. It worked because Sean got all involved in talking about the ropes and stuff they'd be using.

As well as being incredibly handsome, Gavin was smart. He wasn't at all like his father. She didn't care if Mr. Sousa was Mayor, she didn't like him or respect him. Neither did Gavin, he hated his father and what he stood for.

"Money, that's all he thinks about," she'd heard him say. "He should have a dollar sign stamped on his forehead. He's such a jerk, he didn't even ask my sister and me when he sold my grandparents' land to the *WindSpear* company. He just went ahead and sold it for shares in the the goddamned company. He has no soul."

Livy thought that Gavin had a beautiful soul. He loved Nature and he loved the Point just as she did. That was where they had met. Of course she had known him all her life, in the way that all the Island families knew each other. He'd been a year older though, and they had never been in the same grade at the village school. Then Gavin had gone on to high school on the mainland before her. But one glorious day this March break, they met, truly met. She would never forget that magical afternoon, for weeks she replayed the scene in her mind before she went to sleep at night.

It was one of those March days when you could smell spring in the air, even though there were still dirty streaks of snow in the ditches. The crows were cawing noisily above the stubbled corn fields as if they were saying hurry up, farmers, get that new corn planted.

Her mother was busy as usual with some detail connected with the Retreat, so Livy put on her coat and scarf and headed up the road towards the Point. She hated seeing the big sign announcing the *WindSpear* project, so she walked up towards the old fishing cabins. It was her favourite thing, to walk by herself and think about words for her poems. She knew the kids at school thought she was strange but she didn't care. She was looking at the bare tree branches and saying some lines from her latest poem out loud when a bicycle almost ran her down.

"Holy crap, can't you look where you're going?" Gavin said. Those were his first words to her. He had steered so sharply to miss her that his wheel had made a big rut in the muddy lane and he almost fell over.

She was so embarrassed. "I'm sorry," she said, "Is your bike O.K.?

It was an expensive bike, she could see that. Besides, everybody knew what a great bike racer Gavin Sousa was. Last year, he'd won the interschool cross-country championship for Eastern Ontario. His picture was in the newspaper.

She watched as he ran his hands over the wheel. "I guess it's O.K.," he said, looking up. Then he grinned sort of shy-like which was kind of neat because he was a senior and he was so cute and he asked, "I guess I should ask if you're O.K."

She nodded like an idiot.

"What are you doing out here?" he asked.

"Walking," she said. "I like it here, just me and the wind."

"Me too," he said. "I was just headed back."

They fell into step.

"You must be glad to get your bike out again," she said. He wasn't wearing his summer biking gear yet of course, just jeans and a green windbreaker, with a hoodie under it.

"Yeah, I like to ride," he said. "I like the freedom, getting away from it all, all the freakin crap."

She knew what he meant. "The world's a mess alright," she agreed.

When they got near the sign, he looked mad. "I guess you know that my dad's involved with the project."

She nodded.

"I'm not going to let it happen," he said. "I'm not going to see the Point destroyed."

"What can anyone do?" she asked.

He shrugged. "I have my ways."

"I worry about the birds," Livy said. "It makes me sick. They'll come back here next year like they usually do and they ll run into all those big whirling knives in the air."

"That s exactly right," he said eagerly. "Big whirling knives. You said it perfectly."

"It s the beginning of a poem I m writing," she said boldly. And she quoted,

Whirling knives that chop the air
Causing death and fright
Poisoning night.
Feathers falling from those that dare
Peril more than they can bear

"I haven t finished it yet."
"You should."
She felt warm all over. When they got to the main road, she thought he would get on his bike and ride off but he kept walking along beside her, pushing the bike. A soft snow had started falling, blurring the line between fields and sky. She felt she was floating in heaven. She wished they would never get to her house but there it was. Luckily her mom and the others would be in the lodge room at the back, not spying out the front window.

Gavin hadn t said anything for the last few minutes. Now he looked at her long and searchingly. "I feel I can trust you. Am I right?"

"You can trust me," she said.

"Will you help me defend the Point?"

She nodded.

"Good. You're my first recruit."

Livy had thought of the name for their work. *Shawks* for save the hawks.

Gavin had recruited Sean Barr and Kelly Beam. Livy would have preferred just to be working with Gavin but he said he would need extra muscle for some projects. Livy doubted that Sean Barr had joined the *Shawks* because he was much interested in saving birds. He just liked the adventure, the idea of prowling around in the dark and teeing everybody off. And scaring people, he got a kick out of that too.

And Kelly Beam was such an airhead, she had just joined because she wanted to be around Sean. Neither of them were dedicated like herself and Gavin. Dedicated and united in their passion to save the hawks of the Point. Yes, passion. She liked the sound of that.

Gavin was *so* good-looking. She loved the way his dark hair swung over his forehead when he talked, the way his eyes sparked when he talked of their mission. He even looked sort of like a hawk she thought. Dark and proud and deep-souled.

He had such great ideas too. All Sean wanted to do was to go out to the Point at night and make scary noises, like hoots and shrieks. They'd tried it a couple of times but it was pretty well wasted effort. It was always so windy that no one could hear. Then he'd thought of putting some dead birds around on the site, really dumb kid stuff. It was Gavin who had the great ideas. Like making the dummy and hanging it on the fence. Or this new plan to hang up a banner on the demonstration turbine to pay tribute to World Migrating Bird Day in May. How terrific was that? She thought how wonderful the banner would look up there. Mocking those ugly machines and the people who wanted to put them there.

Gavin now got Sean talking about how they would hang the banner. Sean liked that part. Gavin had brought a picture of the tower that showed an outside metal ladder, well not really a ladder, just a series of metal steps going up from the concrete pad about ten feet to to a control box.

"You can just shinny up there Sean with the rope and I'll bring the banner. Then the girls can run the rope around the tower and bring it back to us and we'll tie it up."

The girls would be lookouts too.

Gavin said the tower was sixteen feet around, like the girth of a huge concrete tree, a petrified redwood. Sean would carry the heavy coil of rope. The banner that Gavin would be carrying was heavy too. Livy had painted the banner, big red letters on a piece of painting tarpaulin. *Keep The Skies Free For Our Birds.*

"Good work, Livy," he said.

After the others left, they lay in the grass by the road for awhile longer. Or Livy did, her thoughts swirling in soft hazy drifts like the swooping flight of a redtail high above. Gavin sat with knees up, tearing bits of grass as he talked. He had such a beautiful face, like a Greek statue, only with living eyes. Eyes kindling with inspiration. She liked to watch the spark catch, warming his gaze as he painted his future. The battle to save the Point was just a start. After graduation, he was going to apply for a job with Greenpeace, on the Rainbow Warrior, challenging whaling ships. Or he might even become an eco-terrorist. She didn't dare tell him how she really felt, how she selfishly hoped that would never happen. She didn't want him to go away, ever. Not unless she could go with him.

Now he was talking about his father again, about how he was never going to take any of his old man's blood-stained money. How he would make his own way. She wished he would just relax and lie back in the honey-warm sun of this perfect afternoon and watch the redtail float on the currents of the wind. But he just kept on talking, when all she really wanted to know was what it would be like to feel his lips on hers.

Idly she played with some pebbles in the dirt, forming them into a little heart. In the middle she traced the letters, L & G. But Gavin didn't notice.

7

The wind bloweth where it listeth.

Ragusa shifted restlessly. "Crowd control," he said scathingly, looking at the cars that lined both sides of the muddy gravel road that led to the *WindSpear* site. "I guess watching a bunch of guys putting up a wind turbine makes a change from Saturday at the Bonville Mall or whatever else the locals do for excitement."

Saturday, a damp day at Hawk Nest Point. The sky was grey, the lake the colour and texture of mushroom soup. There had been a drizzling rain in the night and the field surface was muddy and chewed up by the tracks of countless heavy vehicles. Against the grim backdrop a huge industrial crane stood out like a monstrous gibbet awaiting its prey.

But the folks at *WindSpear* were ecstatic. It was the first day in a week that the wind had dropped enough to safely attempt to install the demonstration wind turbine. Because the irony was that the very winds that had attracted the developers to the Point in the first place at times made construction work so hazardous as to be virtually impossible. For most of the week now the giant lifting crane had stood unused in the empty field at a cost of a thousand dollars a day.

Yesterday though, crews had finally been able to erect the seventy ton tower and the nacelle, a housing which contained the drive shaft for the blades. The task of the day was to install and bolt on the three giant rotor blades, each of which was the size of a small airplane and weighed several tons. A wicked amount of weight to be swinging around in the air on the end of a chain. Any screw-ups could be disastrous, in a maneuvre where a misjudgement of only one or two millimetres could mean the difference between success or failure.

"You could be on Main Street, monitoring the burst water main," Pete said . "But hey, instead you're right here at the hub of the action."

"Yeah right." Kevin groaned.

But he stood up straight and flexed his shoulders as a couple of giggling high school senior girls wiggled past him to get a spot in line. Ragusa was third generation Italian, on his father's side. In great shape, fresh from basic cop training, he deplored his slightly chubby baby face. Pete guessed that was part of the reason Ragusa wanted to be a cop, he thought the uniform made him look tough.

Now he was rewarded as one of the girls looked back and said, "He's cute," to her giggling pals.

It looked as if most of the school population was out in force, gawking with the rest of the populace and for once forgetting to pretend to be bored or cool. Burt Sousa had put out a lot of hype about his demo turbine and it seemed his strategy had worked. There'd been a lengthy interview with Sousa in the *Island Record*, followed by a week of paid ads and posters warning of Monday's two hour shutdown of Main Street while three huge trucks delivered the sections of the turbine.

"Keep an eye out for anybody who looks like they're planning a stunt," Pete reminded Kevin.

"Yes, Dad. For sure." Kevin had started the 'dad' dig recently. It was mildly irritating but Pete could live with it.

Despite the weather, there was a holiday atmosphere about the crowd. People laughed and talked with each other and wrapped themselves in car blankets. Pete suspected there were a few nippy bottles in those car glove compartments. And there was nobody happier or more glad handing than Burt Sousa. The Mayor, sporting a size large navy blue *WindSpear* jacket and baseball cap, stood with Vern and the rest of the council members in a self-congratulatory clump to watch the show.

Chief Halstead spoke to Jim Keen, the *WindSpear* site foreman. "Looks like some tricky maneuvering with that crane. I hope these guys know what they're doing."

Keen barely nodded. His features were tense under his company hard hat. Obviously a lot was riding on successfully mounting this demo tower.

He'd briefed the cops on the set-up. Two technicians had already climbed the narrow eighty-foot inside ladder to the top of the turbine tower. Once there, they'd opened a hatch door which let them out onto a small railed platform at the end of the nacelle. Pete could see them up there now, in bright orange safety overalls. They were connected by a radio link to the workmen on the ground and waited with steering guide ropes to catch the blades and lock them into place. The company had placed sawhorse barriers in a wide berth around the action to keep the crowd safely back but people kept pressing closer with their cameras.

Halstead called to Pete. "Better get those people back further."

Curse the digital camera, Pete thought. These days everybody acted like a professional photographer, vying for the best shot.

The crane picked up a rotor blade and tried a trial swing towards the tower as the people in the crowd craned their necks and raised their cameras. There was a collective gasp as an errant gust of wind blew in from the lake and wobbled the huge blade. People moved back anxiously, pushing against their neighbours.

"You're going to have to move those barriers farther back," Halstead told Keen. "Or we're going to shut this down. These people shouldn't really be here at all."

"I said the same thing," Keen said angrily. "But it's Burt Sousa's show."

He hurried towards the barriers, calling in a couple of *WindSpear* workers as he went.

Stephanie shifted her wet feet and pulled up the collar of her jacket. Why am I here, she asked herself when I could be sitting cozily in my new wing chair at the retreat, reading the weekend papers. But of course you couldn't miss the big event. Besides, you're too damned nosy and you have to see who else is here.

Such as that handsome new police officer—unfortunately the exotically beautiful woman next to him must be his wife. Look at that scarf of hers, it's gorgeous.

And here was Pam Gillies, a long-time friend, owner of the wool shop, Knits and Knots.

Pam looked assessingly at the sky. "It doesn't look that great today either. I'm surprised that they're going ahead."

"Are you kidding?" Stephanie scowled. "Look at Sousa over there. If he had to wait even one more day, he'd be hauling those blades up single-handedly with a block and tackle. No mere force of nature is going to hold that jerk back."

Pam looked a bit embarassed. "Actually I feel a bit guilty talking about him that way Steph. I'm just so glad my son Brad has a job this year, I must admit I don't care who he's working for. Brad's going to have a big student loan to pay off for that engineering degree, you know. And the surveying training is right up his alley."

Stephanie patted her shoulder. "I understand, Pam. Anyway now that the damn project is going through and there's nothing we can do about it, I hope some Island residents do get some advantage out of it and some money out of Sousa's ill-gotten profits."

Still it was hard to watch the smug Mayor working the crowd this morning. Radiating benevolence and bonhomie as he smiled and waved, his smoothly coifed wife Elena at his side. A biggish blonde in her forties, of the type once called handsome, she was a match physically for Sousa. Steph remembered Elena as an athletic babe in highschool (volleyball team) and she still wasn't in bad shape. She'd always had a perpetually sulky look though that marred even her youthful features. On her fortyish face, the lines had become permanent brackets.

Now her frozen little smile barely concealed her boredom. She patted her hair constantly, trying to protect the expensive styling job from the chilly gusts of wind.

"I can't believe she's stayed with that philanderer all these years," Pam said.

Steph smiled sourly. "I'm always surprised that more than one woman in this world would put up with the jerk."

"A lot more than one, by all accounts," Pam said.

"Well Elena's not likely to leave now that he's about to become a millionaire from this project."

"That's true enough. And they have the kids too. That Gavin is a good-looking boy. Must come from Elena's side of the family."

"I suppose he's a jock-jerk in training, though," Steph said. "Like his old man."

Pam nodded. "Hard not to be."

"Well thank goodness he isn't Livy's type."

"Little Livy has a type already?"

"Oh you know what I mean, some sensitive, poetry loving type. I'm guessing but she's mooning after somebody. I recognize the signs."

"Ah, these kids. They do grow up."

Pam scanned the crowd. "I wonder if Andy Poltz is here. I don't see him."

"He probably has a pretty good view from his farm. More view than he wants I guess."

"Well it's all pretty exciting," Pam said dryly. "For a bunch of country hicks like us, anyway. I'm told there's already a 'Wind Tower Burger' on the menu of the the Island Diner. And the county website is advertising the unique experience of "Golfing Under the Turbines.""

Steph laughed, a brittle sound. "Might as well get what we can out of the darned things. They're supposed to be putting up six more turbines this month. Lots of jolly jigowatts for all."

The crane operator seemed back in control. The huge blade swung out and up, the men in the tower pulled on their guiding ropes and steered the blade safely towards the nacelle. A cheer went up from the crowd, the clouds cleared of a sudden and the sun shone through as a phalanx of cameras filmed the event.

Even Kevin was impressed. "Wow that's one big sucker of a machine."

Pete had a sudden unpleasant image of the Point, transformed into a forest of the hundred feet high spinning egg-beaters he'd seen in Europe. It did seem kind of a desecration. A wind *factory* as Miranda Paris had put it—

Maybe others were feeling something similar when faced with the reality. After the excitement, a kind of hushed awe had set in over the crowd.

The workers started to repeat the manoeuver with the second blade. People poured more coffee, or whatever else they had in their thermoses, to fill in the waiting time. Then of a sudden the mood changed again, to a surprised roar of outraged shouts, as people scattered in all directions.

"What the hell?" Kevin stared.

Pete saw a blue pick-up truck come bursting through a break in the line of parked cars. The driver banged angrily on his horn as he crashed noisily over a couple of sawhorses and made a bee-line towards the crane operator's cab. Pete caught a glimpse of a head of shaggy white hair beneath a faded baseball cap.

"It's that farmer Poltz! What the hell is he up to?"

It was obvious that the crane operator was at Poltz's mercy. The huge unwieldy machine was going nowhere, especially with a ton of wind blade dangling from its chain.

And god knows where that blade would end up if set loose. There were a hundred spectators on the site.

The two policemen started to run. "You go help the crane guy," Pete yelled to Kevin, as he sprinted for the truck himself. He was dimly aware in his peripheral vision of shouts from the horrified on-lookers.

The truck was making great bouncing leaps over the rutted muddy surface of the ground. He could see Poltz's grizzled old face through the windshield and he didn't look as if he was going to stop, not for a cop, not for anybody. It didn't seem advisable to hold up his hand and say HALT. He was just about to dive out of the way when the truck made a great lurching dip into an oversize rut. Poltz ground the gears till the pick-up roared like a baffled minotaur but the jaunt was definitely over.

Pete took a quick look back to where Kevin stood with the white-faced, shaken crane operator. Then heart pounding with adrenalin and rage, he yanked open the door of the pick-up.

He was so angry he wondered if he could trust himself not to tear Poltz apart with his bare hands. It looked as if he was going to have some competition though, as Sousa came thundering up to join the party. The bulky Mayor moved surprisingly quickly, much as he might have three decades ago on the football field. Angry as a bear who'd had his honey stash stolen from him, he barrelled past Pete and made about to drag the older man out barehanded.

Poltz lurched out under his own steam though and with an angry roar of his own, launched himself at Sousa. For a second, maybe just a millisecond, Pete paused. Why not leave them to it? Let them go at it. Then sighing, he made a grab for Poltz.

"Come on, guys. Break it up."

In the end, it took both Kevin and himself to pull the fighters apart.

Sousa was gasping, he looked like a volcano about to pop. But he sputtered out the words. "Arrest the bastard! Throw the book at him. He's crazy, lock him up!"

As Kevin manhandled Poltz off to the cruiser, Pete, waving his arms like a lion tamer, warded Sousa away. Step by step he forced Sousa back.

"We've got Poltz, we're taking him to the station. It's over."

"That's what you think!"

"Come on, Mr. Sousa," Pete indicated the watching crowd. "You've got a turbine to haul up."

With an effort, the Mayor regained control of himself. He yanked up his windbreaker collar, directed one last virulent scowl at Pete and barreled off to rejoin his visibly embarrassed wife. Elena Sousa looked as if she wanted to sink into the muddy ground.

Pete thought that Jim Keen looked pretty happy though, at his boss's discomfiture. He didn't bother to hide his triumphant grin.

The other turbine blades were hauled up without incident. The motor wouldn't actually be set in motion for another week but the tower stood firmly planted and triumphant against the sky. Despite his earlier concerns, Pete found it was hard not to be impressed by the sheer scope of mankind's inventiveness and engineering accomplishments. The daring and yes the dreaming. To harness the wind, the power of the sun. For once, was it possible that mankind's efforts would actually be a good move for the planet? He hoped so.

The day had turned chilly again and the crowd was dispersing. Pete watched them leave, relieved that the difficult and dangerous task was over. Sousa had cheered up at the applause from the crowd, and seemed pleased enough with the day's result. His wife Elena perhaps not so much. Her gaze was not exactly brimming with love. She stood fastidiously apart from her husband, her face in the shadow of the tower which now lay like an enormous dark sword across the newly greening trees.

The amateur video CKAS television ran of the HawksNest Point drama was a bit jumpy but contained all the pertinent details.

Ali found the footage of the Sousa/Poltz fistfight particularly entertaining.

"My hero, facing down a rampaging pick-up truck," she saluted her husband with a drumstick of take-out chicken. "Rfff, you looked pretty hunky doing your superhero bit."

"Kevin helped too," he allowed modestly.

"What's going to happen to Andy Poltz?" she asked in a more serious tone. "He could have killed someone."

Pete nodded. "He's out on bail. The hearing will be in two weeks. He hasn't done his cause any good either. I doubt anybody will have much sympathy for him or his cows now. The other protestors are probably furious with him."

She frowned, pushing aside the gluey gob of coldslaw on her paper plate. "It's awful the tension building around these wind turbines. Even as a newcomer to the area, I can see they might be a really bad idea."

Pete looked in the direction of the driveway. "Our prickly neighbour certainly thinks so."

Ali nodded. "I noticed her light on last night when I got up to go to the bathroom. I think she stays up quite late."

"Old people do," Pete said. "My grandmother did."

Ali was surprised, Pete so rarely mentioned his family. But he didn't elaborate.

"Have you noticed her chickens?" she asked.

"I waded through them the other day," he said wryly. "Don't you remember?"

"They're quite pretty," she said. "And the chicks are so cute. My grandmother in Turkey raised chickens. I remember visiting her, everybody had chickens in Turkey." She paused. "I was thinking of asking Miranda for advice on starting a flock."

She laughed at the expression on his face. "And you needn't look so horrified."

"I'm not horrified, just practical." He rattled the carton of wings and legs from their supper. "Chickens are for eating, let somebody else do the work of raising them, I say. And killing them," he added. "I can't see you doing that."

Though he found it easy enough to picture Miranda Paris twisting a chicken neck.

"I'd just keep them for the eggs," Ali said.

He started picking up their plates, "I wouldn't start counting your chickens before they're hatched or your eggs before they're laid. I can't see Miz Paris warming up to us any time soon."

Ali looked across the road where Miranda's porch light gave a false welcome in the dusk. She tsked impatiently. "We should be friends! Eileen Patrick told me that Miranda was a teacher all her life. And in some really interesting places. First Africa, then for twenty years in the Arctic, at Baffin Inlet. Eileen said that she has some beautiful pieces of Innuit sculpture and some paintings."

"Really?" Pete had to admit he was surprised. "So what's with the tough old country bird routine?"

"Eileen said she was raised right on that farm. She never married because she wanted to teach. I guess it was harder then, women had to make a choice between a profession and a family. She only came back to the Island about eight years ago."

"So why did she come back?" Pete asked.

"She got terribly sick, pneumonia, then pleurisy. She took so long admitting she was sick, that she almost died and had to be flown out as an emergency case in a blizzard."

Pete glanced across the road. "That sounds more like our Miranda."

"When she came out of the hospital, her doctors said her lungs were permanently scarred and that she couldn't spend another winter up there in such frigid temperatures."

"That's too bad. Must have been quite a blow for her."

"Yes but Eileen said she was sixty-eight at the time, anyone else would have happily taken retirement long before that. The children at the school where she'd been teaching sent her a thank-you album and apparently she has an adequate pension."

"Wow, you sure got the scoop," Pete said sarcastically. "Makes you wonder who's gathering the information for our biography?"

Ali laughed, unfazed. She tossed him a kiss. "Let's just try to make it as spicy as possible."

It was dark outside now, he could see the thin glow of Miranda's light. The dog was woofing at something. "So the world traveller is back in the family home?"

Ali nodded. "Her brother had died and left the family farmhouse—he never married either. He'd always rented out the fields for Andy to grow his feed and Miranda continued the arrangement. Eileen said Andy used to drive her into town until she got well enough to drive herself again."

"You mean Andy down the road?" Pete found it hard to picture the man of the Hawks Point rampage, on such a prosaic errand as driving Miranda into town to a medical appointment or to pick up groceries. On the other hand, it was almost as difficult to imagine Miranda accepting the help.

"I wonder what they'd talk about?" he marvelled. "I can't picture either of them saying much."

"Eileen was surprised when I told her how unfriendly Miranda has been. She says nobody would ever have called her the sociable type but that she's never known her to be actually rude to strangers before now. She thinks that Miranda is having a hard time with getting older. She hates being beholden and dependent on other people. Eileen says there is an active seniors organization in town but Miranda never attends any of the events."

"So we should leave her alone too and respect her privacy. No chicken raising seminars," he teased.

"That's not what I meant!" Ali tossed a sofa cushion at him. "Men!"

He carried out the garbage and stood for a moment under the dazzling star-studded country sky. He found himself a bit humbled by the image of Andy Poltz as a Good Samaritan. A reminder of the unseen weaving of connections that underlay human relationships. A reminder never to be too quick to categorize or judge.

Ali pulled the couch snuggli up around her shoulders. "Umm," she said getting cozy. "My students tire me out so much I think I could fall aseep right here. Do you think Mayor Sousa sends himself to sleep with visions of busily whirling turbines in his head?"

She closed her eyes, let drowsiness begin to drift in. Pete envied her ability to fall asleep at will. She would gladly have shared her sleep with him. She wished she could wrap it up like a gift. *Think of this she wanted to say*, I am giving you a parcel, a gift of a night's sleep. Like a gentle fog softening the busy day thoughts till they became a pleasant colourful blur . . . her young students singing . . . . spring purple dogwood in the roadside ditches . . . . Miranda's chickens, brilliantly coloured and flapping upwards like the gay spirits of a Chagal painting in a cobalt blue evening sky . . . . And one of Andy Poltz's long-horned shaggy cows, jumping over the moon.

*   *   *

"Well that's just dandy," Stephanie Bind said glumly. "That's the kind of great publicity we need to attract clients to the retreat. Berserk farmer tries to run down crane operator. I've lost any sympathy for Andy Poltz, I can tell you. He's crossed the line now."

"I don't think he's so crazy," Livy said. "What's crazy is to build wind towers on Hawks Nest Point. Do you know that in California thousands of hawks die every year when they try to get past the wind towers in the Altamont Pass. Do you want to see that kind of massacre at our own Hawks Nest Point when they come back in the fall to cross the lake?"

Steph was taken aback by the girl's sudden vehemence. They'd been having a fairly decent time for once. Livy had even eaten supper with her. Just frozen fries and burgers—a tofu one for Livy of course. The food wasn't special but the occasion felt like it.

"Of course I wouldn't like to see that," she said cautiously.

"But that's what will happen," Livy said. "I've seen the information."

"There's all kinds of information out there, honey. Sometimes it's difficult to know what's right or wrong and this is a tough one. People need energy to live."

"I know it's wrong to kill birds." Livy said stubbornly

Steph sighed. "Part of the process of entering the adult world is learning what's possible."

"That's pretty depressing mother. You've just told me that I should get used to ignoring what's right."

Steph groaned with exasperation. "You know that's not what I meant. I'm talking about compromise, that's the way to get along in this world. Good grief Livy, even the Greenpeace people settle for compromise solutions sometimes."

"So what's the compromise here?" Livy asked heatedly. "I don't see Mr. Sousa and the wind turbine people giving up anything."

"Livy darling, I know that the world seems unfair sometimes . . . ."

"Most of the time, you mean."

"Maybe you're right but no matter how strongly you feel about this dear, I hope you don't approve of vandalism of private property."

"I guess it depends on your definition of ownership, mom. Who owns land? Who owns lakes? Now people want to own the wind."

A good exit line Steph had to acknowledge, as Livy stomped up the stairs to her room, no doubt to spend the evening with that darn I-pod plugged in her ear.

Steph sighed and turned off the television. She hated all the tension and fighting in the community. She hated the tension and fighting at home. It had been a long and fractious day and the view from her marvellous new (and expensive) patio window was no comfort. The slim tower with its three curved petals looked almost elegant from this distance. Like a poisoned flower. Harbinger of the invasion to come.

*   *   *

Miranda Paris had lived without television for years at the Inlet. Her days were spent teaching and in the evenings there was always something going on at the community hall. There wasn't much television reception available anyway, just a weak signal from the CBC. When she moved back south, she hadn't planned to buy a tv but her brother had left a set in the house. Her first winter back, she had ignored the dark, glassy-faced box till January, then in an access of miserable boredom had got it connected up. Of course it was no answer to her unhappiness and she soon got fed up with all offerings except the public access channels and the news. Often even these programs only provided her with an outlet for crabby comments to Emily Dickinson her dog, a diversion of sorts. She was starting to drink two glasses of wine at night she noticed, not a good sign.

Tonight she watched the report on Andy Poltz with amazement. She had already heard of the drama from the man who delivered her groceries but the television footage was quite shocking. The fool! He could have killed people. This wasn't likely to help the cause much, would set it back more likely. And what of the turbine? It still went up. He had accomplished nothing.

There were others though. She thought of an encounter earlier in the week when Emily had started barking at some passers-by on the road. A boy and a girl on bicycles, coming back from the Point. The girl was Livy Bind, her great-niece. Miranda had grabbed the dog but stayed at the gate thinking that Livy might want eggs. Stephanie occasionally bought a fresh dozen for the Retreat, to wow the city clients as she put it.

Miranda thought Livy an odd girl certainly, not pretty pretty but attractive, what they used to call 'fey'. A wood nymph. Though she doubted nymphs ever scowled so much, at least the poets never mentioned it. Theirs was not a strong connection. Miranda had been away through Livy's growing years and the girl was one of the darker type of teens. She looked on approvingly though as Livy carefully stopped to pet the dog when Emily ran excitedly up to the bicycle. The boy stopped too, but reluctantly.

No smile was forthcoming from Livy, but she did say Hello Miranda and continued making a fuss over Emily. The girl seemed to like creatures, more than people maybe. A trait she and Miranda had in common, so maybe there was a family connection after all. Neither of the young people had made any attempt to introduce the boy who just stood with a bored expression on his face. Miranda recognized him though, Gavin Sousa. The apple never fell far from the tree, and it would be no surprise to her that Gavin Sousa was turning out to be as unpleasant and rude as his father. She could warn Livy but what was the point? The young never listened.

But she had asked Livy politely whether she had seen any trilliums flowering yet up at the Point.

The girl had straightened up abruptly. "I don't know, I haven't been up the Point for ages."

She was obviously not telling the truth but Miranda didn't argue, just held Emily back and watched as the pair cycled away. They'd been up to something, she wouldn't be surprised if they had something to do with those pranks at the Point. She shrugged. She wasn't going to tell. The old folks weren't being very successful at protecting the Point and it was the young people who were going to have to live with the results. Good luck to them.

Miranda patted Emily's silky head. No wonder she preferred her animal friends these days. No wonder she needed that second glass of wine.

Every year she became less enchanted with the human race and its rampaging sprawl over the planet. Even in the beautiful once remote North she'd watched the approaching hordes. Sending down their probes and drills, seeking oil under the ice.

"Someone should stop us," she said to Emily.

Maybe Andy wasn't so crazy after all. This was war after all, a war against the natural world. She poured her third glass of wine.

Vern Byers stopped by the cruiser as Halstead was leaving the post office. The two men talked for a moment about the weather (rain that afternoon) but Vern didn't waste much time getting around to the real point of the conversation.

"Jeez Bud, what was that mess at the Point on Saturday? And now I hear Andy Poltz is out on bail. The Council members are concerned, they say that man is so crazy he's likely to try to blow the tower up. Burt says if we can't guarantee police protection, the foreign owners willl just pull up stakes and move the whole project somewhere else."

"We've obtained a restraining order," Halstead said, waving the brown envelope. "Andy knows that he's not allowed anywhere near the place or he'll go directly to jail."

"He'd better not then," Vern said direly. "This is not the way we like to make the six-o'clock news, Bud. Not a desirable situation at all."

Vern was a good fellow, Halstead thought. But he owned a gas station. He didn't know squat about policing. Neither did that group of sheep farmers and small businessmen who sat on Council. And not one of them had the balls to stand up to Burt Sousa, the wimps. He backed up the cruiser with a squeal of tires, startling a couple of old biddies waiting at the corner. A small satisfaction in a frustrating week.

He stopped by the Bitner's bungalow on the way to the station. Alice opened the door with a warm smile. She had known Halstead's wife Kathleen and after her death had made a point of asking Halstead to dinner a couple of nights a week.

"Fred's in the garage," she said. "He'll be glad to see you."

His former second in command was sorting through his tackle box. Fred looked good, well on the road to recovery from his by-pass surgery, though he'd put on some extra weight through the months of reduced activity. He'd come a long way since that day last December when he'd collapsed on the station parking lot, clutching his chest in agony.

"Getting ready for the season?" Halstead grinned.

"Just sorting through the box," Bimmers said. "See what I want to pack."

"You're going on a trip?"

"Yep, a big trip. We're selling the house, going to take the RV on a swing through the western U.S. Visit the kids in California."

"You're kidding."

"No we're going." Alice had come into the garage, hooked her arm through her husband's. "We figure we've had our warning. We want to go before Fred falls completely apart," she joked.

"So you're leaving the detachment? Taking early retirement?"

Fred nodded apologetically. "I was going to come in and talk to you soon."

"That would have been nice." Halstead couldn't hide his surprise. He was kind of shocked really.

Fred looked even more sorry. "I figured it was good timing, Bud, what with the OPP likely coming in and all. They wouldn't want me with my patched-up ticker. Not as a patrolman anyways."

"Who said the OPP was coming in?"

Alice attempted to backpedal. "You know what Fred means. If they ever do. Someday. Sometime."

"Yeah," Fred said. "That's what I meant." His expression brightened. "We'll e-mail you when we get to California. You could come and visit us.".

"Yeah. I could do that."

He hung around for a few more minutes but his heart wasn't in it.

The familiar strip of Main Street went past in a blur. He knew he was over-reacting. A fellow cop was retiring, not a big deal. But good friends were leaving town, definitely a big deal. A lot of changes and they were all happening at once.

When he was a kid, the police station had been in a house on Main Street and the chief and his wife lived upstairs. When he came back to town ten years ago, the detachment had moved to its current location in the bunker. Now Vern and the others wanted to close up shop altogether. Times were changing even on Middle Island. Maybe he was out of step even to care.

A part of him almost envied Fred for being out of it all. He sighed as he came up to the station, feeling the weight, the responsibility. Once upon a time he had taken that responsibility on with pride but that was ten years ago. He knew that Jane was worried about her job. She didn't say so, in fact always welcomed him with her usual good cheer but he knew it was on her mind. The OPP organization had a central dispatching department, they wouldn't need her.

He got out of the cruiser, his steps feeling as heavy as the empty stone flower tubs. The unexpected smell of cinnamon hit his nose as he came into the station, lending an exotic fillip to the familiar site of Jane's territory of computer desk, phones, the dispatcher line.

"Hey Bud, you're just in time," she called from the coffee maker. "I'm trying a new type of coffee this morning. It's called 'Cinammon Twister'.

Jakes and Parks were already holding mugs. The mugs all bore different coloured logos of traffic signs. Jane was a sucker for novelty items from the dollar store.

"It's good," Jakes complimented her. "I drank a lot of different coffees in Afghanistan. You might like to try adding cardoman some time."

Jane was interested in the suggestion. "Where would I get that?" she asked, as Kevin took a swig and made a face. Halstead took his mug gingerly. He wondered if he could get it into his office before Jane noticed whether he actually tasted the stuff or not.

"You could try the Bonville Metro store," Pete told Jane. "They probably have cardoman."

Kevin looked with resignation at Jane, anticipating the daily assignment list. "What have you got for me this morning? More garbage dumped on the causeway? I knew I should have stayed home this morning and studied for my forensics exam."

Jane grinned. "I've got something real exciting for you here. Another smash and grab robbery at the Island Grill. This time the perpetrators took a couple of pounds of bacon along with the smokes."

Halstead carried his cup (sporting the yellowYIELD sign) into his office. He settled into his chair, form-fitted for aging backs. Looked around at the familiar walls, maybe too familiar. He had left the Island once for five years in the city but Kathleen hadn't been happy there. He'd come back for her and they'd raised a daughter, had a generally happy life. Maybe he should have left again after Kathleen died and not stayed on to be assaulted with memories around every corner.

At first he had dreaded going home to the empty house, then what was worse he'd got used to it. He'd lost the energy or interest to make a move. He ate his weekday meals at the Island Grill, Sunday night dinners at the Legion. On summer weekends he and Fred went out on the boat to fish. Time passed. Four entire years.

Now Fred was leaving. Was he going to slip down the same slide into retirement? Fred and Alice had each other and their plans but what the hell would he do all the time? Visit his daughter and her husband and the grandchildren? They'd soon get tired of grandpa hanging around. He could only fish for so many hours a day and not even that for six months of the year. So, what did people do without work?

He couldn't think of one darn thing he'd like to do.

He was all used up. Maybe young Ragusa was right. Maybe there was no need for the station on the Island any more either. He'd send Jakes and Kevin out to serve the restraining order. At least with Andy Poltz effectively wrapped up, things should be quiet out at the Point from now on.

And maybe Burt Sousa would get off his back for awhile.

10

Ali looked critically around the gymnasium walls. From the open windows she could hear the children playing at outdoor recess under the newly budding old maple in the yard. After a year teaching in dusty arid Afghanistan she felt she could never get her fill of lush green vegetation again. She often felt a pang that her Afghani students couldn't share her luck.

"How does that look?" she asked Eileen Patrick, the school principal. Ali and young Livy Bind, her co-op student helper from the high school, had been working all morning to mount the kids' paintings to decorate the gym. Now they formed a freize above the dangling climbing ropes and other gym equipment.

Principal Patrick's forehead creased nervously. "I always find Parent/Teacher nights a bit tough." Her worry furrow deepened, "I'm not sure the new wind farm was a good theme for the project."

Most of the crayoned pictures from the younger classes were fairly typical. Against a flat horizontal blue line, representing the lake, rose four to six crudely drawn stick-like towers, each topped with a cluster of blades. Ali thought they looked like ugly flowers. But there were some more imaginative pictures from the upper level grades. One grade five student had drawn a night view of a wind tower where the rotor blades stood out like three dark petals backlit by a bright disk of moon. And then there was the one Livy was pinning up now. A grade six student had cleverly dotted her tower with a shower of bright orange sparks to illustrate the electricity it would produce. At its base, squirrels and rabbits bounded away in terror.

Eileen stopped before the painting and looked up the ladder at Livy. "This one for instance," she said dubiously.

"It's excellent work," Ali said. "Colourful and dramatic."

"Oh yes of course, it's just rather unsettling . . . ." Eileen searched for a word. "Provocative really, I'm sure there will be some *comments.*"

Ah yes, comments. School principals dreaded comments.

Actually Ali had to admit that the total effect of the pictures was a bit disturbing. Childish as the artwork was, the display did give a sense of what all those wind towers might look like when they were actually built and bestriding the entire south shore of the island, like eerie one-legged giant sentries.

Eileen sighed resignedly. "I guess there's nothing to do about it now. We can't leave anybody out. Then there will just be more comments."

Livy came down the ladder, picked up the red first prize ribbon and held it up towards the picture with the bright orange sparks and the fleeing wildlife.

"I like this one," she said.

"You can't pick who wins, Livy", protested a little pony-tailed girl in a pink sweatshirt. "You're not a judge."

"Sure I can," Livy said, raising her arms above her head. "I'm the boss. And I'm going to pin this ribbon right on you." Then she started to chase the kids around to the accompaniment of much delighted squealing.

Ali got a kick out of watching the girl. In her dark clothing and Goth pale make-up, she hardly looked like the usual enthusiastic co-op student type. When dealing with Ali and other adults she presented an abstracted remoteness that was close to rudeness. But most of the little kids on the island seemed to know her and were used to her pale face and dyed black locks. And unlike other high school students who slouched through their co-op duties because they needed the credit to graduate, Livy worked hard and enthusiastically with the kids on their art projects. It had been her suggestion that the kids create pictures of the wind turbine project.

But when Ali asked Livy if she had been out at the *WindSpear* site to watch the installing of the turbine, there was that reserve again. Her face closed up, the brief liveliness gone. She started to sullenly fold up the ladder.

Ali knelt to help a little boy do up his sneaker. It was much easier to figure out the little kids. Such cuties. She felt a familiar sensation, the desire to have chidren of her own. Broodiness, her grandmother would have described it. She was ready, but Pete had his doubts.

"With our family backgrounds as an example?" he'd say wonderingly.

He had a point.

Her relationship with Nuran, her mother was mainly by e-mail. She'd received one only this morning, in fact, inviting her to Nuran's new book launching. It wasn't even a personal e-mail, but a press release from her literary agent.

When she was younger, she would have cried but she'd got tougher over the years. Through necessity.

"When is the launching?" Pete asked.

"In two days. In Vancouver!" Two thousand miles across the country. "This book is called *Women Kind.*"

She felt the old rankling, like a scraping along her spine. Nuran never paid any attention or knew anything about her daughter's life. That she had a job, students to teach, that she had responsibilities. Of course the message was short notice deliberately. Nuran didn't need a twenty-eight year old, married daughter showing up at her book launch. It would upset all her theories and her readers too. Of Turkish heritage and still strikingly beautiful in her fifites, Nuran lead a determinedly and ideologically single life.

She'd even managed to avoid attending Pete and Ali's wedding. Nuran would have thought nothing of flying into war-torn terrain for a wedding or any other event, had done it many times before to research her books. Unfortunately she had been doing just that in Somali, or as close to it as she could get.

She'd left a cell-phone message though and said to keep in touch.

Eventually Nuran had met Pete when they'd returned to Canada four months later. Had insisted on taking them out for dinner. Lots of expensive, pretty food and little real opportunity to talk, just the way Nuran liked things.

And maybe it was just as well. For as Nuran had whispered *sotto voce* when Pete left for the car, 'Of course he's nice-looking darling, I would expect that. I'm just so horribly disappointed that you've got married at all. Haven't you been reading my books? I've sent you signed copies of all of them."

Nuran herself had been married briefly to Ali's father, a pleasant American academic type she'd met at university. He'd been no match for Nuran's steam-rolling verve and had faded fairly quickly out of their lives. From the age of thirteen on, Ali had spent her school terms in boarding school and her summers at a language camp in Switzerland. Nuran's visits, usually unscheduled, were intense and exciting and always left a vacuum. But overall, Ali wasn't lonely, she was used to it. The school was good, and she made good friends.

Of course Ali had read Nuran's books, had encountered them in her sociology class as well. They were important documents about the plight of women in the middle eastern world. A group of women in Africa had given Nuran their honorary name for the word 'mother'.

Sometimes she wondered if her mother knew the word in any language for 'daughter'.

Pete's family seemed practically non-existent. He'd released only the barest details. Mother dead when the kids were teens. Ditto only brother, also had been a soldier, killed by a landmine in Bosnia. That left the old man, the only way Pete ever referred to his father and that only rarely. Despite all Ali's sweet cajoling, Pete had never asked her to meet the man, now a retired government employee who lived four provinces away.

"You wouldn't get along. He doesn't get along with anybody."

Against Pete's wishes, she'd secretly searched out an address (next of kin in his army paybook) and sent a notice and picture of their wedding performed at the army chapel in Kandahar. She wore a red robe and carried flowers from her students. She'd never got a reply.

Nuran had never wanted to have children and had made certain she gave birth to only one. So, with no encouragement, in fact nothing but discouragement from either side of the family, why was Ali thinking baby? It certainly seemed that doting grandparents would be in short supply. So Pete was doubtful to say the least, about having kids.

"You and I have seen the nightmare, Ali. We've seen schoolhouses turned into battlegrounds. We've seen what happens when the structure falls apart. When nothing's solid anymore, nothing's safe. How can you be so sure life will be good for the kid? We can promise nothing, it goes against all sense."

She smiled, her mouth a smooth curve and she stroked his cheek. "It's not my mind that wants to have a baby."

$*$ $*$ $*$

She smiled now and tried to spread the warmth to the pale, tense girl banging the ladder awkwardly back into the cupboard.

"Thanks so much for your help, Livy."

"I've got a class," Livy said. "I've got to go."

The girl hurried out, the breeze from her exit rustling the pictures next to the door. The painted turbines seemed to move eerily on the paper.

"Oh dear," Eileen sighed again. "I really wish we had chosen our visit to the museum as the subject for the art display."

"It will be fine," Ali soothed. "Just lay in lots of cookies."

11

Brad Gillies opened the tower hatch and looked triumphantly out over a silvered kingdom. From a hundred feet up, the view was exhilerating, the rocky spear of the Point lying like the sword Excalibur on the moonlit water. Some of that light in the distance could be from New York City, he bet. He laughed and spread out his arms in imitation of the great quiescent, white blades gleaming in the night.

If he got out on the platform, he could probably touch them. But he wasn't sure about climbing out the hatch. Coming up the ladder inside the turbine tower hadn't been as easy as he thought. The metal rungs were hard and sort of slippery even under his safety boots. It was kind of like being in a Star Trek movie or 2001 that movie about living in a spaceship. Where the guy was climbing up a narrow metal tube forever, towards a lid at the top. It was a good thing he didn't have claustrophobia. He'd almost slipped a couple of times too.

But here he was, and it felt like he was at the top of the world.

He wished his girlfriend Leanne could be here with him. Of course she'd never come and he shouldn't even be here himself, he'd be in big trouble if the boss found out. He was just supposed to make a routine security check of the access door at nine before he went home but tonight he couldn't resist coming up to have a look from the top.

He looked happily around his kingdom. He was happy altogether. This was such a great job, he couldn't believe his luck. He never thought he'd be lucky enough to find a summer job right here at home, on the island. And the pay was good too, he wouldn't have to take out a loan this year for his third year of university.

He was grateful for the opportunity, he wanted to do a good job and give his very best effort. Then maybe someday he'd get a permanent job here on the Island and he could marry Leanne.

Yep, she was the one, he was sure. Maybe she didn't understand much about how he wanted to be a surveyor and maybe she didn't want to listen to the the interesting stuff he tried to tell her, about what he'd found out on the site last week but she was so sweet and sexy, it didn't matter.

At the thought of her, he pulled his cellphone out of his jacket pocket. It wouldn't work inside the metal tower but it might out here. She'd be amazed when she found out where he was calling from. He'd send a picture and give her a scare. She'd probably warn him to watch out for the ghosts and all those other dumb stories about spooky noises at the Point. He smiled indulgently thinking of her soft luscious mouth that always tasted of strawberry lip gloss.

*   *   *

"Someone's up there," Kelly gasped.

They were all breathing heavily from the low scrambling run across the rough, rutted ground and the boys were staggering under the weight of their packs. The banner in Gavin's pack even folded up, was heavy and unwieldy. Sean was carrying some tools and the heavy coil of climbing rope.

"Someone's up where?" Sean snarled. "How are we going to do this thing if you keep jumping at every g.d. jackrabbit."

"Up there. In the tower." Kelly pointed and they all craned their necks to look. Eighty feet up there was a pale glowing square, making the turbine tower into a lighthouse in the sea of night.

Sean looked at Gavin, his eyes like sparks in his ski mask. "Who the heck is that?" he hissed.

Gavin yanked off his own mask, his skin pale and waxen in the dark. He was whispering too. "Shit," he spat out. "There's not supposed to be anybody there yet."

Sean threw down his bundle, the heavy coil of rope thudding to the ground. "So now what chief? I thought you had this all figured out."

Gavin stared up at the light. "We go ahead," he said. "It's even better this way, it will make them look like real dopes if we hang this banner up right under their noses."

Sometimes Livy found it kind of chilling the way Gavin said things about his father. She didn't like the creep either, but he wasn't her father.

"Come on, Sean. Up the goddamned ladder. Let's get *going.*"

"Whoever's up there will hear us."

"No they won't. It's too far away."

Still, they worked quietly, like thieves in the night Livy thought. And for once, the winds on the Point were quiet, wouldn't you know it. Tonight of all nights. Luckily there was the moon, almost full, to see by. Even so, the guys were having a heck of a time trying to tape the rope up. Once it fell right across Gavin's face and he almost lost his balance on the steps. But he didn't yell or swear or anything. He managed to keep quiet.

Finally, after what seemed ages, Sean tossed the rope down to her and Kelly. They picked it up and started dragging it around the tower. It flopped awkwardly along behind them like a big dead python. Livy didn't know how they were ever going to get the end back up to Sean. She was afraid to look up to the top of the tower. Any moment she thought, somebody's going to look down and see us.

That's when Sean dropped the bag of tools.

The connection was patchy, even though he leaned out as far as he could towards the platform. Leanne's voice was fuzzy, and her words were all broken up. But it was nice to talk to her anyway. Then he heard the sounds below. He couldn't see anything though, not from this far up.

"Got to go Leanne," he said. *"I hear a noise somewhere down at the bottom of the tower."*

She said something all muddled. He heard the word *ghost* though and grinned.

"It's probably just a loose cable or something flapping around in the wind," he said. *"But I gotta go check. I'll call you later when I get home."*

"O.K. but be careful . . . ." If she said anything else, he didn't hear it, he had already hung up.

They were suddenly bathed in light. The person in the tower had turned on some sort of spotlight.

"Shit!" Sean swore He started down the ladder steps.

"Come on, Gavin. We gotta go!"

Gavin didn't move. Livy could see that he looked really teed.

"Come on Gav. We don't want to get caught." Sean caught his jacket and yanked.

"O.K. O.K." Gavin said tersely. "But be sure to pick up everything. We can't leave the banner like this. It'll look dumb, they'll know we failed. We'll have to try some other time."

He started grabbing up the rope.

It was weird, knowing that the guy in the tower was on his way down, probably even shouting too but they couldn't hear or see anything. The tower just stood blank and silent as ever. It was as if a vengeful ghost was approaching, coming nearer every minute.

One hundred and thirty steps. He was coming down a lot faster than he'd gone up.

Maybe he should stop and have a listen though before he opened the door. It would be pretty dumb to go charging out there into God knows what. In case it wasn't just a cable banging in the wind. Of course that ghost stuff was crap but maybe the real vandals had come back.

Or maybe it would be better to just roar out the door. This big old flashlight could give a good whack to anybody, ghost or not.

The girls hurried to pick up the fallen tools. Sean had crammed most of the rope into his backpack and wore the last few coils around his arm. He and Kelly took off back toward Mr. Poltz's fence. It was the closest way out.

Gavin was still wrestling with the banner.

"Run!" he hissed at Livy.

She wanted to stay with him but he looked as if he would hit her if she didn't go.

"We have to split up, then he'll chase me. I can run faster. Just go!"

But there was no time. She heard the tower door fling open, saw a sudden burst of light spill like yellow oil out onto the white concrete pan.

Instinctively she crouched at the edge of the light, hunching herself around the knapsack. Gavin looked briefly in her direction then set off noisily away. The pursuer took the bait. It was Brad Gillies, she saw his face as he passed her. He was hollering, "Hey stop! What do you think you're doing!"

She hoped that Gavin would be O.K. He had a lead but Brad looked to be a pretty good runner too.

She scrambled to her feet, heart pounding. Suddenly all was silent. The tower stretched eerily skyward beside her in the night. She just wanted to get *away*. She started to run and in her panic, dropped her darn knapsack. Tools and her schoolbooks scattered out all over the dark ground. Near tears now, she dropped to her knees and felt blindly with her hands for metal and paper and pushed them all anyhow into the bag.

Stumbling, she finally headed for the fence.

She hoped Sean and Kelly would still be waiting for her. She hated the thought of riding her bicycle home along that dark road by herself. At the fence, she scrambled over, the wire digging into the arch of her sneakers. She half fell onto the ground. She heard sounds but it wasn't Sean or Kelly. It was Gavin somewhere further along the fence, shouting and whooping which was crazy, was he trying to get caught?

She turned to see the heads of Andy Poltz's cows, their horns sharp against the moonlight. They were surging through the fence.

Brad gasped for air but he was laughing as he ran.

Just some kids and I bet I know who they are. A few years ago, it woulda been me. I'll give them a scare and that should be enough to keep them off the place.

I've got more serious stuff to do.

But dammit what the heck is all this?

They've let out the cows! Shit! Smart little barstards.

Mr. Keen isn't going to like, no he's not.

Brad boy, you're in deep shit now.

Dammit. I'd better close up the tower first so he doesn't know I was up there. Shoot! Is the whole damn herd going to come out?

They found the spot where they'd left their bikes in the ditch. The moon was behind clouds by then and the ride along the dark potholed and rutted road was slow and laborious. And silent except for the laboured panting of the riders. It seemed to take forever.

As she passed Miranda's house, she heard Emily bark.

12

The dream never varied much and in any case, the outcome was always the same.

The road was always dangerous but there was no other passable route to the airport. Pete's unit was in the second vehicle of the convoy, sandwiched between the other two armoured cars. The soldiers were escorting Johnson the diplomat to Kandahar where he was going to catch a plane home after touring the reconstruction projects.

Johnson, a big genial man in his early fifties, was enthusiastic and supportive of the reconstruction efforts, and had been a hit with the workers at the camp. Striding about in khaki shirt and ill-fitting khaki shorts, he had visited the rudimentary medical clinic, reviewed police training exercises and played volleyball with the school children. He was taking back to Canada his report that recommended more funding for the project.

He sat in the vehicle, making jokes about the heat. How by tomorrow evening he'd be splashing in a nice cool swimming pool in Ottawa. He'd be thinking of the Charley gang though, would treat the fellows to a brew when next on leave.

Only the good stuff for you men! Johnson was laughing to the guys at the back when the IED exploded.

At first there was just noise, you couldn't even really call it noise, it was more like a pressure, an unbearable pressure on the eardrums.

As if that was where the explosion was taking place. The drum
membrane swelling and stretched to its limits, trying vainly to keep
the noise out of the fragile brain.

Then the noise came in.

And the dreadful sights. Like the hole in Johnson's chest.

He could hear groaning from the back of the G wagon. Firing
from the other vehicles. In slow motion he moved to Johnson,
crumpling up that khaki shirt to try and stanch the relentless flow
of blood. But the blood kept flowing over his own shirt, his own
hands . . . . *it wouldn't stop, in the dream it would never stop.*

He woke up in a sweat. Ali was reaching for the telephone.

She listened, sat in shocked silence, then turned to him with
wide eyes.

He grabbed the phone.

*   *   *

The first thing Pete noticed was the cows. The shaggy beasts
were heading down the road towards the cruiser, a straggling line
appearing ghost-like out of the mist. There was mist everywhere,
as the cold air from the lake rose into the warming morning. The
surrounding fields were virtually invisible.

Kevin swerved the wheel, as a huge horned head bawled at the
car window. "What the heck?"

"They must have got out somehow," Pete said. "Just keep going,
we'll send somebody back. I'll radio dispatch to warn the ambulance
driver."

They crept towards the site entrance where Jim Keen, the
grim-faced site manager awaited them.

"It's young Gillies," he said, starkly. "He fell. He's dead."

One of the workmen had noticed the tower door ajar in the
morning. Brad's sprawled and broken body had lodged in the tight
gap. The workman had immediately used his cell phone to call for
help.

Pete knelt to test for a pulse but it was only a primal reaction. The dreadful angle of the young man's head confirmed Keen's report. A broken neck for sure. Inwardly he cursed. He'd seen lots of death in Afghanistan and his other tours of duty but he never got used to it. The waste.

Eight a.m. The body had been discovered at seven.

"Has anybody touched anything?" he asked.

"Like you, I checked the kid," Keen said. "I've got the first aid certificate, I had to see if he was still alive. But there was nothing I could do for him."

A father of two young children himself, he looked sick at the tragedy. And Keen had a professional responsibility here too. The accident had happened on his site, supposedly under his supervision.

"Why is the ground all messed up like this?" Pete asked. "Looks as if an army's trekked all over the site."

"Poltz's cows were all over the place," Keen explained. "They must have got through their fence somehow last night. We had to shoo a couple of them away before we could even get to Brad."

"Yeah, we saw some of them on the road," Kevin said.

Keen grimaced. "We haven't tried to round them up, we had too much else on our minds."

"Has anybody got hold of Poltz yet?" Pete asked.

Keen nodded. "We sent somebody over there."

"Where's Mayor Sousa?" Pete asked. That was all they needed, another big buffalo to trample over the place. Still, he was surprised not to see him.

"In Denmark," Keen said. He explained that Sousa had gone the day before to attend a meeting with the Danish owners of the wind turbine company. He hadn't informed Sousa yet of the accident and obviously wasn't relishing the prospect.

Pete shook his head. "Damn, those cows sure made a mess. Hard to tell what went on here under all that trampling."

When the ambulance arrived, he delegated Kevin to help . For once the guy seemed to have run out of wisecracks.

Pete and Keen stood aside.

"So what do you think happened here?" Pete asked.

Keen looked away from the gurney.

"The kid must have fallen down the ladder, missed a step or something. He wasn't supposed to be up there, he's just supposed to check the door and lights at the bottom." He shook his head. "Jeez though, what a fall. Must have done him in right away. Usually, if there are any repairs or maintenance checks to be done, the technicians are supposed to work in teams."

"I guess you haven't got those security cameras up yet?" Pete asked.

Keen looked chagrined. "They're on back order and Sousa says we only need them to satisfy the insurance guys. Like he says though, it would be pretty hard to do any damage to one of these turbines towers, at least from the outside. There's nothing to burn, you'd need a terrorist bomb to do any real damage. And you'd hardly be a threat to the nation by knocking out a few dozen wind turbines on Middle Island. It's not worth any self-respecting terrorist's bother. So there's really not much risk."

Pete grimaced as the ambulance attendants bumped the gurney past them. "Not for the turbines maybe."

Keen had the grace to wince. "This week, Gillies was night security till nine. He had a beeper. He was suppposed to page me if anything came up."

"Doesn't look as if he had time to activate it. Do you think he was coming down to chase the cows away?"

"Looks that way," Keen shrugged helplessly. "Guess he never got here though."

They watched as two attendants wheeled Brad away. A depressing sight. The mist had risen by now to reveal a soft blue sky.

"So what was Brad doing up there?"

Keen looked upwards, craning his neck. "Looking at the view? Playing King of the Castle? He was a kid dammit, bored with sitting in the trailer all evening. I guess he just couldn't resist going up and checking it out. I wish he'd talked to me."

Pete hadn't much sympathy for Keen. Never mind what Sousa said, Keen was the site supervisor, he was responsible for his workers.

He should have overridden Sousa, reported to the company owners and got that security monitoring system installed.

"What's up there?" he asked Keen. "Any equipment? A desk, a computer?"

Keen shook his head. "There's barely room to turn around."

"A phone?"

"Phones don't work inside the tower. The workmen had a special digital radio up there with them the other day to talk to the crew on the ground. Once the motor gets going, the maintenance guys will take their tools up with them."

"I'm going up there," Pete said. "To take a look."

"Watch your step," Keen said.

A slim, smooth cylinder, barely wide enough to contain the ladder. Not a place for claustrophobics. Big red DANGER and CAUTION signs. *Technicians should work in pairs.* He started up, carefully scanning each rung before he stepped on it. But the rungs rose straight and unbroken above him, there was nothing damaged as far as he could see, nothing out of place. All was as slick, metallic and intact as when it was built. There was no sign of the fall. Nothing recorded, no shout of terror still echoing in the stale air, no sign of that last frantic scrabbling at the unyielding walls. The human body had been removed, now the tower was just a cold, empty tomb.

No rung was different from another. When he got about a third of the way up, he looked back down. The entrance looked very far away. A fall from here would certainly have done the kid in. Or from any farther up.

At the top, he climbed out the hatch. Though he had no particular fear of heights, the day's wind was picking up and he took a tight grip on the railing of the platform. The view was spectacular, like the view from a small airplane. It stretched for miles, the vast shining lake mirroring the sky. No wonder Brad had wanted to see it. He felt a kinship for the poor kid, appreciated his sense of adventure, his curiosity. It wasn't fair that he had to die for it.

He made his way back down, watching his step as Keen had warned.

Kevin met him at the door. "The chief called. The kid's girlfriend is at the station with her mother. She says Brad called her last night from the turbine tower. She's got some story that he heard some noises and went to investigate. I told him about the cows and he said to check what Poltz has to say on our way back in."

Pete told Keen to fence off the area around the turbine base. "We'll be back." He wanted to catch Poltz when he was off his guard.

The burly old farmer was on the road, trying to round up his cattle. A workman from the wind site had left his truck at the side and gone to help. They had succeeded in getting about ten of the beasts into Poltz's lane but there were still a half dozen milling about on the road. The cattle were frightened and confused and they weighed about eight hundred pounds each. Plus they each had an impressive set of sharp pointed horns.

Pete pulled the cruiser to a stop and said to Kevin. "Looks as if we can't question our suspect until we can get to him. So now you get a chance to be a real cowboy."

The policemen approached the cows, spreading out their arms and making tentative waving motions. Pete enjoyed the sight of Kevin trying to impress one of the horned hairy beasts with his city streetsmart bravado.

"What do I say?" Kevin asked.

"Try Get Along Little Dogie."

The arrival of two more waving humans actually had some effect and the cattle turned towards the gate. There was no thanks from Poltz of course. In a typical Poltz move, he followed his cattle in then closed the gate and dropped the crossbar, shutting his helpers out. The *WindSpear* worker shrugged and headed for his car. Poltz seemed about to continue following his cattle up the lane, his back to the cops when Pete called out.

"Just a moment sir, I've got a couple of questions."

Poltz snapped terse words over his shoulder. "No time, gotta get these cows penned up somewheres so they don't get out again."

"That's one of my questions sir, how did they get out in the first place?"

Poltz turned, his white beard jutting out beligerently. "Why don't you ask that devil up there at the site. He musta cut the fence."

"You're saying the fence was cut?" Speaking of fences, Pete was feeling at a distinct disadvantage semi-shouting over this one. On the other hand, he didn't want to open the gate and start the cow circus back up again. There was nothing in the policing manual about how to keep your dignity in this situation.

Poltz nodded. "Haven't been out there yet to check but that's my opinion alright. I keep those fences in good shape."

"Are you aware that a young man died at the wind site last night?"

"I saw the ambulance, like to plowed right through my cattle."

"When did you first notice that the cows were out?"

"Six o'clock this morning. I sleep tight."

"It looks to us they were out a lot earlier than that. Several hours at least."

Poltz shrugged his big shoulders. "This weather they stay outdoors in the far pasture. I wouldn't hear anything. They've always been safe enough before those wind people came along." He sent a black look up the road.

Yes, well the night hadn't been very safe for young Brad Gillies either.

"You do understand the terms of that restraining order, Mr. Poltz. If you're caught trespassing anywhere on the *WindSpear* land, you'll go to jail. That means even if you set a foot on the other side of that fence."

Poltz spat on the ground. "Guess you'll have to get one of them orders against my cattle next."

13

Leanne Gauthier, a round cheeked, sturdy blonde girl was probably a cheerful young woman in her normal milieu of island friends and beach party barbeques. A police station was not her normal mileu. Cheeks now tear-stained, she looked anxiously from Officer Jakes to Chief Halstead. Halstead asked Jane to get her a glass of water.

"Just tell us what you know," Halstead said "What was the exact time he called?"

The girl shook her head. "About ten o'clock. My parents were watching the news."

"And what did he say?" They watched her take a big gulp from the glass. She made an attempt to pull herself together.

"First off he tried to make me guess where he was, then he told me he was up in the turbine tower. He said he figured it was a good night to go up because of the moon. He said it was neat, looking out over the water and that he wished I was with him . . . ." Here she looked on the verge of tears again, so Pete asked quickly,

"Then what happened?"

"He said he heard a noise."

"What kind of noise?"

She shrugged pretty shoulders. "He said like a loose cable or something flapping in the wind. I said it could be the ghosts that have been haunting the Point but Brad didn't believe in ghosts."

"Then what did he do?"

"He said he was going to check and that he'd call me later. Then he shut off the phone." Her eyes teared up again and she reached for the water glass. "I didn't know that was the last time I would ever talk to him."

The two policemen waited while she wiped her eyes. Then Pete asked. "What did you think when he didn't call you back later?"

"I just thought he got busy with his work. And I fell asleep," she said guiltily. "Oh God, I just think of Brad lying there when I could have helped him. I could have called 911."

Nobody could have helped him by then, Pete thought but neither policeman said it.

"Did Brad mention anything about the cows?" he asked.

The girl looked blank and uncomprehending.

"Mr. Poltz's cows got out," he explained gently. "We're not sure when."

She shook her head numbly. "It's those ghosts," she sobbed. "Brad should have believed me. There's a curse on that whole Point now."

*   *   *

"First it was a jinx, now it's a curse!" Halstead said disgustedly. "Next they'll be wanting us to round up some ghosts to arrest."

He sighed. "It's tragic but the kid was was up there where he shouldn't be. He's young and cocky, but he's pretty pleased with himself and he wants to show off to his girlfriend. Then he hears those g.d. cows and goes tearing down the ladder to investigate. It's sad for sure what happened but there's nothing mysterious about it. He should never have gone up there alone."

Pete nodded. That was basically Keen's assessment too. "So what are we going to do about Poltz?" he asked. "Are we going to charge him with something?"

"You mean because his negligence lead to Brad's death?—indirectly anyway." He frowned. "We can hardly charge the man with manslaughter because his cows poked a hole in a fence. It was just a lousy rotten set of circumstances."

"Poltz says that somebody deliberately cut a hole in the fence. Sousa, in fact."

Halstead spread his two hands out like a pair of scales. "Poltz has got Sousa on the brain. I'd bet 50-50 even odds either way. Either Poltz wanted to bug Sousa or vice versa. Let Sousa sue for damages if he wants to."

Halstead reached for the phone. He wasn't looking forward to returning a call to the Bonville Record reporter. But Pete still lingered.

"There's one little puzzle, though," he said. "Keen hasn't been able to find Brad's logbook."

"Logbook?" Halstead looked the question.

"He and the man who works the day session keep a log of security checks and any abnormal readings in the equipment. Anyway it's gone. We've searched the stairs and tower well but it isn't there."

"Maybe Brad took it home with him to show his girl. Not to speak ill of the kid and I doubt that he had any harmful intent but he was breaking rules all over the place."

"We've searched his room and his car," Pete said. Then added, "He might have written something in the book, something relevant."

"From the girl's statement it seems that he was in a hurry to get down those stairs. I doubt that he stopped to write anything down."

Pete shrugged. "It's a loose end."

"What does Keen say?"

"He'd like us to find it. Brad wasn't a very big cog in the *WindSpear* wheel but they'd like to have the book."

Halstead had already started to punch in a number. "O.K. take Kevin with you and search the site for the logbook. Sounds as if you're going to have a devil of a time though since those cows plowed through the place."

He scowled irritably, "And while you're there you might as well check out that fence. It wouldn't hurt to remind that pain-in-the butt Poltz that he'll definitely be serving jail time if he gets up to any more of his dangerous tricks."

*　*　*

Steph grinned as she approached the picnic table in the Canadian Tire parking lot.

Greasy cooking smells drifted over from the nearby chip truck. She clapped Halstead on the back, just as he was about to bite into a four inch thick cheeseburger.

"Aha, caught in the act! I can see the by-line now. *Middle-Aged Chief of Police Risks Death by Clandestine Burger and Fries Lunch.*"

Halstead sputtered. "You're the one who would have killed me." He took the bite anyway and chewed with gusto while she sat.

"And who's calling who middle-aged," he asked. "What about you?"

She smiled smugly. "Still four years younger than you." Halstead had gone through high school with her older brother.

"Yeah and you were a nuisance then too. Cute though."

"You thought I was cute?"

"Everybody thought you were cute and you knew it."

A shadow passed over her face. "Yes well that was a long time ago."

He patted her hand, "You're still pretty cute."

He'd been saying such things to her forever it seemed but now she thought he looked at her differently. They were both older, he was widowed, she was divorced. A lot of water had gone under the bridge.

A group of boisterous teenagers arrived, swarming over the other three tables. Wrestling, horseplay, pushing each other off the bench. He could have shut the kids down but today he was just glad to see somebody enjoying life.

"It's kind of noisy here," he said. "I'd think you would have more peace and quiet out at that retreat of yours."

"Not during the ladies' drumming class," she said dryly. "These kids don't even come close to the racket created by a dozen yoga-buffed ladies."

"Can I get you something?" he asked. "I doubt Bill here sells bean sprout hot dogs but I could ask."

"No thanks," she said. "I just had a coffee. So this is where you hide out from the pressures of office."

He nodded, "Nobody to hound me here. Vern and the council members usually eat at the Island Grill."

She nodded sympathetically. "You've been busy these past few months. How are the negotiations going or is that still a hush hush subject?"

"There will be policing for the Island by somebody, that's about all I can say."

"O.K. I get the point."

She looked over at the kids sprawling and laughing at the next table, her gaze sad. "It seems only a few years since Brad Gillies was goofing around like that. I can hardly believe he's gone." She shook her head. "We're all doing what we can for Pam, taking shifts at the wool shop and cooking, but there's no pie or casserole in the world that's going to fix that hurt. Oh I hate this awful wind war. It's been a bad business since the beginning."

Halstead held up his burger. "And yet we want to be able to cook our food, to heat and light our houses. Folks like electricity, Steph. Got to get it somewheres."

"But at such a price!"

He sighed. "I hope you're not thinking like some people that there's anything spooky going on out there Steph. It's just about money, like everything else. The world wants energy, and we'll get it one way or another."

"Now that's an enlightened point of view," she said hotly.

He looked pained. "From a policeman's standpoint, it's a major headache. Rural areas have become a battleground. Wind power, factory chicken farms, factory pig farms. Neighbours taking neighbours to court. Sometimes it all makes me yearn for a simple drug bust or robbery."

"Maybe you should move to the city then and risk getting shot every time you go out on a call."

"No thanks, point taken. Though this week has been pretty grim, even here."

"Terrible," she agreed. He noticed her hair was graying slightly at the temples. Some day all her hair would be the colour of that dramatic streak.

"So is it true what people are saying" she asked. "That Andy let his cows onto the site and that Brad fell when he came out to chase them? Lord I hope not, how could the man live with himself?"

"Is that the word on Main Street?" He marveled. "News travels fast." You'd think he'd be used to it.

"So, is it true?" she pressed.

"The matter is still under investigation," he said in his policeman tones.

She didn't take the hint. "I hear Andy got fined $5000 for the crane stunt and that he had to get a loan from the bank. You can't seriously think he'd be crazy enough to risk another fine?"

He bit into a pickle and repeated, "The matter is still under investigation."

She took a fry, looked at him teasingly.

"I met your new officer the other day. He came by the Retreat to grill me. You can send him round any time."

"He's a nice guy. His beautiful wife is very nice too."

She nodded. "I've heard great reports of her from Eileen. Are they going to stay here? The Island needs some new faces."

"Is that just your sneaky way to get back to the policing negotiations?"

She flounced her hair. "Nope. I've got my own sources. I'll probably know the decision before you do."

"No doubt," he said dryly.

"Must go, I've got errands to run."

"Business is good then? No cancellations because of the *WindSpear* project?"

"The turbines aren't up yet," she pointed out. "Actually I've got a group of birders coming this weekend." She laughed at the look on his face. "Don't worry, they're not planning to mount a demonstration at the site or put sugar in the tractor gas tanks. Just to attend yoga classes and meditate."

"Thank goodness for that. Maybe they can spread a little peace and good vibes around the Island. We could sure use it."

She rose from the table and fished her car keys out of her purse.

"You know that our little burger tete a tete is being being watched of course."

"Of course."

"By this afternoon, the gossips will be saying we're having a red-hot affair."

"Sounds like fun." And it did. He looked up quickly to try and catch her expression and realized he was sadly out of practise. Besides, she was just kidding, wasn't she?

Only later did he remember that she'd looked at him oddly at some point, as if she was on the brink of telling him something. He guessed if it was important she'd tell him sometime.

14

"So, what are we looking for?" Kevin asked.

Pete described the logbook, an 8 by 11 inch journal, soft leather cover, about the size of a school notebook.

Kevin grimaced, seeing only the churned up ground, the wide swath of broken grasses leading across the field. He seemed to be immune to the beauty of the view beyond the bluff. The rough majesty of water, sky and rock. Along the bluff edge, small white butterflies bobbed over a sprinkling of pink and yellow wildflowers and the gnarled old oaks had sent out new leaves.

"And why is this book going to be out here?" Kevin asked.

"Because it isn't anywhere else—not in the tower, not in the trailer office, not in the kid's car or home."

A soft humid morning. They split up, fanning the torn ground surface between them. In the blurred blue sky above, more hawks were coasting in by the hour. Halstead said sometimes there were hundreds of birds arriving in one day. Hovering over the cliff edges, where the water was about a thirty foot drop straight down. At intervals, sections of the cliff broke off into teetering limestone columns the locals called flowerpots. The gaps were of no concern for hawks, but treacherous for humans.

"Watch your step," Pete warned Kevin as the hotshot forged ahead. Both policemen were sweating by now, had taken off their leather jackets.

"Somebody's mended the fence," Kevin said as they arrived at the perimeter of the Poltz farm. There was fresh wire wound about the break and the metal fenceposts had been temporarily propped back up. Kevin moved along the fence, inspecting the work.

"My bet's that nutbar farmer cut the wire himself, just to stir up some trouble."

Pete nodded. "Could be. Or maybe the cattle just knocked over some of these old posts. A couple are rotting around the bottom."

"They'd have to be spooked some way, wouldn't they?" Kevin said the word awkwardly as if he was remembering a line from some old Western movie. "I mean this is their regular fence, they're not charging through it all the time. The old coot must have got them going."

It could have been that way, Pete thought. Poltz and Sousa, what a pair. The one as mean and vindictive as the other.

Kevin stopped for a swig of water from his plastic bottle and wiped sweat from his neck. "So was the army as much fun as this?"

Pete looked out at the great stretch of shimmering lake, that lay like a mirage upon the horizon.

"It was about forty degrees hotter over there, I can tell you that. And we were wearing full combat gear when we were on patrol. Compared to that, this little stroll of ours is a piece of cake."

"So why did you sign up—looking for adventure, like the tv ads say?"

"Sure, something like that."

It was easier than trying to explain. He'd signed up the day he finished high school. It was the quickest way to get the farthest distance from his home town. From the old man. His brother had left four years earlier, after Mom died. Pete would have gone anywhere.

Then he kept on signing up. There were buddies, there were clearly defined tasks, there was officer training. He was young and physically fit and he kept busy. There was nowhere else to go, certainly not home, whatever that was. A cot in the den of his father's Ottawa apartment, and that only offered grudgingly. The army wasn't a home but at least it was a base of operations. Everyone needs a base of operations.

"So it was cool, driving the tanks, shooting the rocket launchers, all that?"

"It was exciting sure, for awhile."

Kevin finished off the bottle and wiped his mouth. "I wouldn't like some sergeant telling me what to do all the time though. Like being back at school. I'd get teed off."

Pete forebore from saying that his own platoon sergeant had saved him from getting his head blown off a couple of times. Instead he said mildly, "Then the army's probably not for you."

Kevin grinned. "Marriage neither. My girl keeps hinting for a ring, but the way I see it, that's just another kind of sergeant. No offense to Mrs. Jakes."

"None taken."

Pete smiled inwardly, thinking of his own delectable 'sergeant'. Now she wanted to talk about buying the house. After living out of a footlocker for ten years, he found the idea overwhelming. There came a time to settle down, people said, but he didn't know how. A combat soldier pretty well just kept on moving, it was safer that way. There were always new orders, another destination to reach. There was a lot of hurry-up involved, not much stopping and resting, never mind putting down roots or staying anywhere. Not like these wiry oaks clinging to the rocky terrain of the Point. These trees had staying power.

"You don't even like this house," he pointed out to Ali. "You're aways saying how dark it is, that the porch steps are broken."

"We can paint the rooms, we can fix the steps."

"What about Miranda?" he said. "Do you want to have her as a permanent neighbour?"

"She'll thaw," Ali said blithely. "Nobody can resist me forever."

"We don't even know what the Council will decide. Whether there will be a detachment in Middle Island, whether I'll even have a job."

"We know enough," she said. "You'll have a job either way."

Besides, she knew what he was really talking about, she knew his fears. Of taking those big risks in life, in love. She knew of the pictures in his mind, the shattered windows of the schoolhouses in Afghanistan, the bullet-peppered stucco walls of Bosnian streetscapes, the patched tent cities of sad-eyed refugees. Places where it seemed the only thing permanent was the impermanence. But even she didn't know how hard it was for him to make a decision. Even his joining the army was an impulsive action, not a considered judgement.

To have a child, such a big decision. Some of his doubts were selfish, he had to admit. Wondering how this would change their lives, their marriage. Whether he'd like having to share Ali's attention. He supposed all men felt a bit like that. Lately he'd found himself looking at kids with a new interest, sometimes amazement, sometimes with approaching near panic.

She had taken face between her warm hands. "Females nest," she said softly. "Birds nest, despite the wind and storms and wars. They don't think about the temporary nature of things. They know that Nature isn't a temporary thing. Nature is forever."

He wished he could believe her. He wanted to to.

High in the sky a solitary hawk made a brief shadow against the sun before diving purposefully down into the scrubby growths of juniper that crowded up against Andy Poltz's fenceline. Hunting for mice or maybe the lucky score of a rabbit. Next he or she would be hunting for a mate. Nesting, as Ali said. Everybody's doing it.

Lucky bird though. Its child-rearing would be over by the fall. Not like dumb humans who had eighteen years to screw things up.

*   *   *

Keen joined them briefly, walking over from the dirt road where he'd left his vehicle. His boyish looks were rapidly fading these days, his expression dispirited as he asked.

"Find anything yet?"

"Just this messed up fence line."

The curious cattle stood staring with their big shaggy heads as the three men moved along the fence line, heads down, looking at the ground.

"It looks as if something's been pulled up out of the ground here," Kevin kicked at the spot. "You can see it's been filled in but it's not a great job."

"Probably a piece of the original fence," Keen said. He straightened up and looked down the line of wire and metal uprights.

"A hundred years ago, these were all cedar rail fences. No nails, no wire, just the wood pieces laid out in a cross rail pattern. They worked pretty well too, stood for years, right into the sixties."

Pete looked at the hole filled with fresh dirt. It looked to be about the diameter of a fencepost. "This one looks dug up a bit more recently."

"Some of the cedar fences lasted even longer," Keen said. "On an old family farm like the Poltz property, they probably just used them as long as they could."

He became more animated as he warmed to his subject.

"The early surveyors back in the 1800s had a heckuva time. They didn't have the equipment we have today, like the GPS technology. They would use fences and trees as markers, or any other geographical feature such as a hill. Then they'd stick an iron pin or stake into the ground and keep moving. When modern-day surveyors tried to re-do the work, they found gaps and overlaps everywhere."

"So could they fix the problem?"

"Not to everyone's satisfaction," Keen acknowledged. "It led to a lot of court battles. But in the main, the decisions went with using the original section corner markers as the starting points for the new surveys, even though they wouldn't technically be accurate. But that was a long time ago. Today we use the GPS technology, it's a lot harder to argue with that. The fences aren't as picturesque though."

The three men looked down the line as if imagining the rail fences of long ago.

After Keen left, Pete and Kevin spent another hour combing the grounds but they didn't find the logbook. Only a lover's heart drawn into the dust of the road. It was ringed with small grey pebbles and contained the remnants of a pair of initials that had been scuffed away.

*   *   *

Halstead wasn't too concerned about the logbook.

"Never mind, it will turn up somewhere. Things generally do. In the meantime, we've got a funeral tomorrow and it's going to be a big one. Folks around here want to show support when a young person's gone."

Waves of shock and disbelief had spread quickly through the close-knit community. By the time Ali and Pete arrived at the funeral, the line of cars at the church stretched around the block.

Stephanie Bind, supporting her friend Pam's arm, heard the comments from her friends and neighbours.

He was so young.

He and Leanne had their whole futures before them.

The Point is jinxed. That wind project is looking like a really bad idea.

Steph was worried about Livy too. Her daughter, tense and chalk-faced, sat at the rear of the church with some other students from the highschool. She was such a sensitive girl! Though Livy hadn't known Brad that well, she took everything so hard.

How had it gone so horribly wrong?

She'd never been so glad to get home in her life. Had managed to sneak in without waking her mother, then got into bed and pulled the blanket over her head. She'd thought that the worst of it was over. But that was before she knew about Brad.

She hadn't even talked to Kelly since. They'd just avoided looking at each other. As if they pretended nothing had happened, the nightmare would go away.

There were audible sobs at parts of the service. Ali, feeling her own eyes tear up, pressed Pete's arm for comfort.

15

Blow wind, and crack your cheeks

Burt Sousa had returned with a vengeance.

He'd flown back from Denmark as soon as he'd heard the news. Had managed to muster up the grace to behave the day of Brad Gillies' funeral. But now he stormed into Halstead's office.

"Keen says you plan to shut the site down for the rest of the week."

Halstead nodded. "Longer if necessary. Whatever time it takes to carry out our investigation."

An angry flush stained Sousa's features. The man should really watch his blood pressure Halstead thought.

"What's to investigate? Look I'm sorry too, for the kid and his family. The company has offered to pay for the funeral, what more can we do? It's a damn shame but life moves on. *WindSpear's* investors have got millions tied up in that site, we've got four more turbines to put up this month, and we can't afford to lose another day."

"We'll try to keep that in mind," Halstead said wryly. "But it's not just the police you have to contend with. There's the provincial safety inspection, the insurance investigation."

"They're all waiting for the police report."

"And we're waiting on them to see if there are any charges to be laid."

"Charges! What charges!"

Halstead looked grim. "You know damn well what I'm talking about Burt. How about criminal negligence? A young man died on your site."

"It was the kid's own fault."

"That might not be the safety inspector's view."

Sousa brushed this aside.

"So how long are we taking about?"

"Could be two weeks—minimum—till the inquest."

Sousa's glance veered, taking in the cramped office, the photo of Halstead's boat the *Lone Loon*, on the wall, the cartooned coffee mug.

"I wouldn't look so smug if I were you, Bud. That Council decision about policing is going to come up this year, you know."

"Are you threatening me?"

"Just a friendly comment."

"Yeah well here's another. While I'm wearing this badge, I'm still enforcing the law around here. And you're just another law-abiding citizen."

Sousa slammed the office door behind him.

The Mayor's visit was followed by a phone call, Vern Byers' reedy voice coming out of the instrument.

"Dammit Bud, you said you could control Andy."

"We don't know he let those cows out Vern."

"It doesn't matter. It's just more bad publicity. And more ammunition for Council. Burt's talking all over town, saying that you can't handle the situation, that we should call in the OPP."

"Tell me something I don't know."

"You have to give me some assurance, Bud, that you can get things under control."

"I hope you're not suggesting that I should lay off the Gillies' investigation, because the Mayor has a say in the policing decision. Last I checked this Island is my jurisdiction, not Burt Sousa's."

"Then you'd better start running a tighter ship, Bud. Remember that September is decision time for Council."

How forget? He pressed *end* on the phone, considered throwing the thing across the room. He hadn't been this mad in years. Did he need this kind of aggravation?

Yes he did by God and it felt good, as anger charged through his long dormant veins. Now he knew what he wanted to do. He wanted to save his police station. He wanted to save his police station, because it was good for his town. Middle Island needed to be rejuvenated and the place needed folks like Pete and Ali, needed them to stay. He liked young Jakes' with his principles and his steady commitment to his work. He liked to see Ali when she came into the station, her big bambi eyes glowing as she sought her husband. She was the cinnamon in the coffee cup of Middle Island, spicing life up and adding zest to the familiar.

The Island deserved a police presence and protection and he was damned if he was going to let some bully take it away from them. If he Bud Halstead was going to leave it would be his own decision, he wasn't going to be railroaded out of his station by Burt Sousa.

In the days following, Sousa stomped through the Island like an enraged trumpeting bull. Tales came from everywhere. Sousa chewing out Vern Byers at council, Sousa berating his salespeople at the business, Sousa badgering the provincial safety inspector till the man wouldn't answer the telephone anymore.

"I guess he's kind of upset," Kevin said, as the Mayor came charging past after yet another angry visit to the station. "People say he's got a lot of money tied up in the wind project."

"Maybe *all* his money," Pete corrected. "I get the impression if he goes down, he's going down big."

Jane came in from lunch, agog with fresh gossip.

"Burt and Elena just had a big fight outside the bank. They were going at it like anything. They didn't care who was listening. There were people hanging out the door of the laundromat to watch."

"Sounds as if they got some bad news from the bank manager," Kevin said.

"You know it," Jane shook her head in admiration. "I doubt that anyone but Elena would have the nerve to tell Burt off like that. She called him a wanna be millionaire. She said if it wasn't for the kids she'd have got a divorce long ago. But now that she'd stuck it out this long, she said he'd damn well better not screw this deal up. Our Mister Mayor was not a happy camper."

Halstead went thoughtfully back to his office. A balked Burt wasn't good news for anybody.

* * *

Miranda hastily pulled Emily to the side of the road, away from the car roaring towards them. Burt Sousa was at the wheel, she could almost feel the anger boiling out the car windows. All that rancor bottled up. She knew that the components of the next four wind turbines had been delivered a few days ago. The trucks carrying the mammoth sections had filled the road to the Point for most of the day. But the company couldn't start construction until the safety inspection was completed.

She wondered why Sousa was going out to the site. What could he do there but sit and stare frustratedly at his stillborn project. She was reminded of a Joseph Conrad story she'd read of a captain who was nearly driven mad when his ship was becalmed in the Pacific for months on end.

Not exactly a comforting parallel.

* * *

None of them got it. None of them knew what it took to get something big like this wind project off the ground. They had no vision.

Take Elena, somebody take her please. She's as bad as everyone else on the damned island. Has to be dragged kicking and screaming through this project, every step of the goddamned way. She'll be glad enough to spend the money though, when it comes rolling in. And so will the kid when I give him the keys to a new SUV, get him off that bike of his. Not that he deserves it.

But for now they'll all just have to shut up and keep out of my way.

And what the hell's the matter with Vern—I told him to put the pressure on Halstead. The insurance company and the safety boys have finished their report—what the hell is he waiting for?

They're a pair between them, him and Keen, another foot-dragger. The kind of wimps who always have to dot every I, cross every t. Keen has no spirit, no gumption, he doesn't understand that the government has to bring in rules and regulations to sweeten the public but business, real business, doesn't have the time for that crap. Nothing would ever get done if the public had their way. Damn committees and protests and all the other hold-ups. Then by god, they scream just as hard if there's a power brownout and their air-conditioners and refrigerators don't work. There's no pleasing the fools.

Keen doesn't seem to realize that the Danish guys don't want to hear about problems. They expect us to handle the problems, that's what we're paid for.

He'd made a mistake hiring Keen, even the promise of a bonus wouldn't tempt the guy.

The dope didn't even realize the money that would pump into the Island economy.

It was damned frustrating, that's for sure. Here was the biggest and best opportunity ever to arrive on the Island and some of the folks were too stupid to realize it. They were like scared bull-calves, digging in their heels and swinging their heads and not moving a foot forward.

Well they couldn't be allowed to stand in the way of progress. He wouldn't stand for it. He had lived on the Island all his life too and if he had to, he would drag the place kicking and screaming into the twenty-first century.

And he didn't care who he trampled over to make it happen. It was for their own good, the fools. Sometimes you had to break a few heads to make an omelet.

The wind awoke my heart

Ali skipped down the rutted driveway. She felt about eight years old. Birds sang in the neighbouring field, a rollicking bumptious sound. Bobolinks they were called, she'd looked them up in her Peterson guidebook. She was fetching the mail, one of the little pleasures of country life that she never would have thought so enjoyable. At the end of the driveway, she stopped to press her face into a sweet-smelling bouquet of lilac blossoms. The blooms were still wet with last night's rain and she laughed delightedly as the droplets showered her hair.

She felt someone looking at her and raised her head warily to see Miranda Paris standing at her own mailbox across the road. Darn! That lemon juice expression was on her face again, as if she was looking at some kind of lunatic. Though it was kind of funny really. She felt a giggle coming on and had to bury her face back in the lilacs. The Gorgon's gaze never wavered though, she could feel it still burning on her back. Eventually, and controlling her sputters with difficulty, Ali stepped over to the Jakes' mailbox and retrieved a couple of envelopes, the local newspaper and a wad of advertising flyers.

She waved across the road and made some dumb remark about junk mail. Miranda Paris said nothing, turned on her heel and walked away. The dog wagged its tail apologetically.

What the heck is with the woman? Ali was going to turn away too. Instead she crossed the road.

"Excuse me, Miss Paris," she called. "Could I ask you something? I need your help."

The woman stopped, apparently not competely immune to some kind of country code of civility. Her look would have frozen lava but Ali plunged on.

"I've been meaning to come over and say hello. Eileen Patrick says that you and I have something in common. She says that you were a teacher."

Miranda stiffened. Oops bad choice of words. "*Are* a teacher," Ali tried to amend. "I'm a teacher too."

"You said you needed some help?" Miranda asked coldly. "Was that with some teaching problem?"

"No, not that . . . . though I'd enjoy talking about that some time." Flustered now, Ali moved on hastily to her question.

"You have such lovely chickens, I've been thinking of maybe starting a small flock for us, at our place. I ordered this booklet," she held it up. "It just arrived in the mail. Plus I've been researching the subject on the Net."

She pointed. "That pretty hen is an Americana I think. I've read that the eggs are a lovely blue colour."

"Andalusian," Miranda said reluctantly, as if her schoolteacher background compelled her to make the correction.

"Oh," Ali said. "I haven't read about them yet. Are they good chickens to begin with?"

Miranda plucked the booklet from her hand. She flipped a couple of pages then read out in a dry, uninflected voice, "Chickens are interesting creatures that can add a country ambience to your yard. The sound of their busy clucking is a cheery background to the total country experience."

Ali cringed. It did sound pretty fatuous, she had to admit.

"Of course I mean to get more detailed information," she said. "I thought you might be able to suggest something. I mean I'd love to have a look at your coop and the nesting boxes. It must be so exciting to collect your own eggs for breakfast."

"I can't allow that," Miranda said. "It would be too upsetting for the hens."

By now definitely daunted, Ali started to back awkwardly towards the gate.

Then Miranda surprised her with a question. "How's that husband of yours coming along with his *investigation*?" The word said scathingly.

Ali hardly knew what to answer. "Fine, I guess," she said inadequately, foolishly. But the woman couldn't expect to hear privileged information about a criminal investigation. "It's a shame the way the community is being split over all this," she ventured. "And that poor boy falling was such a tragedy."

Miranda crossed her arms, her face set in stern schoolmarm lines. "Tragedy happens when men start messing about with Nature," she pronounced. "But Nature will get her own back, never fear. She has all the time in the universe."

And on this note, Ali finally managed her exit.

*   *   *

Miranda called in the dog. Really it was quite embarassing the way Emily fawned over that young woman. And such a ridiculous naïve idea, that she could just order some chicks from a magazine and start a flock without any idea of what she was doing.

She'd never imagined herself raising chickens. But when she came back, there they were. Andy Poltz had tended them after Henry died. She told Andy to sell the flock to be slaughtered but it took awhile because he was busy with the haying. In the meantime, she had to collect the eggs. On her first visit to the chicken coop, she entered reluctantly. The place wasn't completely strange, she grew up on a farm and had collected the eggs with Henry, her younger brother. But it had been sixty years since she'd held in her hand an egg still warm from the hen's feathers.

She stared at the amazing, wonderfully fragile thing. The shell was a soft mottled pink, like a delicate marble ornament. She saw herself at ten, barefoot in a straw bonnet, cautioning Henry not to run and scare the chickens. It was the first time she'd cried since his death. The next morning, she told Andy she was keeping the birds.

Now she looked disapprovingly across the road. If the woman actually ever did seriously consider buying some chickens, perhaps she should give her some advice—for the birds' sake of course. The Andalusian hens would be a poor choice for a beginner. She wouldn't want some innocent birds suffering in a too-cold climate because an amateur was attempting to raise chickens.

But she'd probably never do it. People had all sorts of ideas they never carried through.

$$* \quad * \quad *$$

Livy was seeing Gavin Sousa.

Steph could hardly believe her ears when Pam came out with it in that flat emotionless way she had of talking nowadays, poor woman. Pam had few details, she seemed barely interested in the news nor how it might affect Steph. She was just offering the tidbit as an attempt at conversation.

And how did Steph feel? Surprised of course, make that stunned. And not too thrilled, obviously. But maybe it wasn't all bad. Livy had a boyfriend. That explained a lot, Livy didn't hate her mother, she was just in love. Gavin was a good-looking boy and aside from his unfortunate parentage, a good catch. A champion runner and cyclist in the tri-county triathalon. Some said Olympic material.

Maybe that's what the kids had in common, Livy spent a lot of time out on her bicycle too. Athough Livy was more of an ambler than a speedster. Maybe they liked the same kind of music. Let's face it she amended, most of the time it didn't take anything more than physical chemistry and beneath her Gothic garb and make-up,

Livy was a pretty girl. Though hopefully Gavin wasn't in any hurry to get beneath that garb !

She tried to remember when she and Livy had last had the sex talk, or any talk at all. Best to have a refresher course, sometime soon.

Thoughts scurried through her mind all morning as she checked out supplies for the retreat breakfasts for the weekend. Silly thoughts, such as what if the kids got engaged some day, imagine Burt Sousa as an in-law. Yikes, shades of the Montagues and Capulets ! Livy was only sixteen but then hadn't Juliet been only thirteen? Double yikes. Still, she was determined to look on the positive side. Livy had a boyfriend. Someone to bring her out of her gloomy-viewed, asocial existence.

So, it was good news, really. Steph switched on the coffee maker and turned a neat little pirouette right there in the kitchen. Ballet lessons at ten, a short-lived passion, abandoned at twelve.

"Livy has a boyfriend," she sang to the cat. "No more talk about dying birds and the evils of society. Maybe I'll get my baby girl back. Hip hip hooray."

*　*　*

Livy tossed her bicycle aside and flung herself down on the grass. A mother killdeer rose up as she landed, peeping and adopting her broken wing act to try and lure Livy away from her young fledglings. Birds were nesting all over the Point. Usually Livy would get a kick out of watching the antics of the little running killdeers, perfect miniature copies of their mother, but today she felt too miserable to care.

Why was love so complicated? Love didn't seem worth it if it made you this miserable. She kept seeing Gavin's stony face at the last SHAWKS meeting. The very last meeting, it looked like.

"We have to lie low for awhile," Gavin had said.

Kelly laughed, a sharp, nervous little sound. "We have to lie low forever," she said. "I'm done with this crap. It's too dangerous."

"Me too," Sean said. 'At first it was fun, but this is getting too crazy. I mean Brad *died*. We were *there*. We could be arrested as an accessory or something, if the cops find out."

Gavin's face went tight in that way it did when he was really angry and not letting the anger boil out. His voice was tight too when he spoke, like a stretched wire.

"Get this through your heads. We didn't kill Brad, it was those frigging cows."

Kelly shivered. "But he was running down the tower ladder to chase *us*. The cows weren't out yet."

"Yeah," Sean said. "I heard him come out the door, he was yelling at us. He was O.K. then, so when did he fall?"

"He must have gone back up," Kelly said, pulling her jacket in more tightly around her shoulders. Livy knew how she felt, she thought if she spoke aloud her own teeth would chatter.

"Maybe he had to shut the lights off or something," Kelly said. "It's so terrible to think of him dying there all alone. If he'd fallen the first time he came down, we maybe could have helped."

"Nobody could have helped the poor guy after a fall like that," Sean said. "And we were trying to get the hell out of there."

"Never mind all that," Gavin said. "We still have a job to do, remember. We just have to wait awhile."

Sean stood up and made a sweeping, quitting motion with his hand. "Not us, man. We're done. Kelly and me are outta here."

Gavin stood too. "Then as far as you're concerned, it's really over," he said. "It never happened, you never belonged to any Shawks group, there was never any Shawks group. There was never any dummy, never any banner. And you're never going to talk about this to anybody, ever. Got that? Because if there's ever any trouble out of this, we're all in it together. Trouble for one, trouble for all."

Sean raised his palms and backed away. "Sure, man," he said. "O.K. Be cool. We get it, don't we Kelly? We get it."

So they got on Sean's motorbike and left.

She should be happier now that the others had left the group, to be rid of that airhead Kelly and Sean the goof, to have Gavin all to herself. But it wasn't like that. He didn't want to see her either. She knew things were bad at his house and about his parents fighting on the street but she still was hurt.

"I haven't left the group," she told him. "I still want to stop the turbines and save the hawks."

But he hadn't talked to her for three days now. She saw him in the hallways at school but he always moved on past her without saying anything. She wished she could ask someone for advice but she'd been so solitary this past year she had no close friends. Other kids had found her too serious until she met Gavin and the group. And she couldn't really consider calling Kelly a friend. Even though she'd thought of talking to her about Gavin, that just showed how desperate she was feeling. But she rejected the idea, Kelly would just blab all around school how Livy had the hots for Gavin and how crazy that was.

In the movies, girls talked to their mothers but that was out of course, the way that her mother hated the Sousas. She curled back into the sheltering grass, shrinking from the blue glare of the open sky. It seemed that being in love was like learning to swim. Scary, with lots of flailing around and gasping for breath. When you finally figured it out, it was nice, at least for awhile. But then in no time, you were back in the water and drowning again.

She looked up at two hawks, circling concentrically in the sky, as if attached by some invisible kite thread. Was love any easier for them?

17

Pete Jakes emerged from the dim high-ceilinged lobby of the Bonville courthouse and stood squinting in the bright sunshine of a perfect May morning. Bonville, a town of some thirty-thousand, was a bustling metropolis compared to Island life but most of the action had moved to the mall and fast food strip area at the north end of town. The courthouse, remnant of an older and softer time, was still the hub of several blocks of treed streets and homes of mellowing yellow and red brick.

The Gillies' inquest had brought no surprises.

Death by misadventure.

Misadventure. The legal terminology sounded almost poetic. Nothing like the grim reality of that broken young body at the foot of the turbine tower.

Keen and Sousa had followed him out. The site foreman looked tired, as if he was emerging from more than a few sleepless nights. Sousa just looked pissed off. He glared at Pete.

"Well that was a waste of taxpayer's money. We didn't need an inquest to tell us that the Gillles kid's fall was an accident." He plunged ahead down the steps, almost mowing down a couple of courthouse employees who were coming in from the parking lot.

Keen shook his head, said disgustedly. "Jeezus. What a creep. A dog would have more feeling." He looked almost beseechingly at Pete.

"I wanted to order the alarm equipment from a different company, to speed the installation up. But Sousa said we'd wait, the other company's bid was lower. I called him a cheap bastard, and he was. Maybe if we'd had that equipment installed, the kid would still be alive. But what do I get for trying? The judge reprimands the company and gives me hell all over again. I get to be the fall guy either way."

He gave a hopeless shrug and looked back at the courthouse dooway, no doubt recalling some of the grilling he'd gone through.

"But hey," he said with weak humour. "It's a job, right. A good job too. And that bastard's not going to make me quit."

He went reluctantly down the steps in Sousa's wake.

Pete wondered how much longer Keen would last at *WindSpear*. *Maybe there are some jobs not worth having buddy. Whatever the money.* He sat in the cruiser, mulling over the inquest testimony, and trying to sort out his thoughts.

It was now official. Brad's death was an unfortunate accident. That was the verdict and it made sense. So why was he still puzzling over the events at the tower that night? Unresolved questions still lurked in the recesses of his thoughts, like the shadowy flickering of a candle in a cave.

Who had let the cattle out?

Was it the same person(s) who had made the dummy and the ghost noises? There was a youthful capriciousness to the deeds. These did not seem the actions of a grown man, of an old man. Still less the actions of dogmatic, unimaginative Andy Poltz.

And then there was always the most frustrating question: where was the damn logbook?

Last night he had dreamt that he was at the Point again, searching through the rough scratchy grass. Though it was brilliant daylight, he heard noises, strange ghostly noises. There were presences out there in the grass, presences who had been there all along, laughing and mocking his efforts. Resolutely he shut out the laughter and finally his efforts were rewarded. There it was, he'd spotted the book. He reached eagerly down through the needle-sharp grass blades, saw too late that he had grasped a landmine that exploded in his hands.

*　　*　　*

He carried his thoughts home with him and looked up from his pilaf to see Ali looking at him indulgently.

"What?" he asked, embarrassed.

"I like watching you think," she smiled. "You just stare into space. I can never do that. I have to be doing something, anything. I think better the more boring the task—like when I'm doing the dishes."

He shrugged, "I'm just thinking. Nothing special."

She topped up their wine glasses and bent to plant a kiss on his head.

"Everything you do is special to me, my love." His steady silence had appealed to her from the beginning. So different from her ever-moving, on the go mother. With Pete you could turn around and he would still be there. Standing strong and sure as a beam holding up a school roof.

"So what's on your mind," she asked. "Still the inquest? The case?"

He frowned. "Nobody else thinks it's a case."

"Not the chief? He seems like a sensible man."

"He is. He's a good guy. Sometimes it's hard to get his attention though."

"I guess he's getting older. Retirement coming up."

"He's not really that old, just sort of old before his time I guess."

"I've got something to cheer you up," she said. She produced an array of paint sample strips and fanned them out on the table. "I've marked some possibilities for the living room," she said. "That nice soft yellow. Then a cream colour for all the woodwork in the house."

"We might not even stay here."

She shrugged. "So if we move, the next people will enjoy it. Anyway, I need some light in here now, some spring brightness. And a little more furniture would help too. Something more to our taste."

He looked into the living room. The house had come furnished which was just as well as they had only been perching in the Toronto apartment. The furniture looked O.K. to him. There was a couch, a couple of chairs, they'd bought a television. He and Ali had both been so busy getting oriented in their new jobs that they'd hardly paid any attention to their home surroundings. Or at least he hadn't. But it seemed that Ali had been chafing. And it was true that the only room that really looked like Ali was their bedroom where she'd chosen a turkey-red bedspread embroidered with a gold thread pattern and curtains and cushions to match. She looked wonderfully gorgeous against it.

He looked down at the paint samples. "I know what you're doing."

She batted her eyelashes innocently. "I don't know what you mean," she said. "I'm just talking about doing a little painting."

She loved to tease him, he was so teasable.

About his John Wayne and Clint Eastwood movies for instance. He had bought a bunch of the DVDs at a mall sale. Now he popped one into the player under her indulgent smile.

"All guys like these movies," he protested. "We envy them. Life is so simple and straightforward for Big John and Clint. You thump the bad guys and you win."

He also said the movies helped him think But tonight old Clint didn't seem able to help much. After she'd gone up to bed, Pete switched the set off and sat there still thinking in the dark.

18

The shed door creaked when Livy opened it but that was O.K. You couldn't hear anything when the drumming class was at practice and her mother would be busy there for at least an hour. She stepped inside, waiting for her eyes to get accustomed to the dimness. The windows of the shed were strung with cobwebs that filtered the outside sunlight and some of the glass panes were broken. She could make out the shapes of an old disused lawnmower, loops of dusty garden hose, a cone of wire tomato stakes. Nobody had been in here for ages. Except for her, after that scary night at the Point.

She'd turned her bicycle into the driveway while the others kept going on down the road. Nobody said goodbye, nobody said anything. They just went off like soundless shadows in the night. Or ghosts.

She'd tossed the backpack in the shed, just thrown it down anywhere in the panic of the moment. And then there had been Brad's funeral. It had been a miserable and confusing two weeks. It wasn't till she heard her mother talking to the workmen this morning about tearing the old shed down, that she remembered the backpack, the telltale tools, the paint can and brush. Why hadn't she gotten rid of that stuff long before this? This morning she had to fret till the drumming class began for a chance to get out to the shed unobserved.

Now she pushed the mower out of the way, wincing as a startled swallow swooped past her to the broken window. She found the pack, the fabric damp and a bit slimy from the shed floor. She'd brought a big green garbage bag and planned just to bag everything up with some other junk. Nobody would even know what was in it. She picked the pack up gingerly and upended it . The paint can and brush all stuck solid, tumbled out. Also a roll of duct tape, scissors, her balaclava, she'd completely forgotten about that for god sake, talk about incriminating . . . . and something else.

A notebook. She snatched it up, puzzled. It wasn't one of her own, she wrote her poems in regular school-type looseleaf books. This book had a smooth blue cover and was smaller, more compact. She took it over to the window, saw the familiar *WindSpear* logo on the top. Cautiously, she opened it. The pages were a little swollen with the damp of the shed and the writing was blurry here and there but she could see the lines for entries were filled with numbers and some pencil sketches. She flipped back to the inside cover and saw written in black marker. *Brad Gillies.*

*   *   *

Steph dropped ice cubes and lemon slices into a pitcher. There were also trays of cut raw vegetables, carrots, cauliflower and broccoli spears for the drummers' break.

Oops, she looked guiltily out at the group of women in the rock garden. Better take out the ear plugs, her little secret. Mustn't hurt anybody's feelings. On the whole though, she was very pleased. The rock garden looked beautiful, with soothing paths and tempting benches. Her assistant Mabb had eight local women registered for the drumming class and the yoga class was even more successful. Most exciting of all, she had booked all four rooms for the first summer week-long retreat.

Now if things would only stay peaceful for a bit

She saw Livy wheeling her bicycle down the driveway. She looked a bit intense but then when didn't she?

*   *   *

Livy caught up with Gavin after school at the causeway where she'd waited with her bike.

"Want to go for a ride?" she asked. "We could go out to the marsh, it's a great day for duck-watching." The sun was hot on her metal handlebars and big white clouds were sailing in the sky like tallships.

He didn't look at her, was fiddling with his brake lever.

"I have to get to work," he sort of mumbled. She knew it wasn't true anyway, he didn't work on Wednesdays. The days of heartbreak had made her bold. She turned her wheel. "I'll walk along with you," she said brightly.

They moved along the roadside, stiff as wooden puppets.

Anything she could think to say just sounded dumb. *How was your chemistry test? Did you watch that program on hummingbirds last night?.*

She sneaked a look at his face but his profile was set tight like the face on a coin.

When they reached the park, she stopped and reached into her backpack. "I wanted to show you something."

"What's that?" Gavin asked.

She handed him the logbook. "It was something of Brad's. I must have picked it up that night in the dark."

He took it gingerly, slowly turned a couple of pages.

"Look at the little drawings," she said. "I thought maybe Mrs. Gillies would like to have it. We could send it to her anonyomously."

Now he was turning the pages more quickly. He looked angry.

"Are you crazy?," he asked. "This is evidence that we were there that night. I'll tear it up and burn it."

She was stung at the way he was talking to her.

"You didn't used to be so scared of being arrested," she said hotly. "You even said we might have to get arrested for the cause."

He scowled. "I didn't mean to get arrested on freaking Middle Island. I want to make more of an impact that that."

He looked stiffly out at the Bay where a half dozen gulls were fighting over a bit of bread in the water.

"I have a new plan," he said. "But I'm going to be travelling light for a couple of years. Just me. It's too much trouble trying to deal with other people."

Now she was other people.

She looked out at the gulls too, with tear-blurred eyes.

He didn't even say goodbye, she just heard the crunch of his bicycle tires on the gravel.

After awhile she started home. She felt bad that Gavin had taken the logbook. She wished she had never showed it to him, that she had just mailed the book to Mrs. Gillies herself. She couldn't believe it, but she actually missed Sean. If he didn't like something Gavin wanted to do, he just said so, straight out. And Gavin had to listen. But Gavin didn't listen to her.

He seemed to have forgotten everything. How exciting it was in the beginning with just the two of them. How he liked her suggestion of the *Shawks* name, all their discussions and plans. How they meant to save the Point together.

She'd never felt more lonely.

19

Bayside Road was looking busy for a Wednesday. Soon the tourists would start arriving. Halstead wondered if either Jakes or Ragusa had any experience with boats. Summertime charges of 'Driving under the Influence' were as likely to be laid against boaters as drivers. Most incidents involved daytrippers from farther up the lake. Not a lot of people stayed over on the Island, not enough to be a traffic problem yet anyway. Middle Island wasn't developed enough to accommodate them, a lack that the newly-formed tourist association meant to rectify. For the moment there were only a couple of B & B's and the motel where Kevin was staying. It wasn't really much of a motel, just a few units out back of the Grill. Jonesy also supplied meals for his clients at the restaurant, part of the appeal for young fellows like Kevin.

Halstead supposed there wasn't much else on Middle Island to appeal to a trainee cop. Most of the trainees were just passing through. He wondered if there would be any more, whether the station was ever to get back to regular strength. Whether there was going to be a Middle Island station at all next year. He sighed. He had the feeling that Pete Jakes might be looking for a place like the Island to settle in, even if he didn't know yet that it would be good for him. His wife knew it though. The Island could be a good place for some.

He noted Steph's girl, Livy riding by on her bicycle, black hair streaming out behind her as if she was fleeing devils instead of riding up Bay Road on a June morning. The girl was as pretty as her mother if she'd ever allow a smile on her face. She'd been a sweet child as far as he could remember but now she had a permanent set, wounded look. Probably a reaction to Steph's divorce. Sometimes he thought he wouldn't be young again for anything.

He looked yearningly at the Island Diner as he passed and wondered if he could sneak a double cream coffee into his office without hurting Jane's feelings. She was still on that kick with the exotic coffees. What the heck was it yesterday—oh yeah, cardoman. Jakes had suggested that one, he'd have to have a word with the lad.

The other cruiser was in the station parking lot and the Jakes' hatchback. Good cops, both of them, always on time. Even Ragusa, despite his grumbling, performed all his tasks well. The phone rang as he was coming in the door. Jane picked it up.

"An accident," Halstead heard her say. His stomach muscles tensed and he knew Jane would have a similar reaction. Between the two of them, they probably knew most everyone on the island.

The others were listening intently as well to the one-sided conversation.

"Anybody hurt?" she asked.

She swivelled in her chair, body sagging with relief. "There's an injured cow on the road at the Poltz place," she said. "A collision between the animal and one of the *WindSpear* company pick-ups. The driver's O.K. but I guess the cow is pretty messed up."

Halstead grimaced. "This isn't good. Kevin, you'd better head out to Poltz's and get the details. Pete, you get yourself over to the Sousa place. We don't need another Poltz/Sousa fracas. Maybe you can head him off. If he's hell-bent on going out there, you make sure you go first in the cruiser and lead the way."

The Sousa home was a sprawling ranch style place on one of the town's half-dozen residential streets. Like the neighbouring residences, it backed on open fields and woodlots. There were two gleaming cars in the Sousa crescent driveway—a gleaming SUV and a smaller sedan.

Pete pulled the cruiser in behind the SUV and walked up to the door. The smell of cooking bacon drifted on the morning air, the family Sousa were apparently still at breakfast. It seemed that no one from the site had called Sousa yet about the accident, that was a break. Keen was probably loathe to do so, would rather handle the incident on his own.

He pushed the bell again, heard a woman's voice call. "Hey kids, here's your ride."

The door opened and Elena Sousa looked out. She wore a peach-coloured robe and her face was morning puffy. "Oh it's you," she said with surprise. "The new policeman."

She pulled her housecoat tighter and patted at her hair.

"Burt's in the kitchen," she said, leading the way.

The kitchen was sunny, the table strewn with the usual breakfast debris of empty juice glasses and coffee cups, four plates with the remains of egg and toast crusts.

The Sousa daughter, a high school junior, had already left the table. He could hear her in the hallway, grabbing up books and binders for school from the sounds of it. Mom have you seen my sweater? My I-pod? And all the other junk that was apparently necessary equipment for school these days. The boy was still at the table, absorbed in some textbook. He didn't even seem to notice Pete, his father probably sucked up all the attention in that house.

The Mayor was dressed in jacket and tie, finishing his morning coffee. He didn't bother getting up, just waved his cup. He didn't bother with a good morning either, but went straight to the point.

"You'd better be here to tell me you've finished the investigation and you're opening up the site."

"Afraid not."

Pete tried not to take any satisfaction from the glower on Sousa's face. That wouldn't be professional. However, he didn't exactly mind describing the accident to the man. As he was finishing up, the telephone rang.

Elena took it, listened, then straight-faced, handed it to Sousa. "It's for you."

Obviously the call was from Keen, as Sousa's face reddened and he lumbered heavily to his feet, hands rummaging in his pockets. "Where are my damned car keys?" he demanded of the room in general, then rounded on his son. "You'd better not have them, I told you not to use the SUV."

The boy looked up from his textbook. "I wouldn't drive that gas-guzzling monster if you paid me."

He spoke coolly but Pete noticed the tension in his shoulders, in his hands that held the book. The boy was controlling some deep emotion. Was it fear? Not so much physical fear of Sousa belting him as fear of being overwhelmed again, his self, his personality subsumed. A feeling Pete remembered only too well from his own youth. He'd had a bullying father too.

Sousa looked furious, then growled impatiently. "I don't have time for this. Elena, where are my keys?"

She tossed them across the table, so hard that the clump of metal keys bounced on the cloth. "They were on the counter, just where you left them last night."

She didn't ask where he was going, but had obviously recognized Keen's voice. Just as obviously she wasn't curious about what had happened or about any any of Sousa's dealings out at the wind site. The boy had gone back to his reading with a set, pale face, ignoring his father's rising temper, the stinging words between his parents. The scene was likely a daily, if not an hourly occurrence in that household.

Sousa headed down the hallway, hurling words back at Pete. "When were you planning to tell me what happened?"

"I was just getting around to it. I was going to offer you a ride out there as a matter of fact."

"No thanks, I'll drive myself."

"Then you'll follow me, sir. If you try to pass me, I'll charge you. And when you get there, please remember who's conducting the investigation."

The trip out to the site was becoming a well-worn track Pete noted. He was getting familiar with every inch of the road.

The poor shuddering beast lay sprawled on the road, Andy Poltz and a man with a veterinarian's bag kneeling beside it. There was a gash in the steer's side and at least one of its legs was broken. The steer's brown eyes rolled in pain. Pete felt sick at the sight, he was reminded of victims of land mines in make-shift hospital tents in Afghanistan.

The vet felt with deft hands along the steer's slashed flank while Poltz stroked the big shaggy neck with surprising gentleness. The *WindSpear* driver, white-faced from the shock of banging into half a ton of cow, waited by the company pick-up truck. Kevin looked on from the sidelines and beside him stood another man dressed in the same dusty overalls as Poltz, likely his hired man. Pete was startled to see that Kevin was holding a shotgun, non-police issue. Kevin caught his glance and rolled his eyes. *Tell you later.*

The Sousa car pulled up, rattling gravel. Pete turned and made a motion to hold the Mayor back. For a moment all was silent on the road save for the caw of a crow flying over the cornfield and the soft groaning of the steer.

The vet shook his head. "Sorry, Andy," he said to Poltz. "Can't save him."

Poltz nodded and the vet did his job, quickly, mercifully.

Poltz got stiffly to his feet and gestured to the hired man. "Better get the wagon, Aaron." It seemed to Pete that the old man was stooped more than usual, as if he had literally had some of the stuffing knocked out of him.

Poltz turned, eyeing the others blankly as if he hadn't realized they were there. At sight of Sousa though, his eyes kindled with anger.

"This is your fault," he rasped with throaty rage. "Crowding the road with the vehicles for your evil project. Now you've killed my cow. I expect full payment."

The *WindSpear* driver stepped forward, protesting to Sousa. "I didn't even see the cow. I honked the horn but I guess it it didn't have time to get out of the way." He turned to Poltz. "I'm sorry, I didn't even see it till the last moment."

Sousa made a dismissive movement. "We'll pay. Send an invoice, we'll pay. It's not worth wasting a day in traffic court." He started to walk towards his car.

Pete would never have guessed the old man could move so fast. He barely managed to catch at him as Poltz tried to get at Sousa. As it was, Poltz managed to take a grab at Sousa's jacket collar and half-strangle him.

"Arrest the jerk," Sousa gasped. "Lock him up."

Pete shoved Poltz none too gently back towards his own gate. "There's a restaining order against you, Mr. Poltz. Remember that. You go and quietly bury your cow or we'll be taking you into the station."

"And I guess we'll be hanging onto this shotgun for now too, Mr. Poltz," Kevin said, tossing it into the cruiser back seat.

"We should lock them both up," Pete said when they were done. "I wouldn't want to bet on the winner, if we just left them to it."

Kevin considered. "Poltz has got twenty years on Sousa but Sousa is heavy and out of shape. You know, I think the old guy just might win Even without his shotgun."

"Has he got a license for that thing?"

"Yep, I checked the gun registry. He says he uses it to scare off coyotes."

*   *   *

Pete lay willingly and pliantly under his wife's cool hands. Ali knew what to do for tense shoulders. And for everything else.

He was still thinking about the cow though.

"It was an accident, wasn't it?" she asked.

He nodded. "Though if it was Sousa in the pick-up, I would have had my doubts."

"You sound disappointed."

"Sousa didn't look exactly unhappy about what happened to Poltz's cow. It doesn't seem right. I don't like bullies."

Neither did Ali. She thought of the extremists in Afghanistan who wouldn't let women go to school.

"He keeps such a personal close guard on that *WindSpear* site," Pete added. "It makes you wonder what he's up to."

Ali's smooth cool hands moved soothingly along his back. "Eileen Patrick says it's no wonder Sousa's edgy about the project—he's invested everything he has and borrowed more. If the project doesn't go ahead he could be ruined."

Pete groaned in pleasure as she eased a tense muscle. "Maybe so, but I wouldn't waste any sympathy on that jerk. I could tell he didn't give a damn about the Gillies kid, he only cared that his site was shut down. It would be nice to get him for something, to take him down a peg or two. He's not a nice guy."

"You can't let that cloud your judgement," Ali said. "Or you won't be any good as a policeman."

"Sometimes it's darn hard to stay impartial. You start to think about what John Wayne would do." He sighed enviously. "One thing's for sure, Poltz had better keep a watch over his shoulder these days. Mayor Sousa is an angry and violent man. I've got an awful feeling that the next round with those two, one of them is going to end up dead."

* * *

Miranda was eating her supper, a cheese omelet and a spinach salad. Seniors' magazines were full of articles about the perils of eating on one's own, apparently launching a descent into loneliness and depression akin to the state of drinking on one's own (her other sin). But she'd eaten many a solitary meal throughout her life and a fair number of meals with fools who weren't worth the company. So damn the danger, she'd risk it.

Besides she wasn't alone. Emily was watching every bite.

After dinner she checked her e-mail. Lately, she'd been getting letters from a former student who was now teaching ESL in Costa Rica.

You would enjoy it here, Miss Paris. The school and the students remind me of our little school at Baffin Inlet. Of course it is a lot warmer here! But there is the same great feeling, of everyone working together.

But there was no letter tonight.

"O.K. Emily," she said to the dog. "I admit it, I'm lonely."

On her desk was a soapstone carving of two geese, a farewell gift from her students at the Inlet. She stroked the smooth, cool surface with her her fingers. The inscription read:

To Miranda with love and appreciation from her grateful students. We wish you happiness always.

The dedication was dated six years ago. She was happy then and even better, had made others happy. In one of her favourite projects, she had established an artist in residence program. The residence wasn't much—one of the same prefab cabins in which she lived herself—but she managed to scrape up a modest salary for a musician or an artist to stay each winter for two months to teach the children.

Yes, it had been a fun, useful time.

"Oh, Emily." She felt like crying actually which she hadn't done for years. She needed another glass of wine. No she didn't, in her years in the North she had seen enough of the fate of those who took that route. Best take Emily for a walk up the road instead.

She snapped the lead on and the two of them tiptoed past the hen house where the chickens were asleep on their roosts. She avoided looking across the road, where a warm light glowed from an upstairs bedroom and she followed Emily who had started trotting up the road towards Andy's. It was a beautiful night, the stars almost as visible as in the stunning sky views in the Arctic. She walked more briskly, the exercise clearing her brain of the soppy, self-pitying thoughts. Emily looked back encouragingly. The dog was good for her, she had to admit.

Andy stood at his gate, looking out at the road. He wasn't as rude to her as to other people—they'd know each other since grade school—but she respected his privacy. She was just going to wave and turn back but he looked so oddly dejected, almost sagging there on the gate, that she was moved to speak.

"I'm sorry about your cow, Andy."

She thought he wasn't going to reply, which was O.K. and she turned to go.

"She was a good cow," he said in his rough unused voice. "I've had three prize calves out of her. And there were more to come."

Miranda awkwardly sought words of comfort. "You gave her a good life here on the farm."

Poltz raised his face, his hair a shaggy silver thatch in the starlight. His gnarled farmer's hands gripped the gate rail tightly. "She should still be here, out in the barn. It's not right." His voice thickened with anger. "It's that devil Sousa causing trouble again. It's not right. He must be stopped."

Emily started nervously and Miranda pulled the dog closer, patting her smooth soft head.

"I'm sorry," Miranda said again. The stars twinkled callously above.

A line from Longfellow ran through her head.

The wind is rising, it seizes and shakes.

But she hardly thought the words would be a comfort to Andy.

That night she tossed restlessly. She dreamt that she was in a boat, approaching Middle Island on the Hawks Nest Point side. Sun sparkled on the water, the boat motor chugged cheerfully. From a distance, the spinning wind turbines looked quite pretty, like the great gossamer heads of wild goats beard in seed. There were thirty or more of the machines, stretching in a ragged line the entire length of the Point. As the boat neared the rocky shore, the turbines grew bigger and she felt rather than heard a great, ominous humming. She tried to steer the boat away, she wanted to warn the people on the island. The great blades spun faster and harder. And she watched in horror as in a vision straight out of Jules Verne, the entire island was lifted up off the water and carried away dripping, into the sky.

She woke up shivering, heard Emily whimpering in concern on her mat.

"I should do something, Emily. What am I saving myself for?"

She thought of orange robed monks immolating themselves in fire. Veered away. Burning her bra, who would care? Setting a bomb. Now there was an idea. She'd heard there were instructions on the internet. Something to do with fertilizer, well she had the chicken shit, that was a start . . . . She dozed. After a few moments, Emily settled down too.

No wind is of service to him that is bound nowhere

Joe Pretty, Middle Island fisherman, opened his thermos and inhaled the sweet waft of coffee that surged out. It was almost better than drinking the stuff. Almost, because it sure tasted darn good too, especially out here on the bay at six in the morning.

"Want some, Harry?" he called out to the man at the front of the boat.

But Harry was looking out for the rocks. After forty years of fishing the bay, Harry could probably steer this bit blindfolded, but not Harry, he always liked to keep a lookout along the bottom of the bluff. They never fished here, there were no reeds just the rocks and the meagre pebbly beach. Mostly they fished for walleye pike in the friendlier waters a mile further south. And these days, they didn't get many pike from the bay at all. Joe and Harry were just about the last fellows to own a commercial fishing license in the area. Most days now, they just went out because they liked being on the water. Shore life meant wives and chores, bay life was freedom.

Joe sipped his coffee while the Bonny Belle slipped quietly through the soft chop of the waves. The quiet was his work, he'd always had the mechanical skill while Harry liked to navigate. Though on a two-man boat they could each do a fair job of almost anything that came up. The ragged columns of the bluff slid by. In forty years he'd watched the outlines gradually change as the eroding limestone chunks crumbled thirty feet down to the water's edge. A single scrawny oak tree still clung to the top of the bluff, its roots now sticking out like a reaching hand into open air. Others had toppled over, to add to the scrambled jumble of rocks beneath.

"What's that there?" Harry called back over his shoulder.

"Where?" Joe asked. "What you looking at?" Harry had a sharp eye. Once he'd seen a pelican, way up here at the Point, a thousand miles off course. He looked where Harry was pointing to a place on the broken rocks. And then he saw it.

As far as he knew, no bird every wore a blue nylon jacket.

*   *   *

Halstead was dreaming. Something about fishing, only every time he reels in his line, there's a cellphone on the hook. As soon as it leaves the water, the instrument starts to shriek. He can't control the rod, he keeps casting and pulling up cellphones. He keeps flipping them to the shore where they set up a shrieking, demanding chorus among the reeds. He wishes he could drop the rod and cover his ears but he can't.

The ringing was real. He rolled over and reached groggily for the phone, his own by the bedside table. Wondering glumly who would be on the other end. Vern? Or Sousa, with another demand to lift the injunction. That's how yesterday began, with Burt's new campaign, phoning Halstead at home. But it was Jane, calling from the station. She sounded breathless, her words coming out in short little gasps.

"I'm patching a call through from Joe Pretty," she said. "He's on his boat."

Halstead hopped up and down, trying to shake off his pyjama pants while he listened. The sound, from Joe's cb radio, was scratchy and Joe's voice was hoarse with excitement but he gave a fairly straightforward report. On sighting the clothing at the bottom of the bluff, the two elderly fishermen had chugged the *Bonny Belle* in as close as they could to the rocks. Using binoculars they'd managed to determine that there was a human body there, likely deceased.

Or "All broke up," as Joe put it.

"Can you tell who it is?" Halstead asked, cursing as he caught his foot in his trousers and nearly fell over. "Is it a man, a woman, Christ, it's not a kid!"

Before the *WindSpear* people had fenced off the Point, teenagers used to drive out there to neck. He'd spent some time there himself aeons ago. He sent up a silent prayer, please don't let it be a kid.

"It's a man," Joe said. "Looks like he's wearing one of those blue jackets from that wind place company. We can't see his face." And don't really want to it sounded like.

"Call search and rescue." Halstead told Jane, who was still on the line. "And the ambulance."

Though he doubted there was much use for the ambulance. Joe Pretty would know what he was talking about. He knew that section of the bluff well himself and couldn't imagine that anyone would survive a tumble off the top.

"Stay there, Joe," he said. "We're on our way."

Halstead put his flasher on the cruiser though at this hour of the day there would be little traffic even in town. Close behind, he could hear the whine of the ambulance siren as it pulled out of the hospital parking lot. He stopped at the Jakes house to pick up Pete, who he had phoned directly he'd finished giving instructions to Jane. The younger man stood ready by the mailbox, looking wide awake. Must be that army training, gets the boys up and at 'em in three minutes. Jakes got into the cruiser, carefully carrying a steaming cup of coffee. Halstead had filled him in only briefly but he asked no questions, just sat quietly sipping. They drove the short distance in silence, but the question filled the car like an exploding airbag. *Who is it?*

It wasn't Jim Keen at the bottom of the bluff, because the site foreman came out of the office trailer on hearing the cruisers and ambulance drive up. It was now eight a.m. Truck and bulldozer operators were arriving for work, as well as the two staff members from the trailer. All were gathering to see what was up with the sirens.

Halstead stopped briefly before Keen. "An accident at the bluff," he said tersely. "A couple of fishermen have spotted a body."

"Jeesuz," Keen paled.

"Hop in."

"Burt not in yet?" Halstead asked over his shoulder.

"I saw the SUV when I came in this morning," Keen said in a strained voice. "I don't know where Burt is."

Halstead rocked the cruiser along the road, a barely visible double track across the stony ground. Directly ahead, the rays of a huge red sun streaked the calm water of the lake, like raking claws. For a moment it seemed that the chief was going to plunge the car right over the bluff but he braked to a shuddering halt a couple of feet from the edge. The three men scrambled hastily out.

Turned out it was handy having the site manager along. It was Keen who made the actual identification from the top of the bluff.

"Yes, that's Burt," he said, handing the binoculars back to Halstead. "That's his jacket, it says project manager on the back. It was supposed to say assistant project manager but he did it his way and nobody could get him to change it."

The Mayor was dead. Halstead could hardly believe it. Burt Sousa wouldn't be getting his own way ever again.

They ended up descending to the rocks by land. The coast guard boat, much larger than the fishermen's craft, couldn't get into that forbidding shore either. Several hundred feet aong the bluff from where Burt had fallen, the bluff edge dipped abruptly into a small gully that opened onto the stretch of pebbled beach. It was a bit of a scramble for the stretcher bearers with their equipment but the others got down alright, then had to pick their way carefully over the rocky scree to the spot where the Mayor lay sprawled like some kind of pagan sacrifice on a slab of split limestone.

Halstead doffed his cap. Thank god the man had fallen face down. Still, it was a quelling sight, the sickening angle of the limbs, that unatural final sagging after life had departed. There was no doubt Burt was dead. He walked cautiously around the body, saw no blood other than a small seeping trail from the head area.

The ambulance guys nodded knowledgeably. "He's gone alright. Broke his neck it looks like. Plus most everything else."

"O.K." Halstead said. "There's nothing we can do for Burt. You fellers will have to wait for a bit though. We need to take some pictures and wait for the coroner."

Two hours later, Halstead stood at the top of the bluff, rubbing his brow and frowning down at the scene below. Chris Pelly the doctor from Bonville General who doubled as district coroner when needed, had arrived to conduct his unhappy examination. It had been a long morning and the rest of the day was going to be even longer. So far, since that first scratchy phone call from Joe Pretty's cb radio, the task had been largely a matter of organization and logistics. Now he'd had to put Kevin on crowd control.

Word had spread quickly through town and people had driven down to the Point to watch the retrieval of the body. Above the busy scene spun the blades of Turbine Number One, obliviously cheerful in the brisk breeze. A casual onlooker viewing the crowd gathered in the beautiful June day, might easily have mistaken the gathering for some festive event at the Point. A fair day or a family reunion picnic. People were shocked but curious too.

It's that jinx at work again. The whole damn Point is jinxed.

He was a real mess. Everything broken.

His head was stove in.

It's true, my sister told me. She's married to Joe Pretty, he's the one who found the body.

The fishermen would get some free rounds in the Island pub tonight.

A tan sedan was parked inside the police tape, between the police cruisers and the ambulance. The Sousa family car, young Gavin at the wheel, his mother and sister beside him. Pete could see only Elena's pale, rigid profile, her blonde hair caught hastily back in a slide, her arm around her daughter Ronda. The boy's face was tense and white, his shoulders rigidly set in his school jacket. There were some blatant gawkers in the crowd who stared at the car but most people considerately averted their glances.

Kevin, posted at the top of the trail, looked alert. There was an involuntary gasp from the crowd as the white-coated ambulance attendants staggered into view at the bluff edge, carrying the stretcher and its shrouded burden. Pete glanced quickly towards the Sousa sedan, where Elena moved to shield her daughter from the stares of the crowd, to give her some privacy at this dreadful moment.

*   *   *

Two in the afternoon. All on-lookers had departed soon after the ambulance left. Now the cops stood with Keen at the bluff's edge, not too close. Framed by a stunning backdrop of sky and bay, picture postcard perfect on arguably the most beautiful day of the year so far. It was obvious where Sousa had gone over. Juniper bushes had been bent flat at the spot and an entire section of the loose limestone lip of the bluff broken away.

"So what the hell happened here?" Halstead asked Keen. "What was Burt doing tramping around the bluff in the dark. Was he drunk?"

Looking down at that cruel landing pad of ragged rock, Pete felt his own stomach lurch at the thought. He hoped that Sousa *had* been drunk, that he hadn't experienced a moment of stark, sober terror as he fell out into the emptiness. Keen seemed to experience the same thought. The site manager looked ill, as if all the blood had gone cold in his own body as well as Sousa's.

And no wonder, here was a second fatal accident on his turf. Obviously the company had yet to install any security system. At the very least, there would be a second investigation, possibly another shutdown of operations. The man would have to shape up though, he was now the the senior authority on the site. As if suddenly realizing this, he made a visible effort to pull himself together.

"I don't know what Burt was doing here," he said. "I couldn't stop him from coming back on the property if he wanted to," he added defensively. "No matter what time of night."

"You mean he'd come out here before at night?" Halstead asked.

Keen looked away from the bluff back to the turbine tower.

"I think Burt was a bit nuts about the project. Once when I was closing up I found him just sitting in that big car of his, looking out at the lake. Like he was waiting for the wind to come up. Or he'd come out just to hear those big turbine blades going around. He *liked* the sound, he could never understand why people would object to it. He said he'd be glad to sleep near that sound, it was soothing, he'd sleep like a baby."

Sure, Sousa liked that sound, Pete thought. The sound of making money.

Halstead looked sceptical and Keen shifted uncomfortably. "I know it sounds weird but that's what he said."

Chris Pelly's baseball cap appeared at the top of the gully. He made his way over to the group at the bluff edge and looked regretfully out at the Bay.

"Nice day for sailing," he said.

"All done?" Halstead asked.

Pelly nodded. "For now anyway. I'll have to do the lab report of course."

"Pretty grim, I guess. Landing on those rocks."

"Pretty grim."

"Check his blood alcohol level for us will you."

Pelly looked up. "You think he'd been drinking?"

"Maybe. It's one reason why a man might step off a cliff into thin air. I'd never mark Burt as the suicide type."

Halstead turned to Pete. "Let's see if we can find out how Burt got to the bluff."

There were several trails leading in from the road. Local people had been using them for decades, long before anyone thought of harvesting the wind on the Point. Some were mere tracks in the dust, others showed the marks of dirt bikes. Most of them ended up near the gully, the only accessible spot where people could get down to the water for a swim.

But Halstead chose the trail that looked as if it would lead back in the direction of the site trailer.

"Looks like this is the way he came, all right." Pete said. There were freshly snapped branches here and there, and the sharp tang of crushed juniper needles. He pressed on, pushing greenery back. "And look at the mess here."

At first Pete thought they had reached a small clearing along the trail. Then he realized any clearing had been done by a couple of bears, that's what it looked like anyway. There was a circle of trampled bushes and a smashed sapling practically broken in half.

Pete whistled. "He must have been falling down drunk to do all this damage."

"It looks more like a two-man job to me," Halstead said grimly.

"A fight, you mean."

"Yep. And a real knock-down drag out one, too."

The crushed branches told a tale of a struggle of some kind but gave no useful clues to the identity of the participants. The junipers were growing in nearly pure rock. What dirt the wind let overlooked was dry, just a powdering over the rock that kept no trace of footprints. Still, when they retraced their steps along the track, the picture became pretty clear. Two people had been moving towards the bluff and they weren't having a friendly stroll. Marks of the desperate race continued all along the route. Either Burt had reached the cliff by himself, going fast or two people got there together and struggled till Burt went over.

The two policemen stood looking thoughtfully down at the rocks.

"Shoot!" Halstead said. "I thought things were bad enough. Now it's a whole new ballgame."

21

M*urder.* The word stuck like an unwelcome burr in Halstead's brain. He could feel it there, prickly and stubborn and not going away.

When was the last murder on the Island? He cast his mind over a string of Island passings, mostly from age-related natural causes, plus a few assorted accidents. Ah yes, that drunken brawl at the Island's one pub a couple of years ago, and even that was eventually reduced to a manslaughter charge. A sad case, the victim was the killer's own cousin. But as Halstead was well aware, that was often the case in city homicides as well. Only a small percentage of murders were committed by strangers.

So likely two people would now be permanently leaving Island life. Burt to the graveyard and his killer to the penitentiary.

First though, he had to find the murderer. And he had two rookie cops to help him do the job. He'd sent them out to pick up Andy Poltz. The man had to be questioned, that was a no-brainer.

*   *   *

Kevin switched disgustedly from the country sounds of KABS and back to the local rock station. He didn't like the rock station any better but that way he got to complain about them both. It was all part of the daily railing of how he hated being stuck in hick land.

An ad for the Island Diner came on touting the Turbine Burger, *a new spin for your taste buds.* Kevin switched it off to flop back in his seat and scowl impatiently at the clumps of small yellow flowers that lined the road.

"Well now we know which of those two dopes won," he said.

"You mean Poltz?" Pete shrugged. "I don't know what he won, a jail term doesn't seem much of a prize. Anyway we don't even know if he did it yet."

"What odds do you want? I'll give you ten to one that crazy farmer pushed Sousa over the bluff."

Pete didn't answer, but he wouldn't have taken the bet either.

The Poltz place looked as unwelcoming as ever, maybe more so. Gate shut, window blinds down. Had Poltz done a bolt? Where would the man go, Pete wondered. Who would take him in?

Kevin knocked on the kitchen screen door and opened it cautiously. A used frying pan lay in the sink, next to a cup of coffee dregs. Pete called, walked to the bottom of the stairs and called again but there was no answer.

"Must be out in the barn," he said.

"Better watch out," Kevin warned. "Remember the old guy got that shotgun back."

But they found the farmer going stolidly about his chores, forking out clean straw into the stalls. He didn't look up from his task. "I figured you'd be coming by," was his greeting. He seemed quiet but the two policemen kept a wary eye on him. There was that pitchfork with its four deadly prongs.

"I guess you heard what happened at the Point," Pete said.

Poltz nodded. "Yep, I did."

"Thought we'd find you doing a victory dance," Kevin said.

The old man frowned. "Right was done. It's not something to crow about."

Kevin looked triumphant. "So you think it was right for someone to murder Sousa? Maybe you thought you should do the job."

Poltz turned around at that, still wielding his pitchfork. Kevin took a step back.

"How did you get that big bruise on your face?" Pete asked. "It looks nasty."

The blood had spread under Poltz's skin, his entire right cheek was a blue-black blotch.

"Fell on a rake," Poltz said. "Dumb thing to do."

"When was that?" Pete asked. "I didn't notice it yesterday when we were out at the road with the veterinarian."

"Last night," Poltz said. He tossed another forkful of straw into the stall.

"Seems a dangerous job, farming," Kevin said. "All that barbed wire, cattle breaking out, now you've fallen on a rake. I guess you've got no witnesses, other than these cows."

"That's right," Poltz said. He seemed barely interested in the conversation.

"What else did you do last night?" Pete asked, though he doubted that Poltz was going to come up with an alibi that placed him in the Island Roadhouse with a roomful of witnesses eager to clear his name. In fact he came up with his usual succinct description of his evenings.

"Ate supper, went to bed."

"Was that before or after you stepped on that rake?" asked Kevin.

Poltz ignored him.

"I'm afraid we're going to have to ask you to come into the station for an interview Mr. Poltz," Pete said. He wondered if the man would come easily or put up some resistance.

Poltz sighed heavily, like a football loosing air. "Do you aim to keep me overnight?" he asked. "I got to get Aaron to look after the cattle."

"I don't know," Pete said. "Maybe you should call him."

Poltz jabbed the pitchfork upright into the straw, took a last look around the barn. Even in his stained work overall, the big rawboned old man was an impressive figure. That rigid frame, the shoulders barely stooped. Was his expression resigned, calm, fatalistic? Or just teed off at this tedious break in his routine Was he acting like a murderer? Pete couldn't tell. As a soldier he'd seen a fair amount of killing, some close to the line, close to deliberate. He'd also seen enough to know that it wasn't always possible to predict what anyone would do under certain circumstances.

They followed the old man out of the barn, past the curious gaze of his rough legged, shaggy cattle.

Maybe the beasts could shed some light on the truth. If they could only talk.

*   *   *

Halstead stood outside the interrogation room, scowling into his coffee.

It had been obvious from the start that there wasn't going to be any easy confession coming from Poltz. If he had indeed murdered Burt, he was going to be a tough nut to crack. The man seemed totally unfazed by their questioning. Nor by the fact that he had no alibi and had been witnessed in a violent struggle with the victim only thirty hours earlier. And that half his face now looked as if it had run into a very heavy fist, several times.

Poltz stuck to his story that he had had his supper and gone to bed as he presumably did each and every one of the other three hundred and sixty four nights of the year. It was a pretty good strategy even if hadn't known it. Unless they could find some handy witness who had seen him at the bluff last night, or some physical evidence that placed him there, the cops were stuck for the moment.

But time for a second round. Halstead tossed his mug ungently into the sink.

"Back to the salt mines," he said to Jakes.

The old man sat upright in the wooden chair. He had declined any refreshment.

Halstead sat across from him, said crisply.

"O.K. Andy, one more time, just so's we've got the record straight. When did you last see Burt Sousa?"

Poltz sighed. He was probably genuinely tired. It was nearly six o'clock, getting close to his bedtime. Or maybe he was a bit pooped because he'd been up all night murdering Burt Sousa.

"I saw him yesterday morning in the road, standing over my dead steer," he said. "Same as the rest of you."

"You sure you weren't out making a midnight patrol along your fence line, last night?" Jakes asked. "Officer Ragusa is out there right now having a look for tracks."

Though he doubted Kevin would be lucky enough to spot a human boot marking in the mess of cattle hoofprints.

Halstead leaned forward and said in a confiding, friendly way. "Come on Andy, you can talk to me. I know that Burt wasn't the easiest man to get along with, everybody on the Island knew that. And you had a couple of run-ins with him. Maybe the next run-in just got a little more out of control. Maybe Burt hit you first, caught you smack in the face and you saw red. Anybody would, that must have hurt. So you hit him back, pushed him too hard, and it sent him down the bluff. Is that what happened, is that the way it went?"

But Poltz wasn't having any, in fact seemed to have got his second wind. He crossed his arms and spoke his longest piece yet.

"Maybe I'm not the only one who's gone a round with that devil. Why don't you ask that Keen feller, that site manager, what he and Sousa were arguing about last week? They were yelling to beat the band, right there in the road."

Halstead downplayed his interest. He shrugged. "They worked together, they must occasionally have had differences of opinion."

"They shared one taste at least," the old man said cryptically. The sly expression looked bizarre on his old Testament face, like the leer on a vaudeville actor.

"And what might that be?" Halstead asked warily. He had a feeling he didn't want to know.

"Keen was doing Sousa's wife," Poltz said with sour triumph.

Halstead temporized. "Now how would you know a thing like that, Andy? I doubt you're out on the social scene much."

"My hired man told me. He saw them over at the Bonville Motel a coupla weeks back, coming out of one of the rooms. That Keen feller was even driving one of them blue wind company cars, Aaron said. The ones with the picture of a windmill on the door."

22

*If a man does not know what port he is steering for,
no wind is favourable to him.*

They let Poltz go for now. The old man made the most of his exit, demanding a ride home. Kevin was assigned the task. Halstead leaned tiredly back in his desk chair, making a tent of his fingers on his shirt front.

"If Andy did do it, there'd be no remorse that's for sure. He'd likely be boasting about it."

"He's got lots of motive, though," Pete said. "Then there's that bruise on his face. Maybe it's risky to let him go. Maybe he'll do a bunk."

Halstead laughed dryly and echoed Pete's earlier thought. "Where would he go, the old misery? He's seventy years old and alone, he'll just go home to his cattle."

He reached for the telephone. "I guess we'd better talk to Keen. Find out where he was last night. And Elena," he added reluctantly.

Jim Keen seemed stunned, his cheeks slack and blanched with shock.

"How did you know?" he asked.

Halstead shrugged. "We're the cops. I give you two credit, though. I wouldn't think it was possible to keep an affair secret for long on this island." He was thinking of Steph's comment about their own "date" at the parking lot picnic table.

Keen groaned. Reality was starting to sink in. He began to babble.

"It just happened. It was stupid, dumb. God, does Melanie have to know? Do you have to tell her?"

Halstead ignored the plea and concentrated on the essentials. "So how long has this been going on?"

Keen shrugged helplessly, tried to concentrate. "Not long, since Christmas I guess." He shook his head again in disbelief. "My God—Melanie—the kids!"

"When were you going to tell her?"

Keen looked up blankly. "Tell her? Tell her what?"

"That you were leaving her for another woman. Or were you planning to send her an e-mail?"

"I wasn't going to leave Melanie," Keen said miserably. "It's hard to explain. Elena and me, we just neeeded each other for awhile. She was lonely, I was . . . . I don't know what I was. Bored. Flattered or something. Stupid, that's for sure."

He groaned again, "Maybe I should have just bought a new car instead. That's what most men do, I hear."

"But you say you'd been seeing each other since Christmas?"

"Off and on. But not much. Maybe once every couple of weeks."

"Wasn't it difficult when you were working so closely with Sousa?"

"Elena usually figured things out. Then she'd let me know when to meet her." Keen's mouth twisted in a weak grin. "I kind of enjoyed putting something over on him. The guy was such a bastard. The way he acted when the Gillies kid fell, I wanted to quit. And he'd been fooling around for years, Elena told me." He wiped his face and looked up. "Anyway it's over now."

"You mean since Burt is dead?"

"No, we broke it off a couple of weeks ago. By mutual agreement." He groaned again. "We thought no harm done, nobody would ever know. She had lots of other reasons to divorce Burt."

"Elena was planning to divorce Burt?"

Keen nodded. "She talked about it a lot."

"So where were you, Jim on Thursday night?"

"On Thursday? . . . . Say why are you asking me all these questions anyway? Did Burt off himself or something?" The two policemen watched the penny drop.

"You think he might have jumped off that bluff because he found out his wife was having an affair and he was *depressed!* That's just crazy." Keen squirmed in his chair. "More likely the guy would have taken a punch at me."

"Yeah we think that too. We think you might have given a punch back and knocked him off the bluff."

"Hey wait a minute. I may not have liked, him, I may have wanted to quit the job sometimes, but I didn't kill the guy for gods' sake." He shook his head numbly trying to take it in. "I thought he fell, now you're saying he was *pushed?*"

"You tell me," Halstead said. "Apparently you had quite the argument with Sousa a couple days ago. You were seen at the site, hollering and waving your fist."

Keen grimaced. "I talked to him that way most days. That was the only way to get Sousa's attention, you had to talk the same way he did." He rubbed his forehead hard, leaving an angry red welt.

"And he didn't fire you for challenging him like that?"

"I knew the drill and he knew he'd waste time bringing in a new guy. He didn't want any more delays."

"So again, where were you on Thursday night?"

He looked ashamed. "Home with the wife," he said.

"She'll vouch for you?"

"Yes," he said sadly. "If I'm lucky, Melanie will forgive me—if not, then I'm just another straying arsehole, drinking alone in the Island bar on Saturday night."

He looked resignedly at Halstead. "Are you sure this has to come out? Elena's leaving town, it's all over."

"I'll do what I can Jim but it's not just a case of tongues wagging anymore. Now it's police business. And we'll be checking your alibi with Melanie. She'd better be awfully sure you were home that night."

"I was home. And I didn't kill anybody. Why don't you question Andy Poltz?" he asked rebelliously. "He's been out often enough prowling around his fence with his shotgun, even though we've warned him off the site. There's already a restraining order against the man for God's sake."

"Sousa wasn't shot," Halstead reminded him. "He was pushed over the bluff. Anyone could have done that."

They poured Keen a coffee and left him to stew for awhile.

"Drive him home," Halstead said. "And see if the wife will back up his sorry butt."

It was a short, silent ride. Keen sat slumped in the cruiser passenger seat, the picture of dejection.

"Stop," he said as they neared the house. "Please stop here for a minute."

"You might as well get it over with," Pete said, though he was hardly relishing the prospect of shattering Mrs. Keen's evening, possibly her marriage.

"I'll tell Melanie," Keen said, his expression miserable in the orange sodium glare of the streetlight. "I know I have to do that. But I can't ask her to lie to the police for me. Melanie would never be able to handle that."

Pete pulled over. "O.K. Talk."

Keen looked down the street towards his house, then looked away. He began talking haltingly, then plunged desperately on.

"I was working late Thursday, wrapping up a report. Everybody else had left and I was just getting ready to lock up. Then Burt drove in the lane and got out of the car. He was swaying and lurching around as if he'd been drinking. He was a big guy you know and could be scary. He started coming towards the trailer and hollering out my name. I thought he'd somehow found out about Elena and me. All I could think of was to get out of there fast. I tried to act normal. I figured I'd just keep on walking past him, wave, say goodnight, keep on going towards my car. But he grabbed me and started pulling me back towards the trailer.

"Have a drink with me," he says, real sloppy and slurring.

I said I had to get home but he kept yanking me along.

"For Chrissake have a drink with me," he kept saying. "I'm the boss and I'm telling you to have a drink, that's an order."

There's a fridge in the trailer, always some beer in it, so I grab a couple. I figure I'd better humor him, then try to sneak out when he has to take a leak or something.

"No," he says, "open the champagne." There's a bottle left from the day we put up the demo turbine.

"What are we celebrating?" I ask him. I'm nervous, I'm trying to read his mood, how much does he know? Does he know about me and Elena? Is he playing a cat and mouse game with me?

But then he just gets all gloomy and sorry for himself, you know the way that drunks do.

"I got nothing to celebrate, he says, not a goddamn thing. I just feel like drinking some goddamn champagne."

So I pop open the bottle and pour some out into coffee mugs, that's all I can find in the trailer. I still want to get the hell out of there, though. I don't trust the guy.

But he's whining away about what a disappointment his son is, how the kid might as well be a queer, he's such a wimp. And about how bad his marriage his. How his family doesn't appreciate what he's trying to do for them.

It was creepy, and all the time I was wondering when he was going to jump me from across the desk and start throttling me. He was starting to pour me another drink but then he kind of fell on his face on the desk. He passed out I guess. So I left, I beat it out of there."

He looked at Pete. "But I swear on my mother's life, Sousa was there at the desk with the bottle in front of him when I left. I could see him through the trailer window as I drove away."

*   *   *

"So what do you think?" Halstead asked Pete. He was starting to rely on young Jakes' opinion. He had a lot more on the ball than Fred ever had.

Pete doodled on a scratch pad. A rectangle for the trailer, a dotted line indicating the path to the cliff. Two stick figures on the path, one behind the other. Stick knees bent. Running.

"We've got them both there on the site that night. If Sousa did come hell-bent on catching Keen, how does it play out? Or maybe Mrs. Sousa is there too. Maybe Sousa caught them there together."

"Why would they be out there? The motel would be safer."

"True. So it looks more likely that Sousa had found out somehow, just as Keen thought. Sousa knew that Keen often worked late. So he storms in, Keen is scared and he runs out of the trailer. Only instead of running to his car like he says, he heads towards the bluff."

"Why wouldn't he run for the car?" Halstead asked.

"He's scared, he's not thinking straight. Or maybe Sousa didn't give him a choice."

"So Burt catches up to Keen at the edge of the bluff, they struggle and somehow Burt loses his balance."

Pete looked sceptical. "Keen versus Sousa in a knock-down drag out fight for survival? Somehow I can't see Keen winning. He's younger and in better shape than Sousa was but does he have the chops?"

Halstead nodded but said, "It's surprising—you never know how a person will react in a violent situation."

"Still, if it was a case of self-defense, why wouldn't Keen tell us?"

Halstead rolled his eyes. "I hate to break it to you Jakes but most people don't like to tell the police anything at all. Or they're too scared."

Jakes looked sheepish. "Point taken. The guy was scared that's for sure. And he's not wearing any sign of a fight. Not like Andy Poltz's face."

Halstead sighed. "Maybe Keen's a fast runner. He stayed ahead of Sousa and Sousa tripped on something when they got to the bluff."

"I could see him running away," Pete said. "The guy has no guts. He never takes responsibility for anything."

"I guess next we interview Elena," Halstead said wryly. "You'll find she's gutsy enough for the both of them."

Pete looked back down at his doodle. Now one stick figure was falling off the cliff, headfirst.

One stick person left on the bluff. Standing all alone.

23

The last time Pete had seen Elena Sousa she was wearing a housecoat in her kitchen, having breakfast with her husband and kids. On this so different morning, he expected to see some signs of shock, if not actual grief. The woman may have been planning to divorce her husband but presumably didn't wish him murdered. Or did she? Maybe she thought the legal procedure would take too long and she'd hurry things up a bit.

Actually Elena looked remarkably sef-possessed, Pete thought. If she was suffering any shock, her make-up hid the effects. Her hair was shorter and freshly blonded and she looked a bit trimmer than he remembered but still strong and sturdy in a cream coloured pant suit with a patterned scarf knotted above her impressive cleavage. An imposing presence, she was nearly as tall as the two men who stood up when she entered the office. Pete wondered how Sousa had had the nerve to cheat on her. She looked askance at the chair before sitting down. Halstead had chosen to interview her there, rather than in the interrogation room.

She responded quietly to Halstead's solicitous inquiry about how she and her children were managing. Then she looked straight at him and asked matter-of-factly why they wanted to talk to her. No phony fragility for Elena Sousa. Not for her the role of the helpless widow.

Halstead answered her in the same vein. "We've been talking to Jim Keen, Elena."

She didn't blanch, as her lover had. She laughed.

"So?" she said. "Is that why you called me in? It was nothing, it's over."

"But you're admitting that you did have an affair with Keen?"

She sighed. "And don't go all moralistic on me Bud Halstead. Why shouldn't I have a social life? Burt embarrassed me enough with his floozies." She clucked her tongue dismissively. "But it doesn't matter anymore, any of that. Burt's gone, god rest his rotten soul, and all that's over with. I'll be making a fresh start, making my own way now. And I don't see that my *affairs* are any of your business."

Halstead looked apologetic—did all women, even women suspects, inspire some vestige of chivalry, Pete wondered. But the chief's words were tough enough.

"That's the unfortunate thing, Elena. It isn't all over, maybe not for awhile yet. It looks as if Burt might not have been alone up at the bluff. It looks as if someone might have pushed him over the edge."

Pete had read in books of warring expressions on a person's face. Now he saw the actual phenomenon. In Elena's case, a puckering of the brows indicating puzzlement, followed by surprise and then was that *irritation*? Yes it was.

"Burt was drunk," she said scornfully. "Drunk and boasting to himself how much money he was going to make. He was like that most nights, he didn't need any help to fall off that edge."

"Somebody was there with him," Halstead said. "We know that."

"And you're suspecting me or Jim?" she laughed rawly. "Now that's a wonderful thing. I finally make up my mind to leave Burt and now you want to arrest me for murdering him. Burt would get a real kick out of that. He'd laugh himself sick."

"Nobody's talking arrest here, Elena. We're just asking some questions. So you were planning to leave Burt?"

She smiled sourly. "Yes, but not with Jim Keen if that's what you're thinking. I'm looking for my freedom, not another man to mess up my life."

Halstead nodded. "But just for the record, where were you Thursday night?"

She sighed and leaned back in her chair. "I had an appointment with my lawyer. I filed for divorce a month ago, long before Thursday night, you'll notice."

"How did Burt feel about that?"

She pursed her lips, "I don't know. Burt and I stopped telling each other how we felt a long time ago."

"How did you *think* he felt?"

She bristled. "He said it wasn't good timing financially. That all his money—*his money!*—was tied up in the wind project. I said I didn't care. He might never get final approval for the darn project and I wasn't going to wait."

Halstead looked sympathetic. "Word is that Burt was over-extended financially. That he'd mortgaged everything – the business, even your house. That must have been rough."

"He tried to get the house," Elena said tautly, "but I wouldn't let him. I'm a co-owner and he couldn't legally sign it over without my signature. The bastard would have taken Gavin's college fund if he could have." She smiled grimly. "So you see, it would have made more sense if Burt had killed me."

"And what if the project does come through eventually?"

She shrugged. "Right now I just have a bunch of shares on rocky old Hawks Nest Point. A whole bunch of nothing if you ask me." She picked up her purse. "This is depressing me. Can I go?"

"What did you do when you left the lawyer's Thursday night?"

"I went home. But you'll have to take my word for it. Gavin was out somewhere, he's hardly every home these days and Ronda was doing her homework. When she's playing on her tweeter and I-pod, she probably wouldn't know if I was there or not."

Halstead rose to his feet. "Alright Elena. That's all for now, thank you for coming in. I'd appreciate if you didn't leave town for a bit."

"Then you'd better wrap this up soon. I get a buyer for the house and I'm out of here. I'm gone."

She turned at the door, mulling something over in her mind. "If Jim did push Burt off the bluff, I'm sorry for him and Melanie. But don't go thinking it's my fault. Jim had his own battles with Burt and he was getting more and more fed up with the job. If he finally snapped, it's nothing to do with me."

She adjusted the knot in her scarf and patted down her newly-brightened hair. "No, if Burt got himself killed, it was his own darn fault. He brought it on himself."

The two men stared silently into her wake.

"Maybe *she* tossed him over the cliff," Pete shook his head, looking slightly dazed. "She's cool enough."

"Oh yes, women can kill too," Halstead said. He'd seen a bit of that in his years away in the city. But despite all Jakes' military experience of death, this case would be Jakes' introduction to domestic murder. It could be a shock.

"She certainly doesn't mind tossing Keen to the wolves," Pete said. "I almost feel sorry for the guy."

Halstead sighed. "Life with Burt Sousa has toughened her up. She was a farm girl—Her folks had six kids but not much luck. Burt was a go-getter and I guess Elena thought he'd get somewhere and take her with him. They did O.K. too with the business and him being Mayor. Too bad he wasn't content with that."

Pete pushed his chair back restlessly, scraping at the carpet. "So, do you think she had anything to do with it? She could have lured Sousa there for Keen to do the job. Either of them could have made a phony tip-off phone call, telling Burt to come and catch Keen and his wife in the act."

Halstead frowned. "Elena might go for premeditated but I doubt that Keen would. He had nothing to gain at all and he wasn't ruled by an unquenchable passion for Elena, they were breaking up. He'd hardly kill Burt as a favour to Elena."

"He might have," Pete said. "Keen is such a jellyfish, she could have bullied him into it."

Halstead shook his head, "I don't know what Elena saw in the guy, other than the sheer contrast with Burt. At a stretch, I can see the guy defending himself, but attacking? I don't think even she could whip him up to that."

He looked wishfully at the picture of the *Lone Loon*, envisioned the quiet marsh, leaping fish, dragonflies drying their wings in the sun. A world away from humans and their sordid motives.

"Elena has lots of passion though, passionate hatred at least and that's pretty strong stuff. She might have killed Burt eventually but I don't see how she could have pulled this one off by herself. Even drunk, Burt would be hard to wrestle with, maybe even worse."

He tossed his pencil across the desk. "One thing is certain, somebody pushed Burt off that cliff and we've got some alibis to check."

24

The second big funeral in one month. Once again cars were lined up for several blocks surrounding the church. Burt would have been gratified at the crowd, Halstead thought or more likely he would just have considered the homage his due. Though he doubted that there was much homage being given. More like relief.

Still, the Mayor had been such a *presence*. Big, bullying, raucous even when jovial but *there*, a fixture at all hockey games and sports events, at all town occasions. He would definitely leave a big hole in the tightly-woven fabric of the island community.

He watched his fellow townspeople file into the church, their faces fittingly sober. He knew darn well though that for the past couple of days the local grapevine had been working overtime with the news that Sousa's death was likely a murder case. He could feel the live wire of prurient interest running through the crowd as folks caught sight of Elena and the kids, Jim Keen and Melanie. People knew that they had been questioned.

Keen looked sick, Melanie looked pallid. Elena stood stone-faced as a statue between her son and daughter. The boy looked stoically forward, the girl leaned into the protection of her mother's shoulder. The principal suspect hadn't attended of course. He was tending his cattle.

When the ceremony was over, a long line of cars headed out behind the hearse for the graveyard. In a pastel blue sky, the newly arrived songbirds followed their own pursuits, oblivious to the silent procession below. Meanwhile, out at Hawks Nest Point, Turbine Number One, its blades humming in the stiff breeze, stood as a lone monument to Mayor Sousa's dream of worldly riches.

*   *   *

Vern was waiting for Halstead at the cruiser. The councilman was livid.

"Why'd you let Andy Poltz go? Everyone knows he did it. He wanted to stop the project, he's tried it before and we all know he hated Burt. Now Burt's widow and kids are following a hearse to the graveyard and his murderer is walking around free on his farm up the road. It doesn't look good, Bud."

Halstead elbowed him aside and opened the car door. "There's the little matter of collecting evidence, Vern. And I'd appreciate if you'd just leave us to it."

"You had to issue a restraining order against Poltz because he was so dangerous. What more evidence do you need?"

"I'll keep you informed of the investigation."

Vern leaned in the open window, he wasn't done yet.

"Now we've got those foreigners, the Danish people after us too. I got a phone call this morning. A man asked what's going, on they never expected this kind of trouble. An executive of the company is on his way here."

Halstead shrugged impatiently. "I imagine the Danes understand what happens in a murder investigation. People get murdered over in Denmark too or haven't you read Hamlet?"

He watched with some amusement as Vern took a deep breath, then switched tactics.

"I can understand if it's getting to be too much for you, Bud. You're short-handed, this is hard for you personally, for all of us. Maybe it's time we called in the provincials."

"Maybe it's time you shut up Vern. I've been looking after the safety of the folks on this Island for a long time now. And I plan to finish the job under my own steam. You keep on with your number crunching, I've got to get back to the real world."

As he drove away, he hoped he was right. Had it really been ten years since he returned to the Island.? Was it already two years since he'd lost Kathleen? One thing about a funeral, there was always that reminder that tempus fugit.

*   *   *

Lawyer G. Prentice's office occupied a couple of modified rooms in his home. The window looked out on a side yard where a flowering crab tree had burst overnight into exuberant bloom. From the back of the house came sounds of children playing. Pete was surprised, then realized that Prentice was only prematurely grey. He was probably only in his forties. He wore slacks, a short-sleeved blue shirt and no tie.

He greeted Pete politely, though he was obviously working on a file, and indicated a chair.

"What can I do for you?" he asked. "I trust nobody has launched a charge of brutality against the force?"

Behind his little jibe, his look was wary, Pete thought. Suspicion was probably habitual in the profession.

"We're investigating the Sousa murder," he said. "We had a few questions regarding Mrs. Sousa."

Prentice looked even more wary. "I'm sure you realize that I must respect lawyer-client privilege."

Pete nodded. "Of course. We'd just like you to confirm that Mrs. Sousa had an appointment with you last Thursday and when exactly that was."

Prentice took up a desk diary and flipped back through a couple of pages.

"She was here from seven-thirty until ten o'clock."

"At night?"

"Yes, I often work evenings to adapt myself to my clients' schedules."

Pete raised an eyebrow. "That seems like quite a long appointment." He wondered if maybe Elena had already moved on to another man since dumping Keen. If so, the woman worked quickly.

Prentice shrugged. "It's not unusual. Mrs. Sousa and I had been working on her divorce application. There was a lot involved."

Pete said the obvious. "But now she doesn't have to get divorced."

Prentice nodded. "Not exacty tactfully put, officer. But you're right, now she doesn't have to get divorced."

"Will you still be working as her lawyer?"

"Yes. There's still a lot to work out."

"You were just handling the divorce, you aren't the Sousa family lawyer?"

"That's right."

"So you don't know any details about Mrs. Sousa's current financial position or whether she expects that to change in the near future."

"I only know what Mrs. Sousa chooses to tell me, and again that would come under lawyer-client privilege."

"I guess it would."

In the yard outside, a little girl about five years old ran towards the crabapple tree. She shrieked happily and spun round under the pink umbrella of blossoms.

"Hi Daddy!" she called.

Prentice looked out the window, his smile goofy with love. Pete felt guilty for his suspicions. He guessed that was another part of being a cop.

So what does Elena get?" Kevin asked.

"Prentice couldn't or wouldn't say. He's not the family lawyer."

"Maybe there's nothing left to get."

"The murder works either way," Pete said. "One way she kills her husband to get the money, the other way she offs him because she's teed off there isn't any money to get."

"So what now?"

"Prentice said Elena left his office at ten. The Chief wants us to talk to the Sousa boy. See if he knows what time his mother got home."

Kevin looked sceptical. "What do you expect him to say? What kind of kid is going to turn in his own mother?"

"It wasn't exactly a happy household," Pete reminded him. "Elena Sousa made no secret of that."

"Yeah well, I still say the kid wouldn't rat on his mother even if she was out later that night."

The sound of a vacuum cleaner came from behind the door but after Pete had rung the bell repeatedly, the machine was switched off. A middle-aged woman with grey hair answered the door, her face flushed with exertion.

"Yes?" she asked.

He explained their purpose and she invited them into the hallway, while she went looking for Gavin. From the doorway, he could see the living and dining rooms. There were stacks of boxes, newspaper wrapped lamps and ornaments and other signs of preparations for a move. A recycling box by his feet was filled with styrofoam fast-food trays.

The boy came downstairs reluctantly, his face creased and pale, as if he'd been sleeping. He was about Pete's own height, five ten, but thin as a rail. Thinner than Pete remembered. His hair was dark, as his mother's might be if she didn't dye it. He looked at the two policemen with a sort of dazed hostility. Pete didn't hold it against the kid. He may not have had a great relationship with his father but it must still be a shock to have your parent murdered.

"Your mother's not home?" Pete knew she was in Bonvillle, had chosen this time deliberately.

Gavin shook his head briefly. No.

Pete flipped through his notebook, as if he had something to check. "We just had a question for her but maybe you can help. I understand that your mother was out last Thursday night, that she had an appointment with her lawyer."

The night your father was killed actually and I feel rotten for asking you about it but I'm a cop and I'm looking for a killer.

"I forgot to ask her what time she got home. Would you remember, or possibly your sister might?"

The boy seemed to be having trouble comprehending the question. Pete wondered if maybe he was on some drug to help him through the family crisis.

He answered though, in a lacklustre voice. "Ronda is staying at her friend's house. She doesn't like to stay home on her own anymore."

He paused and they all thought about that sad fact for a minute. Pete was about to prompt the boy but then he continued in the same monotone.

"Mom was home when I came in. The television was on, sometimes she falls asleep when it's still on."

"And when was that?"

"Eleven maybe. Yeah, around eleven."

He looked vaguely around the hall. "I'm going back upstairs now."

The cleaning lady had returned with the telephone in her hand and was looking upset.

"I think I should call Mrs. Sousa."

Ragusa looked at Pete. Better go.

"It doesn't compute," Kevin said when they were back in the cruiser. "She leaves the lawyer at ten, gets home at eleven. That doesn't give her nearly enough time to play any games out at the Point."

"The boy just said he heard the TV, he didn't say that he actually saw her."

"So why didn't you ask him that?"

"I agree with you. He'd probably lie."

25

The coroner's report lay on Halstead's desk. A thin file to sum up the ending of a man's life. The paperwork described a Caucasian male, fifty-three years old, six foot one, two hundred and thirty-five pounds. A smoker and a drinker. Incipient arterial damage that would have eventually led to bypass surgery. Cause of death, massive trauma to the body incurred from a thirty-foot fall onto a surface of limestone rocks.

Estimated time of death, between nine p.m. and midnight.

And yes, the subject had a high blood alcohol content at the time. In other words, he was heavily inebriated. Halstead looked out the window, where a soft June drizzle was gently soaking the hay field. In June, even rain was attractive.

"So, we've got Elena home in bed at eleven. And Keen home with Melanie."

"So they say," Pete amended.

"And Andy Poltz was home with nobody."

"So he says."

"Even if Poltz had been out patrolling his fenceline that night, he's not likely to tell us. He knows he could go to jail for breaking the restraining order."

They'd interviewed Keen a couple more times, gone intensively over his story. He never altered the details and seemed genuinely shattered and contrite at the disaster his deceit had wrought on his wife and their family life.

They'd been over the murder scene too, many times. The unyielding rocks had given up no clues to the killer's identity.

Halstead sighed. "Murder is nasty. And it taints everything and everyone it touches. People lie and cover up and turn on each other. No matter who we arrest, there are going to be ripples in the community. So we'd better goddamn well be right."

"Maybe Miranda Paris did it," Pete suggested facetiously. "She's always going on about the evils brought on by messing with nature."

Halstead didn't smile, just cast another dissatisfied look at the file.

"No matter how many times we go ring round the rosie, we always come back to Andy. He's right there, practically on the scene. He had the best chance to operate unobserved. He knows those trails as well as Burt did and he's strong enough and big enough to toss Burt off that bluff. Just because he's the obvious choice, doesn't mean he didn't do it. He has motive to burn and he has no alibi."

He stopped, as if challenging the younger man. Or himself. Then voiced the hundred dollar question.

"But is it enough?"

Pete was silent.

"I know," Halstead sighed. "It's all circumstantial. What we need here is some hard evidence."

Jane buzzed the desk. Twice, like a fretful bumblebee.

"Roy Trant is here to see you. This month's manager of the bank," she added helpfully.

Trant was thirtyish, pink-cheeked above a shirt and tie. He was one of a series of similar young men sent out from head office on a rotating basis to train at the bank. Halstead barely got to know one, before the powers that be replaced him with another.

The two policemen looked up inquiringly as Trant put a small package on the desk.

"The bank security tape for last week," he explained. "My predecessor left a note on my desk that I should bring it to you."

Halstead looked at Pete, "Do you know anything about this?"
Pete shook his head.

"The section marked is for the morning of Thursday the 16th," Trant said.

Halstead raised an eyebrow, "Then I guess we might better make ourselves comfortable and watch a little TV. You could stay too, if you don't mind Roy, we might have some questions."

The tape showed the interior of the building at 9:30 a.m. The bank wasn't large, there were only two tellers at the counter and some small cubicle offices further in. Halstead ran the tape at a medium speed as a few customers came in, carried out their business and left. Then he sat up straight and hit the pause button.

"That's Andy Poltz!"

Though the camera view was from above, the farmer's shaggy white locks were unmistakeable. They watched as Poltz bypassed the tellers' counter and strode to a cubicle at the back of the room. The middle-aged woman at the desk looked up and smiled a greeting.

"That's our loan officer," Trant said.

Halstead recognized Peggy Stewart, she'd worked at the bank for years. Now she looked alarmed as Poltz loomed aggressively over the desktop. She stood up, mouthing words and obviously trying to calm the farmer down. But Poltz ignored whatever the loan officer was saying. He pounded the desk and made threatening gestures with his arms.

Peggy, with her back to the wall, edged round to the door of the cubicle and slipped out. Poltz pursued her, stopping in the middle of the room to shout some more, his face contorted with anger. Then he left, kicking out wildly at a wastebasket.

Halstead stopped the tape.

"You'd better get Peggy," he told Trant.

*   *   *

"Hi Bud," Peggy said on entering and being given a chair. Jane also brought coffee. No cinammon.

"Why didn't we hear of this fracas with Andy?" he asked her. "Have I been cut out of the local grapevine?"

Peggy laughed and shifted her ample behind. "There was so much going on, Bud. The funeral and all. Besides, if I was to get rattled by every desperate client who was asking for an extension on their loan payments, I'd have to be taking Valium with my breakfast."

"I don't imagine most of your clients get quite as wild as Andy Poltz."

"Maybe not," she acknowledged. "But the man is in a real fix. Raising those heritage cattle is more of a hobby for rich folks and Andy isn't rich. He's aready got two mortgages on the place, then he had to take out a loan to pay the fine for that stunt out at the wind project site. Of course that was his own darn fault but that just makes it worse I'd think."

"So he was in the bank asking for an extension period on his loan?"

"Yep. And I told him I couldn't authorize it myself, that all the loan arrangements are authorized now in Toronto. He got real mad—well I guess you saw it all on the tape. He kept shouting that he wasn't going to lose his farm because of Burt Sousa. He said he was going to go out to the Point and tear down that tower with his bare hands. And that he'd shoot anybody who got in his way."

"And you didn't think he was serious?" Halstead asked.

Peggy shrugged. "Andy said that sort of stuff all the time."

But this time it was on the night that somebody killed Burt Sousa.

He turned to Pete. "Get Ragusa and go arrest Andy Poltz."

"So it was Mr. Poltz who did it," Ali said. She shuddered. "Sometimes I think the local people are right. It seems there *is* a curse on that wind turbine project. Now there's been a murder."

"There's nothing supernatural about this murder," Pete pointed out reasonably. "Two men were fighting and one fell over that bluff edge to his death."

"Did Mr. Poltz confess?"

"He's stubborn, he isn't saying anything."

"Couldn't it just be manslaughter or whatever you call it?" Ali found the actual word even more unsettling than murder. *Slaughter.*

"We can't do anything until Poltz talks. Till then he stays in the Bonville jailhouse."

"But he's got a lawyer to work on his defense?"

"Not yet, he says he doesn't need one. Like I said, he's a stubborn old coot. But the court will appoint a defense lawyer for him whether he likes it or not."

He'd last seen the farmer at the bail hearing. Handcuffed, clad in a blue prisoner's overall and paying little attention to the proceedings. He wondered if the old man had actually gone wacko, whether his rage at Sousa had sent him over the edge as well.

He finished his coffee and kissed Ali's nose, which had paint on it. She had begun painting the sunporch.

"Who is looking after the farm and the cattle?" she asked.

"The hired man I guess."

"Indefinitely?"

"I'm not sure."

"Maybe you should be neighbourly and go and check. Cattle have to eat, you know." She waved goodbye with her paintbrush.

He hadn't been back to the place since they had arrested Poltz two days before. There was a pick-up truck parked at the gate. Not the blue Poltz vehicle, this one was red. Pulling the cruiser up on the dusty verge, he saw that the kitchen door was open, yet he had a distinct memory of Poltz closing it behind him on the day of his arrest. The old man's movements had been slow and reluctant, a shadow of apprehension flickering across that stoic mask.

Now Pete coud see someone moving around behind the screen. He walked across the untended yard and knocked on the door, to be greeted by a muffled hello. Inside, he found Miranda and another woman he didn't know, cleaning out the fridge and mopping down the counter and tables. An orange cat sat on the door sill, lapping milk from a saucer.

Miranda didn't acknowledge his arrival but the other, younger woman looked up from her scrubbing. She seemed to know who he was.

"My husband Aaron is out in the barn," she said, "tending some calves."

Miranda added reprovingly, "The animals have to be fed, Whether their keeper is a murderer or not."

He stood awkwardly in the kitchen, while the women went on with their work. Eventually getting the message that he was unwanted and unnecessary, he returned to the cruiser. He was impressed by the women's unquestioning commitment to help a neighbour, even such a neighbour as Poltz. As far as he could tell from conversations overheard at the Island Diner, the general concensus in the community seemed to conclude that Poltz was guilty or at least capable of killing Sousa. There were the previous incidents of aggression, the man had no verifiable alibi, he had a hot, ungovernable temper and he had shown plenty of motive. And there was the bank video. Even if people hadn't actually seen the video, they'd certainly heard of it via the Island grapevine. Plus, Poltz had few friends in the community and was seen as a miserable old grump whose wife took their daughters and left him years ago. Apparently the community held no grudge against Poltz's beasts, though.

He drove away, feeling strangely deflated and discombobulated. It had all turned out so differently from what he thought would happen. He felt he could no longer trust his instincts or his own judgement. It seemed for weeks now, he been braced for Burt Sousa to erupt, to cause violence. Instead he had become its victim. He hadn't liked the Mayor, far from it, but it was still hard to believe that such a forceful personality as the Mayor could just be *gone*. Like a tornado that had wreaked a certain amount of havoc then had moved on, simply blown itself out.

On an impulse, he kept on going towards the Point. The *WindSpear* site was quiet, shut down again after only being re-opened for a couple of weeks since the Gillies investigation. How Sousa would have stewed over this! The future of the entire project was under review, Pete had heard. There was speculation that the project might be shut down altogether, that the Danish parent company felt they were meeting too much opposition in the province. A company representative was on the way.

Keen was probably still manning the trailer office but Pete didn't want another encounter with the man today. Instead he drove up to the old resort and walked in along the track to the site. A gull rose effortlessly on an air current above the bluff. It was such a pretty spot, so naturally peaceful on a summer day. The killdeer was out this morning too, now that the backhoes and tractors were stilled again. He knew the world needed energy—it was the prime issue of the age—but surely it was a shame that human needs must always be supplied at the cost of nature. Above his head, the sun gleamed on the white metal arms of the great turbine blades, spinning quickly today. Its energy was going nowhere as yet and it was now unlikely that transmission lines would ever be dug.

He thought of his climb up to the top of the tower, the spectacular view of the entire Point. Burt Sousa's domain no longer. He remembered the man's speech, his vision. A ruthless vision. *This project will put Middle Island on the map. The money will pour in.*

Nearer the ground the breeze was gentler, soft mats of poplar pollen floated to land like drifts of summer snow on the concrete pad. Idly, he stooped to pick up a clump, marvelling at yet another example of Nature's versatility, the myriad ways in which plants distributed their seeds. The life force continuing, in spite of murder, in spite of war, in spite of all the dreadful things. Nature was so optimistic really. Like Ali. Wanting a child, seeing good things ahead, rather than risks. She was good for him, people like Ali were good for the world.

He put out his hand, blew gently and watched the poplar snow sail away into the wind with its precious cargo. New life.

27

Halstead lay back comfortably in his office chair, closer to peace than he'd been in a long time. Outside his open window, the sound of a combine buzzed in the field—taking off the first crop of this summer's hay. There were fresh peas and strawberries at the Island market stands. He'd seen new lambs yesterday when driving back from Andy Poltz's arraignment.

A killer caught and life goes on.

On his desk lay the Bonville Record with the story of the arrest and a quote from Chief Halstead of the Middle Island Police Detachment. That should shut up Vern and the other nay-sayers on Council for the moment. He felt a fleeting remorse that the biggest nay-sayer of all was gone for good, but there came a point when a man made his own fate And Burt Sousa had certainly contributed to his own end.

It wasn't a happy solution, there wasn't one. He felt bad for Andy too, who faced prison even if the verdict was manslaughter, but Andy had also helped create his own fate. Overall, he felt satisfaction. There was sadness yes, at the rift in the community but he had acquitted himself, he had maintained the honour of his police station. He might even get up the nerve to ask Steph out for a drink.

Benevolently, he turned to welcome young Jakes who had entered the office. Jakes had the makings of a good cop, with any luck he'd decide to stay with the Island force.

"What's that you've got?" Halstead asked expansively, then wished he hadn't.

Jakes put a plastic bag on the desk and dumped out the contents. A pile of rags, looked like torn up household sheets and dish towels.

"Stuffing from the dummy," he said. "I thought I'd have another look at it."

The dummy. It seemed ages since that spring day Sousa had called to complain about finding the thing hanging from the *WindSpear* fence. Yet the summer had barely begun.

"I thought I'd have another look at it," Jakes said.

Halstead didn't ask why, merely waited. *And?* Jakes was smart but he did have his hobbyhorses. Like that damned logbook thing.

Jakes sorted through the rags and pulled some strips of fabric out in his hand. Shiny strips of purple and gold, dangling like ribbons from his fingers. A scrap of name tag with a few washed-out letters. F E R

Halstead recognized the local school colours. "Boy's gym shorts, basketball. Bonvillle high school."

Pete nodded.

"So some kids made the dummy," Halstead said. "That's interesting, but . . . ?"

"It means Poltz didn't hang that dummy on the fence."

"Maybe he didn't. But what does it matter?"

"It means these kids have been hanging around the site," Pete said. "I think they were there the night that Brad died. I think Brad heard them messing around and ran down to chase them away."

"Could be," Halstead acknowledged this. "But Gillies is dead and buried. Why get a few kids into trouble now?"

But Jakes was like a dog with a bone. He wouldn't let go. "Maybe the kids saw something. Maybe they saw Poltz let the cattle out. Maybe *they* let the cattle out."

"Again, what does it matter?" Halstead temporized. "Andy Poltz is in a lot worse trouble now. He's in jail for murder you may remember."

"It's a loose end." Jakes looked hesitant. "It could be more than that," he added.

"More?" Halstead asked.

"I've been wondering about Gillies." Jakes said in a rush. "I've been wondering whether there was something wrong about his death too. The boy had already shown he was pretty sure-footed. Maybe somebody pushed him too."

"Ah." Halstead leaned back in his chair, "Go on."

Pete shrugged. "Two deaths at the wind site within a few weeks of each other. There might be a connection."

"Which would be?—Just for the sake of argument. No, first please tell me why anyone would want to murder Brad Gillies." Halstead twisted his pen impatiently. He didn't like the way this was going.

"What the heck would be the motive? The kid's girl and family were devasted at losing him. He wasn't old enough to have made any serious enemies. Or do you figure he had some deep dark past? That maybe he was a drug dealer at university and someone came all this way to settle an old score, pardon the pun."

Pete frowned. "No, nothing like that. I just think he was unlucky, that he might have been at the wrong place at the wrong time. Maybe someone killed him because they wanted to mess up the project."

"Someone like Andy Poltz, you mean. First you're defending the guy and now you want to book him for another murder."

Jakes said stubbornly. "There were others who were opposed to the project."

"To the point of killing Brad Gillies? Who—Miranda Paris, Steph?" Briefly, Halstead felt an icy grip on his heart.

Jakes looked for a minute out the window where the combine was making another swing through the grass. "I'm just saying it could have happened," he said finally. "Those cows made quite the diversion, maybe someone let them out for just that purpose. The killer could have taken advantage of the confusion. Waited till the kids left, then killed Brad. Or maybe the killer didn't even know the kids were there."

Halstead waved a broad, dismissive hand. "Again, back to motive. I can't see Poltz killing a kid simply to delay the project. That's a mighty extreme act. His temper may have led him to kill Sousa in the heat of the moment but the man's not a monster."

"Maybe Poltz mistook the kid for Sousa." Pete suggested, even though he didn't like the idea.

Halstead stated the obvious. "That would be pretty hard to do, even in the dark. Gillies weighed a hundred and thirty pounds soaking wet. Burt was over two hundred."

"Then maybe Poltz didn't kill either of them."

Halstead looked distastefully at the messy pile of torn fabric that Jakes had dumped on his desk. He hoped the gym shorts had been washed before being ripped up for dummy service, doubted it.

"Don't tell me you're suggesting the kids killed Brad?"

"I hope not," Pete said fervently. "But they might have seen something that could tell us who did."

Halstead sighed, seeing the look on the younger man's face. Dogged determination, or pigheadedness? The fine line between good police work and the obsession to prove himself right. He'd seen it go either way.

He reached reluctantly for his phone. "I guess you'd better go scout around the highschool then, that piece of name tag should narrow things down. I'll clear it with the principal, but step carefully, dammit. The last thing I need is a bunch of parents up in arms complaining about police brutality."

He watched Jakes leave, wondering if there was anything to the younger man's thoughts, something he had missed himself. Mostly he hoped there wasn't. He liked that good feeling he had enjoyed only a half hour ago. That rare sense of being on top of his game. He didn't want to go back to the unsettling insecurity of the last few months. Dammit he thought he had the case wrapped up.

But maybe his own instincts were getting old, seizing up like his body, no longer reliable. Maybe Vern and the others were right to doubt that he was fit anymore to run a police station. He rubbed his shoulder and wondered if he was getting bursitis. Or arthritis. Or whatever else was out there, the magazines and newspapers were full of dire warnings. Maybe, like Fred, he too should be thinking about retirement. But what the hell would he do with himself? He could only fish for so many hours a day and not even that in the winter. He'd read stories of people who'd retired and fallen into a deep depression. He didn't think he was that type but there was always the possibility. Or maybe he'd just become an alcoholic.

Big things to think about. And maybe premature, maybe the twinge in his shoulder would turn out to be exactly that. A twinge.

He'd rather think about what he'd say when he called Steph to ask her out for that drink. Or could his instincts be wrong about that too.

S ean Ferrell.

Pete tapped the school register with his finger. "Looks like this could be the boy," he said. "Does he play basketball?"

John Scott, principal of Bonville High School nodded warily. "He's our centre forward. A good strong player." He had already identified the scrap of cloth as material used in the sports uniforms of the school.

"Now what?" Scott asked with the weary resignation of an administrator anticipating yet another tricky situation in his already busy day. "What are you going to do?"

"I'd like to talk to Sean please."

"He's only seventeen, a minor. I think I'd better call his parents."

"Sure. They can meet us down at the station."

Oh man. Sean squirmed in the cruiser seat. *Pulled out of school in a cop car. It should be cool but it isn't. What's mom going to say? What's DAD going to say?*

He looked uneasily at the cop. The guy didn't look so bad, he wasn't old or anything. If he'd met him at one of those school career days, he would have asked what it was like, how you got to be a cop.

The cop didn't say anything, he just drove. The silent treatment, Sean knew about that. They always waited for you to crack, to blab out something incriminating. So he wouldn't say anything, he could be silent too.

That's what Gavin had said. *Keep quiet. Or we're all in deep shit.*

Maybe the cops didn't even want to ask about that stuff at the Point anyway. Maybe he'd gone through a stop sign or something else with the car.

The cop cracked first, said. "So you play basketball Sean."

"Yeah," he said, all cool like, not giving anything away.

"I bet there's always lots of girls hanging around the basketball court Sean. Or is there somebody special?"

It was hard not to talk. He felt like a dope, like a stupid cow or something.

"I got a girl, yeah."

They were approaching the causeway to the Island. The cop stopped at the light and looked out at some sailboats on the water. "I guess you and your friends have lots to do around here. Swimming, boating, that sort of stuff."

"Yeah, I guess so. It's O.K."

"Gets a bit boring sometimes though doesn't it? I know, I grew up in the country too."

"Yeah sometimes, I guess."

They moved forward. "Sometimes you have to make your own fun," the cop said. "Maybe even cause a little trouble. Nothing big, just for fun. I've knocked over a few mailboxes in my time."

"No kidding?"

"Sure. You have to shake things up once in awhile. Though we never thought up anything as good as that that dummy we found hanging on the fence at the Point awhile back." The cop laughed. "Now that was funny! It started everybody talking about ghosts at the wind farm site. I'd like to know who thought that trick up. Somebody real smart I guess."

You're pretty smart, Sean thought, but not smart enough. I'm not falling for it.

*   *   *

The parents were more trouble than the kid. Halstead finally got them to sit quietly on the sidelines.

Sean looked at the gym shorts, the piece of name tag. *Fer . . . .*

"Yeah, so? Maybe they're some other guy's shorts. Lots of names begin with that."

"Give me one."

The boy looked sullen.

"So they're your shorts," Halstead said. "And they were part of the stuffing in this dummy." On the desk were a half dozen coloured photos of the intact dummy with the sign around its neck.

"Somebody else could have put them there."

Halstead ignored this feeble defense.

"Do you take the art class at school, Sean?" he asked.

The boy looked puzzled, then scornful. "Nah, that arty-farty stuff's not my thing."

"Or the sewing class?"

"Frigg, no. What do you think?" *Don't swear at the cop, the old man had the nerve to say. Even though he swore all the time at his friggin lawnmower and crap like that.*

Halstead picked up one of the photos. "This a pretty fancy piece of work," he said. "A nice sewing job. And this cartoon of a hawk. Somebody knows how to draw."

He tossed the photo under the boy's nose. "If you didn't do the drawing or the sewing, Sean, who did? Who helped you with this stunt?"

"Nobody," the boy said sullenly. "I did it all myself."

"We could get you a piece of paper and a pencil, Sean. And you could draw us a picture right here, right now."

So he'd blabbed about Kelly. Told them about the Shawks.
At least he didn't say anything about Gavin.

They made Sean wait while they fetched Kelly, a tensely wired girl with dyed red hair and seven small silver rings in her right earlobe. She was a tougher nut to crack, Pete could see that right away. She was smarter too, and she was furious at Sean, glaring at him as she came into the room.

But they admitted finally to making the dummy and hanging it up on the fence. They wouldn't admit to anyone else being involved though.

"So it was all your idea," Pete asked Kelly. "Just you two, nobody else? And you call yourselves the *Shawks*."

She nodded cockily. "What's the big deal? We didn't hurt anybody."

"And you did this because you're so concerned about the environment and the birds at the Point."

"It was a kick," Sean said helpfully. "Like you said in the car. Just some fun to start people talking about ghosts and shit."

Kelly glared at him some more. *Shut up, you dope.* "It was that environment stuff too," she said to Pete. "The birds and all that."

"So you wanted to scare the neighbours," Halstead said. "You went out there other nights too, when you howled and made spooky noises."

Sean looked at Kelly. "Maybe a coupla times," he acknowledged.

"What about the night of May 17th?"

The kids looked at each other. Sean shrugged. "Dunno. What night was that?"

"Kelly?" Pete asked. She shook her head. "Dunno. That's ages ago."

They were probably being honest about that, Pete thought. Teenagers didn't keep much track of actual calendar dates.

"That was the night Brad Gillies fell. Remember?"

"Oh yeah," Sean said. "Poor guy."

"You didn't happen to be around playing ghost that night, I suppose."

The boy should never play poker. His expression now read Oh Oh watch out. Danger ahead. Even Kelly stiffened in her chair.

Gavin's warning echoed in his head, like the boom of thunder. Keep your mouth shut. Don't say anything.

"No we weren't out there," Sean said finally.

"How do you know? You said you couldn't remember where you were that night."

"We'd remember that," Kelly said, her cockiness back.

"Brad told his girlfriend Leanne he heard noises. He ran down to check."

"I heard about the cows," Sean said. "They coulda made a big racket."

"Somebody let them out."

"Well it wasn't us," Kelly said. "We weren't there."

"When was your last trip out to the Point?"

"We stopped after hearing about Brad. It wasn't fun anymore."

Kelly, likely a student of many a TV cop drama, cut to the chase. "Are you going to charge us with anything for making that dummy?"

"I don't know yet," Halstead said and then came up with a pretty good line himself. "But don't make any plans for summer camp yet, kids."

* * *

Halstead made a face at his cold coffee.

"I can't see that pair planning and executing the dummy project. There must be more kids in the group, a leader certainly, but these two aren't ratting. They're either loyal or afraid but they're not talking."

Pete flipped through the dummy photos once more. "I think they're scared. I think they were there the night that Gillies fell. They know something they're not telling."

Halstead agreed. "They know a lot they're not telling. But what are you saying? That someone in the *Shawks* group deliberately killed Brad Gillies?"

"That kid Sean looks a tough enough customer. If Gillies caught them in some act of sabotage, Sean might have attacked him."

Halstead shook his head. "I'm not buying it. There was no indication that Brad had been in a fight. He was O.K. when he went back up the turbine."

"But you agree they were there? That they might have seen something?"

Halstead nodded. "Poltz was there, the kids were there, the cattle were there. Who else? Next we'll find the whole damn town was there."

"So what are we going to do about them?"

"We've given those two a scare and we'll keep an eye on them, try to find out what other kids were in the group. One of them's got to spill the beans sometime and it sure would help to have a witness or two who saw Poltz that night."

He thought he'd enlist Steph. She had a daughter in high school, maybe Livy would know something.

29

Ali was horrified. "You don't think those children have been killing people? That's terrible. You can't be right."

"Maybe not," Pete said. "But I think they may know something about who has. Besides those 'children' as you call them are seventeen years old, they're nearly adults. Kids a lot younger than that are killing people in countries all round the world."

It was a relief to be doling out apple slices and boxes of raisins to five year-olds this morning. The children were rambunctious, high-spirited and yes downright naughty at times but still sweet-faced and shiny-eyed with childhood innocence—at least most of the time.

"Where is Livy?" asked a little pony-tailed sprite. "Tuesday is a Livy day."

Yes it was. Ali looked at the clock. Livy was more than half an hour late, which was unusual. Despite the girl's determinedly unconventional style, she seemed to take her co-op duties with the kindergarten class seriously.

She settled the children down and sat munching her own apple slice. She couldn't stop thinking about what Pete had said about the highschool students and the secret *Shawks* group. She thought again about Livy and her comment about the wind tower pictures at the art exhibition on parents' night.

'I like this one,' the girl had said, placing the first prize ribbon on the picture of the tower that stood like a sinister black flower on the landscape.

Could the girl belong to the *Shawks* group? She had to admit, Livy could be a likely candidate. She was a sensitive soul, concerned about birds and other wildlife. But it was hard to picture the girl in dark balaclava, attempting to storm a wind turbine tower. Surely not. Livy was more the type to write letters, or even poems.

But here she came, rushing in the door and apologizing to the children. The morning passed busily with sandbox and craft projects. At recess Livy helped the children into their sweaters and jackets to go outside. Usually Livy left then to go back to the high school but today she wandered idly around the classroom, picking up a notebook here, a pencil there. She paused at last before Ali's desk, almost as if she wanted to talk. Now that would be *really* odd.

Ali offered what she hoped was an encouraging smile.

"Thanks for the help Livy," she said, "is there anything else?"

She realized though she'd worked with Livy a couple of mornings a week for the past four months, the girl had hardly every looked her straight in the face, eye to eye. Now she thought that Livy looked even paler than usual. Her eyes were wide and shockingly miserable behind the gloomy Goth white make-up.

She said nothing, seeming to have difficulty deciding whether to speak. Then she blurted out, all in a rush,

"You're married Mrs. Jakes. How did you know you were in love with your husband. How do you kow you're really in love with a boy?"

Ali blinked. Well the girl certainly didn't beat around the bush.

Livy's voice rose, almost desperately. "Oh I know what the songs and the poems say. But I want to know what love is really *like*."

Wow, Ali thought. A big question. "Of course there's attraction," she said cautiously.

She'd wanted to jump Pete's bones the first time she saw him. Even among all those other young uniformed men in prime physical condition, she noticed him.

You looked cool, she told him later. You were trying to anyway.

I was just another soldier. A guy in camo shirt and trousers.
I'd have noticed you in a gas mask. Those shoulders.
She had laughed at his expression. "You complemented me," she
said. "I'm brash and gabby and a show-off. You're cool and handsome
and reserved—a fitting setting for me."
He'd pushed her over. And you're modest too.

"A sense of humour always helps," she added. She saw the disappointment on the girl's face and realized she was sounding like an advice columnist in a women's magazine.

"It's a wonderful feeling," she said simply. "It's like finding out that the whole world makes sense at last. And it's *fun*." She patted the girl's hand. "And please call me Ali. I've mentioned that before."

"But how do you *know?*" Livy asked again. "How do you know when you can trust another person with your love, with your heart?"

Ali smiled. She was right, there was a budding poet in this intense teen. "You know when you're comfortable with a person. It just feels right. But if it doesn't feel right yet, then it probably isn't."

The girl looked stricken, as if the words had struck home.

"You're young yet," Ali soothed. "There's lots of time and lots of fun in the search."

Livy muttered something, Ali didn't catch and started half-running towards the door.

Ali stood up. "Livy, come back!" she called. "Let's go to the lunchroom and get a pop or something. We could talk some more."

But Livy disappeared into the corridor. Ali sank back into her chair. Had she misplayed that somehow? The girl said she was looking for someone to trust. To trust with what—her heart, or something else?

She sighed and looked round the empty classroom. Some of the wind turbine pictures were still there. She should take them down, they seemed inappropriate in the wake of the recent deaths. She started to remove the tacks from one of the paintings, a typical rendering in the bright primary colours of the schoolroom palette.

A half dozen white towers rose like giant primitive lilies from a green stripe of land. In the background, a wobby blue stripe of paint represented the lake. An innocuous picture, even kind of pretty. Why then, in her fancy, did the blades in the picture begin to spin like frantic pinwheels. Spinning faster and faster as they cut the paper to shreds.

*   *   *

"You look very fetching tonight," Halstead said.

"Fetching?" Stephanie batted her eyelashes.

"I've been watching old movies on TV. Maybe I should have said cool."

Though he wasn't really comfortable with that either. There must be some word between the vocabulary of his mother's generation and the rapping kids on the street. *Snazzy? Hot?* The kids said that too.

"You look very pretty," he said finally. She wore a red dress of some clingy material and her wonderful hair gleamed even in the low lighting of the restaurant.

She swirled her wine and smiled. "Fetching was O.K."

He had phoned her earlier and asked if she'd like to meet him for dinner. Said that he needed her advice on a feature of the case.

"Sure, if you don't mind eating early," she said. "I have to be in Bonville by seven for a meeting with my web site designer."

There wasn't a big selection at the Island restaurant but if the food was routine, it was also routinely good. He ordered steak and a beer, she chose a pasta salad and white wine.

"One glass," she laughed to the waitress, "I'm driving and I'm having dinner with a cop." He sipped his beer, content. He could almost pretend it was a real date.

"So, what did you want to see me about?" she asked.

"Chit-chat first, Miss Nosey Parker," he used the childhood name for a snoop. "No case talk till dessert. Tell me about the Retreat."

"It's going well, I'm really excited. I've got the local women coming for yoga and drumming classes and I've got the first weekend session practically all booked."

"That's great," he raised his beer in salute. "You had a good idea and you've made it happen."

She grinned mischievously. "We've got men's yoga classes too. You could sign up. All your officers could come."

He grimaced. "I'll run it by them."

They ate companionably, keeping up an easy dialogue of local news and tidbits. Stephanie was a social being and an active presence in the community.

When the waitress asked if they wanted to order dessert, he ordered vanilla ice cream but she passed.

She looked at him expectantly. "I hope I don't have to wait till you finish before I find out what you wanted to see me about. Is it something about Andy's place? I saw Miranda the other day, she and Gudrun did a big clean-up of the kitchen. I told her I'd take on feeding the cat if they needed me."

Her mobile face showed conflicting emotions. "I wonder what's going to happen to the farm if Andy doesn't come back? It's hard for me to picture Andy as a cold-blooded murderer. It must have been an accident, Bud. Involuntary manslaughter or whatever they call it."

He reached for his coffee. "It's out of our hands now, Steph. Up to a jury. They'll hear the case sometime this summer."

She fidgeted with her cup. "At least all the scary noises and nonsense have stopped at the Point. That dummy of Andy's was pretty creepy I have to admit."

"It turns out Andy wasn't responsible for any of that," Halstead said. "We know now that some highschool kids have been pulling those stunts."

He explained about the interview with Sean and Kelly. How they'd admitted to hanging up that dummy.

"No kidding!" She sounded surprised and something more. Almost shocked. "Kids did all that? Not Andy?" But he sense a hollowness in her protest.

"No," he said. "Definitely younger people. Young, agile, nimble people. Not Andy or any of the rest of you old-timers in the anti-wind farm group."

"Gee thanks. I don't know whether to be glad to be exonerated or insulted at your description." But he thought her attempt at humour was shaky, a bit flat.

"We think there were more kids in the group. They call themselves the *Shawks*," he said. "Have you heard of them?"

She shook her head. "Nope, this is all news to me." She drew back against the bench seat, almost defensively he thought. "Why are you telling me about this stuff anyway? You're're usually all tight-lipped about your police investigations."

"I wondered if your Livy had mentioned anything to you about the group?"

"No," she answered cautiously, "but why would you think she might?"

He shrugged. "It's a small school, a small student population, particularly in the higher grades. You could ask her," he said.

Steph laughed sadly. "I'm afraid we don't communicate much these days, Bud. She hardly talks to me at all." She leaned forward, said earnestly.

"But my goodness, Bud, why so serious about a couple of teenage pranks? We'd have done the same in our time."

"What about the threat to Burt Sousa, pinned on the dummy?"

"O.K. maybe that wasn't so pleasant but surely you're not taking it seriously."

"This isn't just kid's prank stuff anymore. We're into public mischief charges at least. Maybe even an accessory to murder charge. And I'd just like you to ask Livy for some information, it's not as if she's involved."

He was a cop though, experienced at reading the reactions of witnesses and suspects. Experienced at reading the signs he now saw in Steph. Increasing anxiety, agitation, a desire to get away. Especially at his use of the word *murder.*

She started to gather up her purse and briefcase. Said hurriedly, "I've got to get going Bud or I'll be late. Thanks for dinner."

He pushed away his ice cream.

Steph drove up to the house but didn't get out of the car. She'd barely got through her meeting, hadn't been able to concentrate on details of the website Sandra had designed, which was a shame because the woman had worked so hard on it. Now she was dreading this chat with Livy. Her daughter had been so happy lately, lit with the glow of first love.

Steph sighed and got out. It had to be done.

"Hi Livy I'm home," she called up the stairs. She expected no reply, thought she'd have to plod up the stairs and request entrance to The Room.

Instead she heard a small "Hi Mom" from the kitchen.

Livy was standing at the stove—surprise, surprise—stirring a pot.

"Want some cocoa? I made some."

Fresh from the shower, in her pyjamas, with her hair bound up in a towel Livy looked adorable, a description she would loathe. Steph was taken back sixteen years to that moment when she first held her little baby girl in her arms. How time flew by!

"Marshmallows?" Livy asked.

Dazed, Steph accepted the steaming mug. The marshmallows were multi-coloured and bobbed cheerily in the drink. Livy sat on the couch, legs drawn up and crossed with a natural ease that would have made the Retreat's middle-aged yoga clients envious. Steph found it hard to read her mood. Subdued maybe. Lonely even. Trouble with the boyfriend? she hoped not.

Livy looked up from her cup and asked, "So how was your date, Mom?" She actually seemed to care.

"It wasn't really a date." Steph protested. "Bud is an old friend."

"It's O.K for you to have a date Mom," A little smile. "You're allowed. And Chief Halstead is a nice guy."

"Well thanks dear, I'll keep that in mind."

Livy stared intently into her cocoa, as if there were the answer to some secret in the sugary depths.

"How old were you and Dad when you met?" she asked suddenly.

That was a surprise too. The ex and his new wife had moved to B.C. a year ago. Steph knew that Livy and Ted exchanged regular e-mails and that her father had promised there was an open ticket any time she wanted to visit, but they hadn't talked about him for some time.

"I was nineteen. A little older than you are now," she added prudently. "But we didn't get married for another three years."

"What brought you together?" Livy asked. "I don't mean where you met, I mean what did you do together, what did you talk about?"

Steph almost made the obvious joke but stopped herself in time. Livy would have just become impatient or grossed out at the thought of her teenage parents making love. She did wonder though whether Livy was doing the deed yet with Gavin. They had 'the talk' a couple of years ago but practical application was a different thing atogether.

Now she thought about that long-ago time with Ted. There were a few good memories, and of course Livy, the one wonderful lasting result. So it hadn't been all bad. But what had they talked about? She tried to remember conversations before the sniping of those last sour years.

"We talked about music and movies and going out, like most couples I guess," she said. "But we also talked about what we wanted to do. We planned to have our own business right from the start. We loved to talk about that. Later, we talked about the motel mainly. Rude people, nutty people, the crazy requests we got. We were busy," she shrugged. "That worked for us."

And finally, they didn't talk at all.

Livy was looking at her almost pleadingly. "So there's no way to know how things are going to turn out? Ever?"

Steph sighed. "I wish there was." She risked an endearment. "Sweetie if there's ever anything you want to talk about, I'm here, you know. I'm always here for you."

"I know Mom." But she didn't ask anything, just rose from the couch and took both their cups. She yawned widely like a kitten, "I think I'll go to bed."

Steph had almost forgotten what Bud had asked her to do. She hated to risk ruining this brief unexpected peace. Wanted dearly just to say Goodnight Honey, relax on the couch and bask in the sweet cocoa warmth of the past few minutes. But she had to know, not for Bud's investigation but for her own peace of mind. Livy's passionate words kept ringing in her head.

"What's crazy is to build wind towers on Hawks Nest Point. Do you know that in California thousands of hawks die every year when they try to get past the wind towers in the Altamont Pass. Do you want to see that kind of massacre at our own Hawks Nest Point?"

And what had she said about vandalism of private property?

"I guess it depends on your definition of ownership, mom. Who owns land? Who owns lakes? Now people want to own the wind."

Better to give a warning now, rather than risk trouble later because she hadn't.

"Actually Livy, Chief Halstead was wondering if you could help him out with some information."

Livy stopped on the bottom step. "He wants to talk to me? What about?"

"Some activities involving some high school students. He wondered if you or your friends knew anything about a group called the *Shawks*."

Did the girl pale? When she was little, Steph could always tell when Livy was trying to hide something. She would stick out her bottom lip and look away. The telltale signs, though less exaggerated, were still there.

Steph sighed and plunged ahead. "I sincerely hope you aren't involved with any of this activity dear. Even if you desperately, heartfeltedly believe your cause is right, it's never the way to go about things. You could run into trouble with the law and worse, you won't accomplish what you want."

There it was, that sullen, closed look was back on her daughter's face. "What if the law is no help," Livy said. "What are you supposed to do then?"

She hadn't denied knowledge of the *Shawks*, Steph noticed. Now really concerned, she pressed on. "I think you were out at the Point a couple of weeks ago, Livy. I think you might have had something to do with that horrible dummy thing."

She watched expressions chase across Livy's face and knew with a sickening feeling that Livy was choosing a story, that she was going to lie to her.

And here the answer came. "I wasn't there, Mom. I've got nothing to tell Mr. Halstead. I heard that a couple of kids in grade twelve had to go to the police station but I don't even know who they were."

When Steph said nothing, Livy went on. "I wouldn't do anything like that Mom. I want to help the birds but those kids are too extreme for me. I just want to finish highschool and get away to college. Anyway I'm sure it's all finished, they won't dare do anything now that the police know about the Shawks—or whatever that name you said."

Steph thoughts raced. Livy was lying. And yes, it was possible that Livy knew something about the *Shawks* and maybe she had even been involved. But the group did seem effectively broken up by now. The police had ensured that. And if Livy no longer had anything to do with those kids, surely there was no need to involve her in the investigation. Bud would no doubt point out that this was faulty, not to mention morally twisted logic. But what was a mother to do? She would think about facing Bud Halstead later, if it ever came to that.

She wondered if she should tell Livy that she knew about Gavin, knew that she was seeing the Sousa boy. Better not, at least not right now. Livy had her hackles up already. And besides, the boy might actually be a good influence in this case. Maybe that was another reason why Livy was glad not to be associated with the *Shawks* group. It would have been a barrier between her and Burt Sousa's son.

Besides, when it came to a loyalty battle between Romeo and mom, Romeo always won.

Steph nodded wearily. "Good night Livy. Sweet dreams."

31

Middle Island Marina. the sign said. *Motorboats and Canoes for Rent.*

About a dozen boats bobbed from the ropes that tethered them to the dock. Gulls wheeled above the sun-glinted water. Ragusa actually looked excited.

"This could be O.K., you know. Look at that police boat." He pointed to a launch with the Middle Island Police logo painted on the side. "I bet it can get up some speed."

"Have you ever driven one of these?" Pete laughed.

"Sure," Ragusa said. "Up at my uncle's cottage. I'm a real waterbaby, been waterskiing since I was eight."

"Yeah well the job is to give out tickets to speedsters. And to arrest DUI's on the water."

Kevin grinned. "Doesn't mean we can't have some fun at the same time."

It was good to see Kevin excited about something. Even though his interest might drop off a bit when he realized the job also entailed such mundane tasks as enforcing life jacket regulations and checking that summer boaters were carrying out proper disposal of sewage water from their watercraft.

"Yessir," Kevin put his foot on the police launch bow and lightly rocked the boat. "That'll be me out there in a couple of weeks. Just call me Middle Island Vice."

Pete nodded judiciously.

"There's a certain ring to that."

"Yeah and I don't care if I see another goddamned cow for the rest of my tour of duty here."

Pete hadn't mentioned where he'd been this morning. At the detention centre in Bonville, visiting Andy Poltz. Ragusa would probably think he was nuts. So would the chief but it was those loose ends. Loose ends drove *him* nuts.

The guard had lead Poltz into the visiting room. On seeing Pete, the prisoner stopped abruptly and tried to turn around.

"What's this about? I don't want to talk to him."

But the guard pushed him to sit.

The old farmer seemed unchanged but on closer scrutiny, he looked tired. Hard work hadn't felled him, but inactivity and life away from his fields was sapping his strength. His face was sagging too, like a neglected tombstone.

He's already seventy, Pete thought. If he's convicted, he'll be eighty-five before he even qualifies for parole.

"Why are you here?" Poltz asked finally.

"I have something to tell you, news that might affect your case."

"You mean *your* case. The one you cops have cooked up against me."

Pete waited. The man can't be so stoic, that he isn't even curious. He'll have to ask.

But he didn't. So Pete leaned forward and spoke.

"We know now that you weren't responsible for the noise campaign at the site, and that you didn't truss up that dummy. We found the high school kids that have been doing all that."

Poltz shrugged, barely lifting his shoulders under the blue detention centre shirt.

"And how is that news for me?"

Pete spoke urgently now. "If you know anything more about those kids or what they've been doing out at that site, you'd better let us know. Even though you might support those ideas, those kids are no help to you now."

Poltz was truculent. "I know the kids was out there some nights, making their noises."

"Were they at the site, the night Brad Gillies fell in the turbine tower? Were they out there the night Sousa died?" Pete asked intently.

"I don't know. I generally stick to my own business."

"Come on, man. You have to give me something to go on. You don't seem like the type of man to just sit meekly by while a judge sentences you to prison. Don't you want to go home, back to the farm?"

A flash of despair leaped across the rugged features, like a thin bar of lightning splitting the dark. Then his expression hardened again.

"I don't know if the kids were there those nights. But the kids didn't do in Burt Sousa and I didn't neither. I told you it was the wife and that foreman guy."

"Do you have any proof?"

"That's your department, copper."

The guard led Poltz away. Pete wondered what sustained the old man now that he was deprived of his farm, his cattle, his pitchfork, his daily tasks. But would he crumble eventually and collapse like his own aging front porch?

He went gratefully out into the sunshine and breathed deeply of the fresh air. But he had learned nothing. At least Poltz hadn't tried to pin Sousa's murder on the kids. He still believed that Jim Keen had killed the Mayor. Was he right?

* * *

Elena Sousa was in her bedroom packing. Tearing clothing from the cupboard racks and throwing things into boxes any which way.

Burt's stuff. Good suits, shirts, sweaters, socks, underwear. She had called the Goodwill people to come on Thursday to pick the boxes up. The clothes would all be too big for Gavin and she doubted he'd wear them anyway. It would be a good haul for the local charity. She was also donating the expensive duvet and all the bedding and the curtains. She wanted nothing to remind her of this room. She wanted to start fresh.

She didn't hear Gavin come in but felt his presence at the door of the room. Her son was like that, he had a kind of disturbing aura about him at times. Like now, when he stood there in the doorway saying nothing, just watching her. She didn't turn around, but kept on filling up the boxes. She didn't want to get into another argument. Finally though, she spoke. Gavin could always outlast her in the silence struggle, even when he was a toddler.

She didn't mince words, it wasn't her way and besides there was no point.

"The real estate agent called today. She said I can have the house in Vancouver. There's a good girls' school for Ronda and you can go to university there in the fall. The agent says there's a great basketball team. You've probably heard of it."

His face twisted, she knew that expression too. She'd been seeing it a lot lately.

"What do you care where I go to university?" he asked rawly. "You're just glad to have me out of the way. Just like you're glad to have the old man out of the way. Now you can do what you want."

She didn't answer. They'd been covering approximately the same ground for the past week.

He quivered in the doorway. "Maybe I don't even want to go to university anyway. Maybe I have different plans."

She balled up a sweater, crammed it angrily into an overflowing box.

"We're going to Vancouver," she said through gritted teeth. "I am not staying one minute longer than I have to on this god-forsaken crummy Island."

He went slamming down the stairs. She didn't know why he was so upset now anyway. He and Burt had never really got along.

Just another of Burt's failures, his relationship with his son. He'd always criticized the kid, ridden him. It didn't matter that Gavin had always got good grades, that he was a champion cyclist. It was never good enough for Burt. He thought cycling was a sissy thing, wouldn't even call it a sport, though Gavin rode every day and had leg muscles like iron. Burt taunted Gavin because he wouldn't go hunting with the men. He'd even said to her a couple of times that he thought the boy might be gay and if he was, he'd better not tell them or he'd throw him out of the house.

And now Burt was gone and he'd left her with the problem of this bitter angry kid. That was typical of their whole marriage. Burt had never been interested in what happened at home. He just went out the door in the morning with never a thought for the rest of the day about the kids or her. He was off to his business world, the important world, the money world.

Now he was dead and who had his money?.

The bank, not his family.

Thank god she'd managed to hang on to the house.

32

Livy hadn't talked to Gavin since the day he took Brad's logbook. She wasn't mad anymore about that. She just wanted to tell him that she cared about him and that she missed him and how sorry she was about his Dad being killed. She knew Gavin and his dad fought a lot and that must make him feel even worse now. He didn't come to school much and when he did he looked terrible, his face all tight and miserable, even his dark brown hair had lost its shine. She didn't dare call him at home.

She e-mailed him finally, even though it didn't really feel right, putting those feelings in an e-mail. Then he didn't answer anyway. So when she saw on her laptop this morning that there was an e-mail from Gavin, she was so happy she almost cried.

Then she couldn't believe what he asked her to do.

And when she said she wouldn't help him, she couldn't believe what he wrote to her. That she was scared, a coward. That she wasn't committed and never had been. The cruel words flew off the screen like poison arrows into her heart.

As if she didn't want to save the hawks as much as he did. More even. She just didn't want to risk hurting anybody else. But he wouldn't listen to her anymore. That magical March day at the Point seemed such a long time ago. She wished that they had never let the others in. That Gavin hadn't got all bossy and weird. She wished she'd never shown him the logbook. He'd been kind acting kind of crazy ever since. Now he was going to hurt himself. Or somebody else.

She knew what she had to do now.

She had to go out there, to Hawks Nest Point. She had to stop him.

She just didn't know how.

*　　*　　*

Ali put down her pen and and snuggled into the pile of pillows on the couch. A poor substitute for Pete. It was silly but she missed him even for a night or two. He'd been away in Toronto, visiting with an army buddy who was home on leave.

She could think of him though, always an enjoyable passtime. He was like a puzzle box to her, she had to keep pressing him at different spots for the key. And even on those rare occasions, he let out only the tiniest bits of the puzzle.

"I wish I was more mysterious for you," he protested once at her questioning. "But I'm not."

But he was. A quietly reflective man, always watchful and alert. Not just a result of his miitary training, it seemed inborn. Fortunately she was willing, not to say eager, to spend a lifetime on her fact-finding mission. She would relive their meeting at times for the sheer deliciousness of remembering. Then scare herself, imagining what a lucky chance it was they had met. Or thinking that he might have met some other lucky woman before her. He was as reticent about past romances as about any other detail of his past life.

No tattooed names on your arm, she teased.

I'm a combat engineer he laughed, not a Viking. And you are tattooed on my heart.

For a reticent man, that was pretty romantic.

She eyed the pile of unfinished report cards with reluctance. She loved to teach and to work with the children, but she had never been a fan of the paperwork. Had never found it satisfactory to try and describe a child's development in the few lines provided. She would much rather talk in person to the parents. That glass of wine with her solitary dinner hadn't been conducive to the work ethic, either. Still, the reports had to be tackled. Maybe a cup of coffee would help.

She carried her plate and empty glass to the kitchen. A quarter to eight and the day was just now waning. She loved summer hours. A bit of a breeze stirred the maple tree leaves, sending a soft soughing sound through the open window. Was rain predicted? She couldn't remember. She did know by now that in a farm community it was a cardinal sin to complain about rain. Even the tourist operators who relied on sunshine for business, kept their opinion to themselves. Just in case, Ali went meekly around the house, closing windows. The farmers said you could smell rain coming. She leaned out the window, sniffing and thought she could. It smelled exciting and whirling and stirring and *green*.

A half-hour and eight marked report cards later, she registered the sound of barking from across the road. She had been hearing the racket unconsciously for awhile, she realized. In Ali's experience, Emily was usually a sensible dog, she barked to announce when people or cars approached along the road, then retired in a ladylike manner to her post on Miranda's porch.

But she was definitely barking now. Was Miranda not there? She rarely went out but why wasn't she shushing Emily? Maybe the dog was barking at a fox. A fox prowling around the chickens, that wouldn't be good. Maybe she should go out in the driveway at least and check. It was almost dark by now, in the kitchen she hunted out the flashlight before opening the door. The wind had strengthened too, a gust caught her hair and whipped strands across her face.

Emily was still barking, an uncharacteristic, high-pitched hysterical yelp. Something was definitely amiss. Ali made her way cautiously down the dark driveway and followed the thin, bobbing beam of the flashlight across the road. She could see a light on in the living room but why wasn't Miranda coming out? Had she fallen?

There was a banging, slamming sound, a thumping below the yelping of the dog. The wind seemed to have blown open the door of the chicken coop. She looked in at the birds huddled and cowering in their nest. It wasn't easy pushing against the wind but she managed to shut the door and pull the wooden bar across. Then she ran toward the house and charged in, not bothering to knock. Emily leapt excitedly at her legs, panting and whining anxiously. Warily, Ali entered the living room calling out, *Miranda?*

She let out her breath, there was no crumpled figure on the floor. Still calling, she made a quick search of the two upstairs rooms, the dog at her heels. No Miranda there either. Despite the circumstances, she paused at the sight of an exquisite soapstone sculpture of a dancing polar bear. There were paintings too, all down the stairway. It looked like a beautiful collection. The dog was still whining though, she almost tripped Ali up. They staggered together off the last step into the kitchen.

"Where is she, Emily?" Ali asked a little desperately. "Where has Miranda gone without locking up her chickens and turning off her lights?"

Emily whined at the door and looked expectant. Ali thought of cop television shows (that Pete liked to mock), of tracking dogs. But weren't they specially trained? It had to be worth a try. She took a leash from the coat rack and looked dubiously at Emily. The dog had always seemed friendly but what would she think of a stranger approaching her and trying to tie her up?

"Emily's a good girl," she said, kneeling on the floorboards and speaking in the tones she'd heard people use when talking to dogs or small babies. "Would you like to go for a walk? Let's go look for Miranda."

Emily submitted. Ali congratulated herself and then hung on tightly as the dog charged eagerly out onto the door. It was dark as soot on the unlit road and she had to jog to keep up. She was afraid to let the dog off the lead in case she lost her. Or got lost herself.

Mir-a-a-anda, she called, and felt her words blowing away in the wind.

*   *   *

Miranda felt in the dusk for the posts of Andy's fence. Ahead of her, Livy moved quickly over the hoof-pitted ground. The girl couldn't hear her because of the wind and Andy's cattle were already spooked and made restless by the girl's presence. There was no reason for her to turn around. Miranda doubted that Livy would be noticing any external details right at the moment. She moved as intently and single-minded as a zombie. Like a girl on her way to an appointment with destiny.

Miranda scrambled to keep Livy in sight, her thoughts burning with self-recrimination. She cursed herself for not having spoken up sooner. She was a stubborn old fool. She should have told Bud Halstead what she suspected. About what she knew. About seeing Livy with that Gavin boy and the others on their way back from the Point that night.

She should have spoken to Livy too. The girl likely wouldn't have listened to any warning but at least she would have tried. Or she could have talked to Steph.

Now what was she going to do though, what on earth was she going to say to Livy even if she did manage to catch up to the girl. How could she make her understand that she was in danger? She didn't trust that boy.

Nine o'clock on the longest day of the year. But the light was fading now, the girl just a fairy-like silhouette in the gloaming ahead.

*   *   *

Steph pawed clumsily through Livy's desk drawer. She had tossed aside her parental ethics, her guilt. She was frightened, she had to do this.

Livy had lied to her tonight. She wasn't where she was supposed to be. Steph found out because Livy's friend got her wires crossed and phoned to ask where she was. A classic teen mistake, the stuff of television sitcoms. Only this wasn't funny.

The wind sighed eerily past the house at that moment, Steph felt it like a howl in her own soul. She knew that Livy hadn't sneaked off to some rock concert at Bonville. That wasn't Livy. She knew in her bones that Livy had gone off to meet those kids in the *Shawks* group. Livy's backpack was gone, also the flashlight. She knew she'd been fooling herself when Livy said she'd quit the group. Dear God, what were they up to, what reckless act were they planning now? How had she so lost communication with her daughter this past year, that Livy had involved herself in this secret, dangerous life.

There was nothing in the drawer to give her a clue to where Livy was going. Only a jumble of hair clips, random pens and markers, a newspaper article on wind turbines, and a picture of Ted, Steph, and a three-year old Livy in a heart-shaped frame. No handy datebook or diary. If Livy was like every other teenager on the planet, she could try calling her on her cell-phone. But Livy had eschewed the gadget, along with driving a car. She would ride her bike even in the rain.

She did however, allow herself use of a computer for her school work and her research on the accursed wind turbines. Steph had no idea of her daughter's password of course. She looked despairingly at the blank eye of the laptop on the desk. It looked like a box of secrets, she saw no point in even turning it on.

One last wild look around the room. The white dresser that had been Steph's own as a teenager, the mirror now hung with windcatchers and a black jet necklace. The collection of stuffed animals on the shelf made her want to cry. She sank down on the bed, trying to think what to do. She smiled tearfully at the tucked in bed sheets, and Grandma Bind's quilt, folded tidily at the foot. Livy was personally as neat as an infantry private on inspection, always had been. Fondly, nostagically, Steph lifted a corner of the mattress to check the perfect sheet corners. And there found Pandora's box.

A slim sheaf of printed e-mails.

Livy, my keen lieutenant ! Together we will win the battle to save the Point. The birds are depending on our efforts.

My father is such a jerk. I can't believe I'm related to him, it makes me sick whenever anybody asks me if I'm Burt Sousa's son.

I heard the monster man on the phone last night. They're starting to dig the foundation holes for the next six turbines. We have to stop this!

And the most recent letter, the most chilling of all.

I'm disappointed in you Livy. I thought that you were different from the others. That you were brave and that you understood the supreme act sometimes required of us brave ones. That at times, we must sacrifice ourselves to gain our goals. But I guess you won't be journeying with me to bring down the turbines once and for all. I will be going on my way alone.

The sheet of paper slipped from Steph's nerveless hands. She had to snatch it back up, to stare again with disbelief at the e-mail address. *islandgavin.*

She reread the e-mail, her mind flooding with new terror as she tried to assimilate this shocking new information. How could Gavin Sousa be the writer of this wicked nonsense? He seemed to be plotting the destruction of his own father's property. In the words of a deeply disturbed mind. But what had Livy thought when she read those words? Steph clutched her chest. Please God, that Livy hadn't run away with that disturbed boy.

She strove for calm. She had to keep a clear head so that she could think. So that she would be able to outthink Gavin. With shaking fingers, she picked up the telephone.

"Bud! I don't have time to explain. Livy is in danger from Gavin Sousa, now, right this minute. I think he might be about to involve her in a suicide pact. Bud, we have to go after them. We have to find her!"

Her voice quivered with panic.

"Where did they go?" Bud asked tersely. "Do you know where they went?"

She glanced at her watch. Eight p.m. on the longest day of the year. It would be light for another hour at least.

"To the Point," she whimpered. "Oh God, the bluff."

"I'll pick you up on my way," he said. "I'll be there in ten minutes."

Steph grabbed her sweater. By the time Halstead arrived in the cruiser, she could ony babble and was fighting back tears.

"There's no time for crying now," Bud said. "We have to concentrate. Keep looking for the bicycles or some sign that they went off road."

Steph fought for control. The boy's head would be flooded with panic, too. But the thought was little comfort.

33

Emily pulled steadily and strongly on the leash, Ali was hard pressed to hold her. They had passed the darkened Poltz farmhouse a few hundred yards back, when the dog suddenly left the road and began to follow the fenceline that separated the Poltz property from the *WindSpear* site. In the near distance Ali could see the great turbine tower rising starkly against the waning light. The wind was picking up as they neared the Point.

"*MIRANDA,*" she called, feeling it was fruitless as she did so. "*MIRANDA.*"

Shaggy haired cattle faces stared at her from the other side of the fence. She shivered, despite the lowering sultriness of the evening air. *Where was Miranda?* Maybe she should go back and get some help in the search.

She stood indecisively in the now rapidly dimming evening, while the dog raised her muzzle to sniff at the air. Stubby clumps of cedar trees made dark, lurking shapes in the field. She shivered, for the first time thinking of who might have made that awful dummy the boy had found hanging on the *WindSpear* fence. Someone had crept around in the dark, daubed the gruesome thing with red paint and hung it up on the rope. Someone who might be out there now.

At the same moment, woman and dog heard the faint, feeble cry. It seemed to be coming from a nearby stand of cedars. Emily ran forward, tearing the leash utterly out of her hand and disappearing into the dark brush. Ali ran too and found her neighbour pushing vainly against an ecstatic bundle of fur.

"*Down, girl. Down.*" Miranda gasped. "My ankle," she said to Ali. "I think I've sprained it."

Ali tugged the dog off, it took a few more commands from Miranda to get her to sit.

"Here," Ali said to Miranda. "Let's try to get you up."

Miranda was bony but heavy enough as a dead weight. Ali could feel her wince with pain as they struggled to get upright. She was favoring one foot.

"You can't walk on that," she said. "I'll have to go get help. Maybe someone is working late at the *WindSpear* trailer. I could use the phone." The older woman's hair stood up in wild white tufts of disarray. She looked like a beleaguered dandelion, gone to seed.

Miranda put her foot down, testing the pain. "I've just turned it," she said. "We have to keep going."

She walked another step then gasped in agony. She collapsed back down and the two women crouched for a moment in the cedars.

"I'm going to get help," Ali said.

Miranda grasped her sweater. "Help for me can wait. You have to help Livy. That boy will hurt her."

*   *   *

She'd found him at the turbine. Just outside the door, on the concrete platform where they said Brad had died. The door was open this time too, Gavin must have found or stolen a key. She could see him framed in the doorway, a dark silhouette against the square of light. Above him stretched the tall white column of the turbine tower, its three gigantic blades moving majestically like the rotor of an ocean liner in the air.

Ka bumpf, ka bumpf, ka bumpf.

"Gavin!" she called.

She had startled him. He jerked around in surprise and peered out into the dusk. Then he smiled, almost the way he used to. Briefly she was happy, then she realized he thought she'd come to help him.

"Gavin," she said again. "You can't do this. It's wrong. We were all wrong. There has to be another way."

His face changed again.

He wasn't the Gavin she'd known. His eyes were kind of blank and staring, his voice flat, like the line you saw on a hospital monitor in the movies when someone had died. It was horrible to see. She wondered if that was what people meant when they said a person had gone mad. It was more like watching a person's soul die.

Worst of all, he didn't seem to be able to hear her what she was saying. She sent her words out to him but it was as if the wind whipped them away down the Point. They never reached his ears.

But she could hear him. She wished she couldn't. His voice wasn't flat now. He was yelling at her through the wind.

No Livy, the others were wrong. We were right.

Remember your poem Livy. The whirring, cutting knives. Remember the blood. It will be our blood now, Livy. You and me. We'll go up there and we'll leap into the wind. They'll put our story on the Net around the world and they'll never forget.

Others will be inspired by our courage. They'll rise up and save the planet.

He grabbed her arm.

*   *   *

There were ducks on the causeway. A mother bird and one, two, three, make that eight ducklings. Pete waited patiently till the little troupe had disappeared down the far bank of the road. To the west, the sun had almost finished its descent, leaving pools of gold and red like paint slicks on the water. He tapped his fingers to an old rock song on the radio. He still had a bit of a hangover. Not so much from the booze, although he'd managed to drink his share of beer last night. More from the experience. It had been an odd couple of days. He and Rick hadn't had that much to talk about, once they'd got done with catching up on the news of the other guys in the unit. They talked of new equipment and the progress of the war which seemed as uncertain as ever. Rick was thinking of re-enlisting when his tour was done but he didn't seem entirely sure. Pete saw himself in his buddy, himself several years ago. Kind of lost, at loose ends. Signing up just because you can't think of anything better to do.

He was glad to be out of it, he realized. Now he wasn't lost at all, he was a man driving home to his wife. Maybe someday not too far in the future, he'd be a man driving home to his wife and kid. He couldn't wait to tell Ali that he was ready to embark on the kid plan. Still a bit scared but ready.

He drove on into Main Street, humming along with the song. The tourist shops were closed but there were several cars parked outside the Island Grill. Something was going on there, it looked like some kind of scuffle, a couple of fellows going at it. He stopped, though Jonesy the owner was usually quite capable of handling his own bouncer work. He grinned to himself. He wasn't in uniform but maybe he could charge the detachment overtime for this.

"Having trouble Jonesy?" he asked. The burly owner stood at his doorway, casually holding some sputtering youth in a hammerlock.

"No trouble," he said breezily. "Just doing your work for you cops. This guy here is mad because I won't sell him a beer and he started to kick up the place. Looks to me as if he's had enough booze already tonight."

The kid was Sean Ferrell, not quite falling down drunk. But any time soon.

"I'll drive him home," Pete said.

Once in the car, he regretted he wasn't in the cruiser and hoped the kid wasn't going to puke.

Sean looked up blearily. "I remember you," he slurred. "You're the cop who came to the school." He smirked. "You guys thought you were so smart but we didn't tell you a thing."

Pete shrugged. "You've got your secrets, I've got mine."

Under the influence of the booze, the kid couldn't handle his facial expressions. His disappointment was obvious, almost clown-like. Pete just had to wait. And here it came.

Ferrell looked at him owlishly. "Betcha you'd like to know this."

Pete made an elaborate pretence of looking for the road sign. "Is this where you said we turn?"

"Yeah sure," Ferrell said. "But hey, it's not me you should be wasting your time with. I'm not the crazy guy who's gonna blow up that freakin turbine someday."

Pete kept looking straight ahead at the road. "Yeah sure," he said. "Some kid in your little gang is going to blow up a wind turbine. Give me a break. The best you could come up with were some noises and a stuffed dummy."

"Don't believe me then, a-hole. But you should check out the shit that Gavin Sousa has stored in his garage. Gasoline and everything. That guy's a real wack-o. He started the whole thing."

Then Ferrell slumped against the passenger window and started to snore.

Pete felt as if he'd been hit by lightning. He kept driving, his reflexes operating on cruise control, while his thoughts battered against his brain like trapped bolts of fire.

What the hell?

Gavin Sousa?.

Sousa's own kid was the leader of the *Shawks*?

The one who had tried to scare people away, to start rumours of ghosts, to shut the *WindSpear* site down.

The one who had painted on the dummy *'Burt Sousa you're next.'*

And now this little puke in my car here says that the Sousa kid is planning to blow up the turbine, even though his father is already dead.

Wow, he knew the boy hadn't liked Sousa but this was a lot more than that.

This was hate. Crazy hate.

The kid must be out of control. Maybe his father's death had unhinged him completely.

He switched on his cell and called the station.

"Jane, call the chief and tell him to meet me over at the Sousa place. I think there may be some explosives in the garage. Tell him to watch out for the Sousa kid too. He could be mentally upset and dangerous."

Jane was strangely silent. He wondered if there was something wrong with the radio, if she hadn't heard him.

Then he heard her voice not her usual cheery, I'm on it handsome! but subdued with worry.

"The Chief isn't here," she said. "He's out with Steph Bind. They're looking for Livy, she's run away. Stephanie thinks she might be going to meet Gavin Sousa at the Point."

He turned the car around, stopped at the station only long enough to deposit Sean hastily on the cot in the holding cell and toss the keys to Jane.

"Call his parents, if you get the chance."

*　　*　　*

Ali had reached the turbine. The solitary tower rose three hundred feet high from the rough landscape, like an eerie white obelisk to a foreign deity. Following a primitive instinct, she crouched down out of sight behind a low-lying scratchy bush. In the light from the tower doorway she could see the two figures, Livy and Gavin. She could hear their voices but couldn't make out any words. Both voices were high and frantic though, like a dreadful hysterical duet.

What to do? Miranda hadn't expained her fears for Livy but her tone of voice was enough. *That boy wants to hurt her.* Ali couldn't see if Gavin had a weapon. Should she show herself or not? Would that help Livy?

Cautiously, she edged a bit closer. There was no danger of the kids hearing her approach, the rhythmic swoosh of the giant turbine blades was too loud for that. She could only hope that neither of the kids turned around. Now she saw that Gavin had hold of Livy's arm, that he was trying to tug her forward into the tower. The girl was pulling back but Gavin was stronger and he was winning.

As they drew closer to the door, Ali felt a rising panic. She had to do *something*. All she had going for her was the element of surprise, she would just have to launch herself at the boy. She tried to to recall what she'd seen in the movies, what would James Bond do? He'd probably have some wonderful gadget to save the situation, but she didn't. Best to go for the boy's feet or legs, and knock him over. Anyone puts a hand out if they're falling and that would give Livy a chance to wriggle free of his grip.

She felt a giggle bubbling up in her throat. Hysteria, that was no good. She bit her lip hard enough to hurt. Mustn't succumb to panic now, she must stay alert.

She wished desperately that she had stopped to call Pete or at least left him a note.

*   *   *

Steph leaned tensely forward, staring out the windshield of the cruiser. Halstead, watching her, swung into the site road, narrowly missing another car. Both vehicles came to a shuddering halt.

It was Jakes in the other car. "Chief!" he hollered through his open window. "I think Gavin Sousa's out there at the turbine. I think he means to blow it up !"

"Oh God!" Steph mumbled beside Halstead. He felt her crumple back into her seat.

"He's got Livy," Halstead hollered back. "Jane's radioing Kevin, he's coming too."

Pete's car spat back gravel as he started it up, the cruiser following closely behind. The cars sped up the road to the turbine pad. Pete got there first, saw the group at the tower. The Sousa boy, Livy Bind and . . . how could that be Ali?

His stomach turned to ice.

* * *

Ali heard noises, saw lights slice through the dusk. She turned in bewilderment to see cars and people. And there was Pete! Miraculously, as if he'd somehow heard her wish. It was as if the tower had drawn them all here, herself and Miranda, the two young people, Pete and Chief Halstead and Stephanie. The wind had sucked them into its vortex and brought them onto this barren stage to play their parts. She and the boy and Livy were the show unfortunately, the others were only the audience. But there were no footlights and everything was getting darker fast.

Gavin didn't seem to have noticed their arrival, he just kept on dragging Livy towards the door. Ali would have loved to go to Pete but she had a job to do. She was the only one who could help Livy right now.

She launched herself and ran desperately towards them, throwing her whole weight against Gavin's shins. The boy staggered but managed to keep hold of Livy. Ali held on with all her might and the threesome lurched awkwardly forward. Before she could react, Ali felt herself falling with the other two, through the doorway. Then they were in the tower.

34

Pete was running, harder than he'd ever run in his life. Harder than his final test at basic training. Harder than the time he'd seen the grenade coming his way in Kosovo. But he didn't make it in time. He couldn't believe it when the tower door closed. His eyes couldn't believe it, his mind couldn't comprehend it. He continued forward and came to a slamming halt, his hands pressed against the cold, unyielding metal.

It was as if a trap door had closed on his life, on his existence.

He knew the door wouldn't open, but he watched his hands work on remote control, expertly as a safecracker, exploring each useless option. There was no window, the hinges were inside, not outside. Physical force was useless, the metal slab swung out, not in.

He turned to the others, Halstead and now Kevin too, had caught up to him.

Halstead was breathing heavily. He held out his cell phone and managed to get out the words.

"I've got Melissa Keen on the line. Keen's out in the yard, she's gone to get him. He'll have the code for the lock."

There was nothing to do but wait and count the seconds. It was now almost completely dark except for the flashing red aircraft warning light at the top of the tower.

"Organize some lighting," Halstead told Kevin. "Break into the damned trailer if you have to. And keep Stephanie away, tell her not to get out of the car until I say so."

*   *   *

It was stunningly silent inside the tower, an utter absence of noise, a thick silence that pressed against the ears. Ali wanted to huddle into it, like a blanket. But things were happening.

They'd all fallen in together but Gavin had quickly scrambled to his feet, yanking Livy up to hers. It was crowded in the little space, he had to step over Ali, still sprawled on the floor. He started toward the metal stairs pulling Livy after him. But the girl resisted, hanging desperately back.

"Gavin, stop!," she cried in a tiny, scared voice. "I'm not going. I don't want to die and neither do you!"

Ali's blood ran cold. *Die? What was the boy planning to do? To kill Livy?*

Gavin didn't answer. His features were set and frozen, he was a man with one objective, to get to the top of the tower and to take Livy with him. Brutally he twisted her wrist, his grip super-humanly strong. Livy yelped as her ankle banged against a stair.

Ali's thoughts raced. *Why does he want to go up there? He'll never escape. There's nowhere to go.*

Yes there was. He could go down. Way, way, down.

And take Livy with him.

Frantically Ali reached up and sought the door bar with trembling fingers, scrabbling on the metal for a grip. She pushed the bar. Nothing.

She pushed again. Nothing.

Gavin must have set a safety lock.

So, no hope for help from the outside.

Gavin had already pulled Livy up a couple of steps. Still on hands and knees Ali scooted over to the ladder. She straightened in one quick surge, and managed to grab Livy around the waist. Livy flailed harder at Gavin with her free hand. Ali hung on until Gavin kicked her in the face, then she fell back to the floor, reeling from the blow. She tasted blood in her mouth.

Groaning, she staggered back up.

* * *

Outside the two policemen waited, their attention centred on the little gadget in Halstead's hand. The seconds passed excruciatingly slowly. Pete consciously tried to slow his breathing, to regain the necessary cool control of the battlefield. He'd almost lost it a few minutes ago and that would be no help to Ali or the girl.

Finally, a tinny ring sounded in the night. They could hear Keen's voice, nervous and questioning. Impatiently, Halstead shot his questions down.

"Just give us the code, man. For god's sake."

Pete punched in the numbers. 1298645

* * *

Livy seemed to be transfixed by the violence of Gavin's kick.

"Mrs. Jakes," she moaned, looking back from the ladder.

She was no longer offering any active resistance but it was still a struggle, maybe even a harder struggle for the boy to drag her sagging weight up with him.

Ali leaned dizzily against the wall, gathering her strength for another attempt. Then the door fell open and a man burst in.

Pete.

He grabbed her up, she fell against him. It was a wrench to pull her head back from the protection of his shoulder and speak.

She pointed to the ladder. "Up there. He's got Livy. Go! I think he's going to jump!"

"Get out of here," he said. "Go outside and stay there."

"Be careful," she warned. "God, please be careful."

He started up the ladder. He could see the kids about ten feet ahead of him, like a dark clot filling the narrow artery of the tower. He couldn't make out any details, could only hear their panting with the effort of climbing.

"Let her go, son," he called up. "You don't want to hurt her."

If he got too close, the boy might drop her and it was a long way down.

There were light bulbs in cages about every ten feet up the stairway. Pete thought about switching the bulbs off to slow Gavin down. But that would slow him down too and add considerably to the danger. Gavin might be suicidal but Pete wasn't.

Someone's foot slipped. The girl's, he heard her frightened moan. Then the boy's grunt as he strained to hold the extra weight.

Now the girl was screaming, "Gavin, hold me! Hold me!"

He could see her legs frantically fishtailing above him as she tried to regain the step. Then with one last despairing wail, she fell straight towards him.

Pete had only seconds to react and in that narrow space, there was almost no space to manoeuvre. He moved back the few inches that he could, and as the girl collided with him, he pressed her tight against the ladder with his body until he'd stopped her descent. She went limp, he wondered if she'd fainted. He looked down. Halstead was in the doorway, Kevin part way up the ladder. He handed Livy carefully down to Kevin.

Then he kept on climbing. The boy had a greater lead on him now but they both were travelling light. Gavin reached the narrow landing at the top of the ladder and began banging at the hatch door. Pete felt the rush of air as the door fell open. He made a mighty surge upward, pulling himself onto the landing. The kid was already almost through the hatch. When Pete tried to grab at the door, Gavin slammed the metal door down hard.

Pete winced and hastily drew his hands back, just in time. But the kid had no way to fasten the door shut, the handle was on the inside. When Pete tried again, he was able to get through. He stood for a moment, half out of the hatch, taking in big draughts of fresh air and looking around cautiously for the kid. The great swooshing rhythm of the rotor blades filled the night. And there was Gavin, he'd crawled out on the transmission housing and was now lying spreadeagled along the smooth and slippery flank, his cheek pressed to the metal. Ninety metres below lay the ground, far away and now invisible in the dark. As Pete watched, a whale-sized turbine blade floated eerily by at its stately pace, oblivious to the human drama being played out on the platform.

A narrow metal catwalk ran along one side of the housing. Pete was loathe to step out on it though, in case he spooked the kid. He leaned out the hatch and called, "Hey Gavin, why don't you come back in? It's way too dangerous out there. I'm not going to hurt you. Nobody wants to hurt you. We just want to talk."

The kid made no acknowledgement, Pete doubted he'd heard. He was staring out at the moving turbine blades, and seemed to be in some kind of a trance. As if he wasn't hearing or seeing anything other than that hypnotic movement.

He wondered if Livy was down below too, watching.
She was the one person who seemed to understand
And then she didn't, she changed
He felt a pang of fear, of doubt, of loss.

But he had to keep going, he had to finish his task.
Otherwise the nightmare he had every night would come true.
The frantic, butchered birds
Falling in pieces to the rocks
All their life and beauty broken.
Brutal humankind triumphant once again.
Ruining the planet, ruining everything

He could see the tower below him, cold and white and evil.
The great blades raised and cutting through the cloth of the night.
It must be silenced, it must be stopped.
His sacrifice would stop the evil.
His death would stop all the others.

Pete had to go out there, he had to get closer. He stepped out onto the catwalk, talking slowly and calmly to Gavin, as he inched along the metal track. Directly above him, another turbine blade moved regally past. He could feel the flow of air on his face.

"Come on kid, this is no good. Why don't you come in and we can talk about it? You haven't done anything too bad yet. Nothing that can't be fixed up."

He stared out at the softly swinging blade as it came round again. Like the great white wing of a gigantic albatross. Ka-bumf, ka-bumpf. He remembered a movie he'd seen when he was a little kid. Some Disney thing where mice travelled on an albatross as if it was a passenger airplane. It was a funny movie, the albatross was kind of a goofy bird. He had to lurch and stumble down a long runway before he could take off and even then the mice were never sure it was going to happen. All the little kids in the audience were shouting and cheering him on and they gave a great whoop when he finally left the ground.

His mother had taken him to the movie. His father never took him anywhere. He was too embarrassed that his son didn't like to hunt or fish like real boys.

The albatross was rescuing the mice, he couldn't remember why. From something bad that's for sure. There was always lots of bad stuff, even in cartoons.

It would be nice to be rescued, from all this confusion, from everything. From all the crap of living.

But it was all up to him, nobody was going to help him. He was alone. He was the albatross and now he was finally off the ground.

*   *   *

Kevin had managed to rig up some lights. A big emergency battery-operated flashlight from the trailer, plus the powerful police spotlight.

Ali stood with the others, anxiously looking up. "Can't we do something? Anything at all!"

Livy had told them Gavin's plan to jump. Steph was clutching Livy tightly. She had wanted to take her daughter to the car but Livy wouldn't leave.

"I wasn't going to kill myself with him, Mom. I was trying to make him come back down. I was trying to stop him."

Steph stroked her hair, "I know sweetie. I can see that now. I was just so worried."

Livy looked up, "Is Gavin going to be O.K. Mom?"

By now, Keen had arrived and was upwards like the rest of them. The lights didn't reach the top of the tower. They could only guess what was going on. And wait.

"Can't you stop the damn blades going around at least?" Halstead asked. "That might help Jakes."

"It's not like a ferris wheel," Keen snapped nervously back. "And I'm not a carny operator. There's no switch or lever down here marked 'STOP'.

"What about the electrical box?" Halstead said. "Can't you just shut off the power?"

Keen looked up to the sky, where the wind was picking up speed.

"It's the other way round remember? The wind is turning the blades and feeding the electricity into the transmitting wires. That's the whole damn brilliant idea."

*   *   *

Pete took another step, edging closer. But Gavin seemed to sense the movement. He turned and looked at Pete with a blank stare, then shinnied farther out along the housing.

The cop was talking again. He keeps saying they can fix it, they can make it better.

He doesn't know. He doesn't know what I did.

He doesn't know that no one can fix it, ever.

Oh oh. Pete tensed. The kid was moving, pulling himself up to a sitting position. Christ was this the jump? But no, he was just sitting there, as if he was on a chair at home. Instead of clinging to a slippery metal tube, ninety metres up in the air. His face was a white disk glowing eerily in the faint light from the hatch door. And he was talking, saying something.

Pete cupped his ear to show that he couldn't hear the kid above the wind, that he was coming closer. But the kid started to wave his arms frantically. He was yelling now.

"Stay back! You don't understand. I can't ever come back. I have to die. I'm a murderer—I killed my father ! He killed Brad and I killed him."

Now he was half-standing on the tube, half leaning over the catwalk, his position the most desperate yet. Pete could see one of the big blades coming up behind him, looming softly like an object in space. The soft swoosh startled the kid, he leaned back and lost his precarious balance.

There was no time to think. Pete leapt forward.

*   *   *

Kevin was at the hatchway, had been standing silently by and unseen for several minutes. He helped Pete wrestle the kid down to the landing.

They fell in a tangled melee on the platform but there was no fight left in the kid. He lay curled in the foetal position on the cold metal, limp and sobbing. They pulled him to his feet.

"It's alright, Gavin." Pete said. "You're safe. It's going to be alright now."

The kid sagged between them, his face smeared with snot and tears.

Kevin looked confused. "What did he mean about killing his father?"

Pete looked grim. "I guess we're going to find out."

They flanked him going down the ladder, Kevin going first.

Gavin babbled and sobbed all the way down.

*   *   *

The ones who waited on the ground watched the trio emerge from the tower. Gavin had his arm over his face, while the two officers winced in the sudden glare of the spotlight.

"Gavin!" Livy called, but Steph pulled her back.

Ali forced herself to wait while Pete and Kevin took Gavin over to the one of the cruisers. Then she ran over to join him.

"Are you alright?" She ran her eyes and her hands over him.

He kissed her. "I'm O.K.," he said. "What about you? You've been doing some pretty crazy stunts of your own tonight."

She touched her bruised cheek. "I'm O.K. But I'm not about to take up police work any time soon."

"You're a brave lady. You just might get a medal." He kissed her again, then said apologetically.

"But for now, do you mind if I get Jim Keen to take you home? I've got to go into the station."

"Of course you do," she said, her expression sobering. "That poor boy! What happens now?"

"I'm not sure. There's a lot to figure out."

She waited with Steph and Livy while the cruisers left. Livy looked utterly stricken and silently followed her mother into Keen's car.

"Oh my goodness," Ali stopped, she was about to step in. "I completely forgot about Miranda!"

Pete wondered if it was always like this. He'd read the scene in books, watched it play out in countless movies and television shows. The torrent of confession. He supposed it was a relief for the guilty, that was the theory anyway. But Gavin didn't look any less miserable. He spoke in a muted rambling monotone, his body slumped forward in the hard wooden chair, his head down.

I killed him. I killed my father.
He was a monster. He killed Brad.
Brad found out the survey lines were wrong and that was going to stop the project.
So he killed him.
I knew it as soon as Livy brought me the logbook and I saw Brad's notes about Andy Poltz's place, his drawings of the old survey marker stakes.
I rode out on my bicycle to the site office, one night when he was staying late. He was drinking, like he always was, every night.
I told him I'd seen the logbook. I told him I knew what he'd done.
That Brad didn't fall when he was chasing us. He went back up the tower and then my father the monster put something on the stairs that made Brad fall when he came down the second time.
He said that he was only trying to make money for his family. I told him I would never have spent a penny of his blood-tainted money and

I never will. I told him that it was me and my friends who had been vandalizing his fences and that we had left the dummy.

He called me an ungrateful bastard. He said that he'd never really believed that I was his son. That my mother fooled around all the time. That I didn't look like him or act like him. That he was ashamed of me. Then he started to chase me. I ran into the woods towards the bluff.

He stopped here and shivered violently. At the station, they'd put a blanket round his shoulders and brought soup and coffee but he hadn't touched either. Seventeen years old, Pete thought, and his eyes looked seventy, as he journeyed back to that other desperate night.

The two cops were silent, Halstead's look conveying the message. *Don't break the mood, don't interrupt the flow.* Pete leaned against the wall, picturing that frantic, pounding run along the dark path, cedar branches clawing at the boy's face. His own father in deadly pursuit, smashing down saplings and branches like a crazed bear. The thought turned his stomach.

Gavin started speaking again, so faintly the cops had to lean forward to hear.

I got to the bluff first. It was lighter there out of the woods. There was some moonlight shining on the water.

I saw him come bursting out of the path.

I said 'Dad, Dad, don't hurt me' but he didn't pay any attention. He just kept on coming at me like he didn't even hear me.

I could have run some more, but I knew it wouldn't make any difference. He would just keep coming after me. It would never end, for the rest of my life.

So I just stepped out of the way.

The kid stopped again, seemed to wonder at his own voice, at the horror of his own words. Again the cops waited.

He kind of roared as he went over. I could hear him all the way down. Then it stopped. I didn't try to help him, I didn't call anyone. I just left him there.

He was a monster. He would have killed me to protect his project. So I killed him instead.

Now the kid started to cry again. "I'm a murderer too. I wanted him dead. I'm as bad as him."

*   *   *

"That problem must have been building for years," Halstead said.

Pete nodded. "He hated his father already, after years of fear and being bullied. And then Burt was going to destroy his favourite special place, the old resort where he'd spent happy times with his grandfather."

"Any jury will take his age into account and the circumstances. Probably bring in a verdict of self-defense."

"Yeah but will the kid ever let himself off the hook? That's the question. He sees himself as a murderer. Maybe he always will."

Halstead sighed. "Maybe the shrinks will be able to do something for him. He's got years of therapy ahead of him, that's for sure."

Four a.m. They'd waited for the ambulance to come and take Gavin over to the psychiatric ward at Bonville General. There was nothing open in the village, and no milk for the coffee, so they drank pop and found Jane's stash of chocolate covered granola bars. Halstead opened one of the foil-wrapped bars, sniffed it suspiciously before taking a bite.

"So it *was* the mysteriously disappearing logbook," he said. They'd discovered it in Gavin's jacket when they searched. He said he'd meant to take it with them when he jumped so the cops would find it with his body.

"You were right, Jakes. You're a smart cop."

Jakes didn't actually blush but he fidgeted with embarrassment.

Halstead let him off the hook and asked, "O.K. I've seen the drawings. Tell me what it all means."

Pete turned with relief to the relevant pages. "It's interesting stuff. These sketches are of some stakes that surveyors in earlier times used to mark off property lines. You see, Brad's drawn the date on them, 1889."

He explained what Keen had told him that day they'd been inspecting the fence-line. Too bad they hadn't recognized the significance of that newly dug hole at the time.

"So where did Brad see these old stakes?" Halstead asked. "In the Island museum?"

"Actually there are some there," Pete said. "I checked. But Brad found these three stakes or at least the tops of them sticking out of the ground along Andy Poltz's fence-line."

"Why were they turning up now, after all this time?"

Pete shrugged. "Likely the cattle hooves have been gradually chewing up the ground under the fence." He turned the page. "Brad was a surveying student. He would have realized immediately what the markers meant. After finding the first marker, he walked aong the fence line and found the others. Look here, he's made the sketches and put the co-ordinates right here in the logbook."

"But I thought Keen said they wouldn't matter."

"This is different. Most of those old stakes were discovered decades ago and the areas long since re-surveyed. And even when there were major differences, the problems were resolved eventually. In a case like this, the company would normally pay something reasonable or even generous for allowing the amendment or property variance or whatever. But we're talking here about Andy Poltz. He was so opposed to the wind project, he would have loved to have a hold over the company. And with the discovery of these old stakes, Poltz could demand a new survey of the entire property. It would only take a marker or two to cast the required legal doubt. Even if he lost the court battle, he could tie up the project for months, maybe even a year or more."

Halstead whistled. "The *WindSpear* people wouldn't have been too pleased with that. Or with Burt. He was responsible for getting title searches from affected landowners. Now he'd have this marker mess and another big construction delay."

Pete nodded. "Even worse, the wind company might not wait, they might move on somewhere else altogether and drop the option on his property. Then he'd lose everything. The land sale and all he'd borrowed on the strength of that."

Halstead winced. "So Brad showed his findings to Burt? Jeezus. It's pretty easy to imagine how Burt felt at the thought of giving Andy Poltz such a weapon. He would literally see red."

Pete nodded and quietly closed the logbook. "Too bad Brad didn't go to Keen about the surveying inaccuracies, instead of to Sousa. He'd have been alive today."

Halstead smiled sadly. "He was a local kid. As far as he was concerned, big Burt Sousa was the boss. The poor guy probably thought he was doing the company a favour, pointing out a problem before they made a mistake. He didn't realize he was giving Burt a hell of a scare. Burt knew he had to move fast before the kid gabbed about his findings to anyone else. The whole project could have been shut down for non-compliance."

He made a face as if he'd bitten into something healthy like a raisin, by mistake. "So he rigs up something on the turbine ladder step and that's it for young Brad. You never found anything out there?"

Pete thought of the times he'd been out tramping over that wind-scoured stretch of bedrock. "Kevin and I went all over the place but we didn't know what we were looking for then. Maybe we could find something now, but it's doubtful. Sousa could have used anything—a hunk of log, a piece of rope that he removed later . . ."

"So he kills the kid, then just goes out calmly sometime, pulls up the old stake markers and fills in the holes. Jeezus." His face darkened. "I can't get over how Burt killed that kid. I knew he was capable of cutting a few corners, but murder . . . .

"He was probably planning to do it some night before Keen had the security system installed. He was keeping an eye on Brad, maybe he even suggested the kid for the night watch. When he saw the confusion and the escaped cattle that night the *shawks* kids were there, he grabbed his chance. And if for some reason the accident theory didn't fly, nobody would suspect Mayor Sousa because he had left the country that night."

"Only his flight wasn't till midnight," Halstead added grimly. "He had time to wait till the kids had gone, time to booby-trap the turbine steps and kill Brad, and still make it to the airport. Then he could sit over there in his hotel in Denmark and wait to hear the sad news."

"He must have thought he was in the clear," Pete said. "Brad was dead and couldn't talk. Though he would have had some bad moments wondering where Brad had left the logbook."

Halstead unwrapped another bar. Live dangerously. He could really use a coffee though. "No wonder Burt was in such a hell of a state when he got back from Denmark. We thought it was because the project was halted for a couple of weeks but he was likely also going crazy wondering when that logbook was going to turn up. He must have finally figured like we did, that it got lost or trampled on that night."

Pete nodded. "Then later on, Livy brought Gavin the book. Gavin was a top math student, he realized the significance of those sketches and surveying notations. He came to the same conclusion as his father did. And he guessed what his father had done."

Halstead balled the wrapper up and threw it in the trash. "And we know how all that turned out."

Outside the window, the sky was lightening. Details of the landscape emerged slowly out of the grey light, like a photo developing in a pan. A few early-rising seagulls were already foraging on yesterday's newly-turned furrows. In another hour or so, the farmer would be out with the seeder. Farmers rose early. So did policemen.

"Jeez." Halstead shook his head. "I wonder whether he actually meant to kill Gavin, his own son."

"I hope not," Pete said. "I hope greed can't do that to a man."

Halstead hit the desk a hard thump with his big hand. "The damn fool! All he accomplished was to hold up his damn project for a couple more weeks." He looked wearily down at his desk. A daunting task, to summarize up the night's events in paperwork.

"Vern and I and the others should have seen that Burt was in way over his head this time. Fighting with Elena, mortgaging the business. All the signs were there. Well he's beyond earthly punishment now."

"You're sorry for him?" Pete couldn't believe it. "The man was a bully, a killer. He killed the Gillies kid, he wrecked his own son's life."

"I'm sorry for everybody," Halstead said. "I'm sorry I couldn't stop the train wreck. It's a cop's lot, get used to it, son."

He stood up. "Vern should be pleased. At least the county won't have to cover the cost of Burt's trial. His son saved the taxpayers that expense."

"There you go," Ali opened the door, watching anxiously while Miranda hobbled into the kitchen. The walking cast made her progress awkward. It didn't help that Emily was whining wildly from the den, where she was temporarily shut up.

"You needn't hover," Miranda snapped. "I can manage."

But she sank gratefully into a kitchen chair, Ali noticed. And her thin cheeks looked grey with the effort. It was too bad Miranda hadn't consented to stay at the hospital.

"I'll get the groceries from the car," Ali said. "And your pills." When she got back, Miranda had let Emily out. The dog was sitting with her muzzle pressed lovingly on her elderly owner's lap.

"Yes, you're a clever girl," Miranda crooned. "You found me. You're a good, clever girl."

Ali went quietly about the room, putting items away in cupboards and the fridge.

Miranda sighed, leaning back tiredly in her chair.

"I do thank you," she said crisply. "It's been a strange time and you've been a big help."

Ali smiled. "I'm not going far. I live across the road you know. We're neighbours."

Miranda winced, "Yes we are my dear, I'll try and remember that."

"I'll go feed the chickens, then."

The dog whined and Miranda resumed her petting.

"There's no fool like an old fool, Emily. I'm the living proof of that."

During the wait in the emergency room the other night, Ali had got her talking about life up north at the inlet. It passed the time and took her mind off her throbbing ankle as they waited for the doctor. Miranda told the tale of her arrival at the inlet all those years ago, to replace the former teacher who had been taken out on an emergency flight with a burst appendix. She told of her total unpreparedness for the weather, the ill-equipped classroom, the short days and long lonely nights when she wondered why she had ever marooned herself in the god-forsaken arctic. She doubted that the regular teacher was every coming back—who would?

But by the end of that first month, Miranda was hooked on the North and its peoples, especially the children.

'That's a wonderful story,' Ali said. 'And so inspiring. You should write it down, I'd love to read it.'

'What do you think, Emily?' Miranda asked the dog. 'I do have all those pictures. And it would help pass the time.'

Emily wagged her tail.

*   *   *

A fine morning summer morning on Middle Island. The tourists on Main Street wielded ice cream cones, traffic was busy on the causeway. A flotilla of sailboats bobbbed gaily on the Bay. Halstead walked briskly up the steps to the town office, the *Bonville Record* in hand. *LOCAL COP MAKES DARING WINDMILL RESCUE,* read the headline.

He found Vern in the clerk's office.

"Morning," Halstead said, tapping the newspaper against his hip.

"Morning, Bud. You're bright and early." Vern tapped some papers on his desk. "I've got the contract right here, if you want to look through it."

"Oh I think we went over it pretty thoroughly yesterday, Vern."

The wording was overblown as in all things legal but the underlying meaning was clear. Council had decided to keep the local police detachment. Four officers, plus a dispatcher. With the Mayor gone, it turned out that the other councillors had never truly endorsed a switch to the provincial police force.

Vern handed Halstead a pen and he signed the contract at several indicated places.

The clerk shook his hand. "Congratulations. You did a good job there, Bud."

"Thanks, Vern. Burt had so many enemies, for awhile there I thought I might have to detain myself as a suspect."

He grinned. "What about you, Vern? How are you enjoying the job of acting mayor? Planning to make it permanent the next election?"

Vern looked shocked. "Hell no, I've got a gas station to run."

So, a good beginning to a new day. A new beginning altogether. Driving up Main Street towards the police station, Halstead saw his town through refreshed eyes. The veil of grief he'd felt since Kathleen died was lifting. Memories were forever but life goes on. He'd heard the bromide since childhood, now was reminded once more that it was true. He felt like eating a maple walnut ice cream cone, like getting his boat out on the weekend, like whistling.

He slowed to let a girl on a bike turn the corner and thought back to that day when he'd seen Livy riding along the waterfront. He had no idea of the torment in her mind then, had just seen a pretty young girl on a bike. That brought up thoughts of Steph and his meeting with her yesterday. She wore shorts and her legs were long and tanned. She smiled under her glossy hair.

"I'm taking a couple of weeks off from the Retreat, leaving my yoga instructor in charge. Livy and I are going on a little trip, just the two of us. We're heading off in the car and we'll see where the whim takes us. Just have some fun and be together. Then she'll fly out to see her Dad in August. The change will do her good."

Her smile wavered a bit, as if she was trying to convince herself and it wasn't quite working.

"Livy will be alright," he said. "It might take a little while, but I know she's a strong person underneath. Like her mother."

Then Steph kissed him on the cheek.

"I'll be here when you get back," Halstead said.

"I know," she said.

And that was worth whistling about. As he entered the station, Jane looked up from her desk.

"The news is good, Chief?"

"The news is good. Though it might be a bit cramped in here during the renovations."

Her eyes widened. "You mean we won't have to use the pails when it rains? The news is *very* good."

"I brought you a little something to celebrate," He deposited a pound of unadulterated coffee on the desk. "No cinammon."

To sit in his chair was like coming home. From the open window came sounds of field sparrows and the sweet scent of ripening corn. He left the ringing phone to Jane, he could use a few more moments to savour the peace.

But she poked her head in the door anyway.

"It's John at the motel. A couple of the motel bicycles are missing."

Halstead, put his feet back up on the desk.

"Send out Ragusa," he said. "The kid's still got a couple more months here in the sticks."

*   *   *

There were two vehicles in the Poltz driveway. The old blue pick-up truck that had sat idle for the weeks that Poltz was away and a maroon sedan. Halstead had mentioned that the daughter had brought the old man home from the detention centre. Maybe a reconciliation developing there? Pete wondered.

He hoped that the old tyrant would have been softened somewhat by his recent harrowing experience. That he'd mellowed some with gratitude at the way his neighbours had pitched in to tend his animals and clean his house. Or at least have cheered up at the news that the *WindSpear* company had cancelled the wind turbine project at the Point.

In the chief's words, "Goddamn, won't old Andy do a jig when he hears that."

But it was more likely if the old man did feel any triumph, he'd be too ornery to show it. That he wouldn't admit to any change at all.

And in fact, there he was, Poltz the indominatable, back on his manure pile with his trusty pitchfork. In his green overalls, crazy white hair sticking up all over the place, his cattle bawling and milling around as if they were glad to have him back.

Pete tooted the cruiser horn and risked a wave as he drove past.

There was a new sign where the road turned down to Hawks Nest Point and a gate with a padlock.

Danger Keep Out. No Trespassing.

He got out of the cruiser and looked to the left towards the Sousa property, the old fishing camp. The bank owned the place now, he'd heard. Elena had lost the place when the bank called the mortgage in as collateral for Burt's now useless investments in *WindSpear* shares. As reported in the Bonville Record, the Danish parent company had abandoned the project because of a lack of community support. And too much unwelcome publicity no doubt.

He put a leg over the locked gate. There was no operating security system, as he knew only too well. The company trailer was still there in the parking lot, weeds already growing up around the wheels. He glanced in the dusty window, saw that the computer equipment was gone. A couple of abandoned maps were still taped to the walls. He didn't bother going inside. The wind was soft today, the great blades of the turbine hanging idly, like limp sails in the sky. There was a legal requirement that the company remove the turbine at some point but Pete doubted that would be any time soon. It was much more fun to erect a seventy ton turbine than to take it down.

He squinted against the blinding flash of the sun on the lake. Out on the water, he could see a fishing boat, perhaps the Bonny Belle whose owners were the first to discover Burt's body on the rocks. Life goes on. Fish keep biting.

He left, climbing once more over the gate. But there was really no need for the No Trespassing sign. The company had been the trespasser here at the Point. The wildife were the true home owners, the folks in residence. Someday all that would remain of the ill-fated wind project would be the demo pad. Just a big slab of concrete, a dance floor for the wild creatures that would now come cautiously creeping back.

37

Wisdom sails with wind and time.

September. Ali lounged on her newly painted porch, laptop open, reading an e-mail from her mother. Nuran, having wowed the Western provinces with her book tour, was now headed for Toronto. Ali supposed she'd better attend. Maybe she could spend the night at the hotel with Nuran. Let her have a couple of glasses of wine before giving her the news that she was going to be a grandmother.

She felt the stirring in her womb. Yes that was the word for the sweetly unsettling feeling. Of course it was months too early for any actual detectable movement but there was definitely an exciting disturbance in her universe. She hugged herself with sweet expectation.

She'd finished her lemonade. She tinkled the ice cube left in the glass, looking for her keeper. That's what she called Pete these days, he fussed over her so much, wouldn't let her do a thing. Ah well, might as well enjoy the pampering while it lasted. In another few days, she'd be teaching again and things would be back to normal.

Actually her keeper was already shirking his duties. Right now, he was across the road talking to Miranda, getting some pointers about how to barbeque a trout for supper. Miranda and Emily were bringing the salad.

EPILOGUE

The hawks are leaving now. Heading south, two thousand miles to the Texas border. Approaching the lake, they can smell the water ahead. They're wary though, there's something fearsome in their memory. There's a tall strange object ahead, some new kind of tree.

But it's OK, it's not moving. The strange tree is a dead tree, with dead limbs, with no power to hurt.

And the warm air thermal currents are rising off the water, just as they always have, as long as hawks have been flying.

Waiting to take the birds safely across the lake.

—The End—

Quotations

Title, William Shakespeare, from *The Tempest.*
p. 34, William Shakespeare.
p. 42 The Bible, John.
p. 93 William Shakespeare.
p. 99 Robert Louis Stevenson
p. 122 Henry W. Longfellow
p. 123 French proverb
p. 139 Seneca, Roman philosopher
p. 226 John Florio, Elizabethan poet